THE DEVIL'S DECEPTION

DEVILLE BROTHERS

WENDY VELLA

To my readers a huge, big, massive thank you!
Because of you I can do what I love.
Wendy xx

OTHER BOOKS BY WENDY VELLA

The Lady Plays Her Ace
The Lady Seals Her Fate
The Lady's Dangerous Love
The Lady's Forbidden Love

Regency Rakes Series
Duchess By Chance
Rescued By A Viscount
Tempting Miss Allender

The Lords Of Night Street Series
Lord Gallant
Lord Valiant
Lord Valorous
Lord Noble

Stand-Alone Titles
The Reluctant Countess
Christmas Wishes
Mistletoe And The Marquess
Rescued By A Rake

The Notorious Nightingales
The Disgraced Debutante

PROLOGUE

The year was 1709, the monarchy was under threat, and the queen's advisers worried. Danger came from many different quarters, and something had to be done. A council was formed by Anne, Queen of Great Britain, and she gathered ten of her most powerful nobles. Men she trusted to pledge their allegiance to her and none other. Each was given a ring, the gold band forged from goblets said to be used by William the Conqueror in 1066 when he won the Battle of Hastings and took the throne. The men would protect the ruling monarch, and the council would be known as Alexius. *The Defenders.*

Over the years their numbers would grow as members would be enlisted for courageous acts undertaken or loyalty to the throne. Others inherited the position. Brothers, cousins, all united in their quest.

Veritas scutum tibi erit would be their pledge. *The truth will be your shield.*

CHAPTER 1

"We are to leave in one hour, Theodore."

"Yes, Uncle."

The man gave him a look that suggested Theo could be something stuck on the heel of his polished leather boot and not a grieving nephew. Someone who carried his blood but he'd never met until the week after his parents were murdered.

"Be sure you are ready."

Theo nodded, and his uncle walked from the room, closing it behind him with a decisive snap.

Theo loathed him. His father's brother, and now his guardian. A man who felt he should be the new Lord Montgomery. Not some thirteen-year-old boy who had very little knowledge of the world he would one day walk in.

Tall, overbearing, and pompous, his uncle was everything his brother had not been. His father was the best man Theo knew; his uncle was the worst.

A year had passed since the day he'd found his parents brutally murdered. A year of hell. A year that had changed Theo into someone he no longer knew.

He was becoming his uncle. Cold and emotionless. But it was either that or walk into the lake he and his parents had rowed all over and let the water take his pain away. Let it stop the deep, aching grief that was relentless and threatened to destroy him.

His father and mother would have been ashamed had he done that, so Theo had learned to cope. He'd shut himself away from everything he'd once loved.

And now, for the final act, he would leave the only home he'd ever known. His uncle was sending him to Eton. Away from his family's staff, the people who cared for him. Away from Iris, his friend. Once, he'd spent his days with her here, riding or playing.

He hadn't laughed with her in a year. Theo didn't think he'd ever laugh again.

He opened the note she'd sent him and read it once more.

I have not seen you in many months, but I can feel your grief. Yesterday I learned you are to attend Eton and can only imagine your pain at leaving the home you love.

Hold your memories close. Know always that your parents loved you with all that they were. They taught you to be strong. Never forget those lessons. Stay strong, and one day it's my hope the pain eases and we meet again. Know that I am your friend, my dearest Theo, now and always.

Iris xx

He'd seen her from a distance but not spoken directly to her in a year. But she'd written to him every week, and he'd read each word carefully. He'd then folded the notes and placed them in a small chest under his bed.

Theo never replied because he didn't know what to say. If he spoke of his loss and the suffocating grief, he may never put himself back together. Never be able to get out of bed and be the cold, hard boy he'd turned himself into to survive.

He'd been mourning his parents for a year, and now it

was finally acceptable for him to leave his house. Iris had tried to visit with him. Tried to get inside over the past twelve months. Theo's uncle had not allowed it. He'd spent the year being a prisoner in his own home. Walking in the gardens was acceptable, but little else.

Thankfully, the staff had not allowed his uncle to intimidate them. They'd come to his rooms to play cards and bring him food. Had it not been for them, his life would have been hell.

But now he was going away. It was almost a relief. Finally, he could leave here. This place held so many wonderful memories that were now all destroyed. Shattered by senseless murder and his emotionless uncle.

He'd heard his uncle talking to the magistrate. No one knew why the late Lord and Lady Montgomery had their lives ended so brutally in their beds. But one day, Theo would find who had done it and make them pay. Vengeance had burned and smoldered into a hard determination inside him.

He looked at his bed. Under it was something he wanted no one to see. Something he'd uncovered when he'd walked into his parents' rooms and found them dead. He could allow no one to find it. Theo knew it would be safe here until he returned.

Someone would pay for what happened to the two people he loved most in the world.

A tap on his door had Theo looking around his room one last time. A place that had become his prison when once it had been anything but. He didn't have any tears left and wasn't sure he'd ever cry again.

He felt empty. Hollowed out and emotionless.

His uncle had told him Lord Montgomery does not weep. That he needed to be the man his father had expected him to become. He'd then talked at him every day for hours about his responsibilities and actions. His uncle had said Theo's parents failed in their job to prepare him to be the lord he would one day become. Theo had not stood for that. Something in his eyes must have warned his uncle to never go there again because he hadn't.

At thirteen, Theo was now a man, according to his uncle.

"Are you ready, my lord?" his butler said.

"I am, thank you, Stephens," he said to the man who was standing in his doorway. His father's butler, a man who Theo felt was almost a grandfather.

"Come along then. Your uncle awaits you in the carriage." A hand settled on his shoulder, and it took every ounce of his strength not to turn into that body and let Stephens hold him. Let him tell him his life would one day again make sense. That he would laugh and find happiness and know what it was to be loved again.

Stephens kept his hand on Theo's shoulder as they walked through the house. The staff were lined before the door waiting for him. Some were weeping.

He shook all their hands, because his father always said he needed to be kind and humble with them. His mother had insisted he know their first names.

They said things like "God be with you" and "your parents loved you."

Theo nodded, dry-eyed, and then walked out the front door with Stephens. His uncle sat inside the carriage.

The butler opened the door.

"Hurry it along, Theodore. We have many miles to cover," his uncle snapped.

"Goodbye, Stephens." He shook his butler's hand and then climbed inside.

"You don't touch staff," his uncle snapped at him.

Theo was mostly quiet and respectful, except when

someone challenged what his parents had taught him. "As they are my staff, I can do as I wish."

His uncle's mouth tightened into a thin line at the reminder. He then fell silent as the carriage rolled away from his family's home. Theo did not look back. Pain lay behind him.

He was looking out the window as they reached the village a thirty-minute walk from his home. Theo knew this, as he'd walked it many times with his parents and Iris.

He saw her as he reached Prism's Bakers. Iris stood outside, watching his carriage.

How had she known he would pass at this time?

She moved closer, so close he thought the carriage could hit her, but it simply passed her by. It was close enough for him to see the tears tracking down her cheeks, though. He pressed a hand to the window, and she raised hers, and then she, too, was gone from his life. The three people he loved were no more.

Theo had a feeling as the carriage headed toward Eton and a new life, that, in fact, she would never be part of his life again. No one would because he never ever wanted to love someone as much as he had his parents and her, then lose them.

Theo decided as he looked across the carriage at his uncle, who was reading the newspaper, that he would become a coldhearted bastard just like him.

CHAPTER 2

*S*ixteen years later.

Lord Theodore Montgomery rode through the streets with his hood pulled forward far enough to cover his face. It was likely no one from his world would recognize him even if they saw him, as he appeared vastly different from the man who walked in society.

It wasn't excessively late, and darkness was only just lowering its cloak over London. Lamps were being lit, and soon the city would be cast in a yellowish glow.

Halting, as a large, lumbering coach pulled out into the road in front of him, he heard the roll of wheels as a carriage stopped at his side. Looking at the window, he saw a lady. She was staring out at the street. Something about that face jolted his memory.

Did he know her?

Her eyes caught his, and they stared at each other for long seconds, and then she was rolling away from him.

Monty pressed a hand to his chest. Why was there a burning sensation there? He felt like he knew her, but then he knew many women in society, and some out of it. However, something about that one stirred a memory inside him.

Odd.

Nudging his mount into a trot, he turned right down the next street. He rode for fifteen minutes further and then halted near a church. After dismounting, Monty tethered his horse to a tree.

Pulling a chain out of his shirt, he then undid the clasp and slipped off a ring. After tucking the chain into his pocket, he slid the ring onto his third finger.

Monty walked the worn path past the church, blackened by fire on one side, and the other covered in a creeping vine. Old, it had been a place where the secret alliance of Alexius members had met for centuries. A group that had protected the monarchy for hundreds of years.

Raising a fist, he hammered on the scarred wood of the door four times. He then opened it and entered. A man sat at a table. There was a single candle burning, which offered little light. The setting had not changed in the many years he'd been coming here.

Traditions, Monty thought. He'd never understood them.

"*Veritas scutum tibi erit,*" the man, Geraint, said.

The truth will be your shield, Monty interpreted as he always did. "*Veritas scutum tibi erit,*" he replied.

Tall, well-built, the man he knew only as Geraint was solemn and serious-minded, as he had always been.

Removing his hood, Monty sat. He then stacked his hands on the table, showing the ring he wore. His father's ring. He had just not realized the significance of it until he'd become part of Alexius.

Pushing that thought aside, as emotion had no place in

his life anymore, he focused on Geraint. Soon it would be his turn to speak, but for now, he would listen.

"I have called you here today alone to discuss something that has come to my attention," Geraint said.

"I, too, wish to speak with you alone," Monty said.

The man nodded, like he was the bloody king he worked for.

"A rumor has reached us that one of the monarch's most trusted advisors, Sir Stephen Ackland, is, in fact, a traitor."

"A traitor how?"

"He is a devil worshipper. A courtier alerted one of the king's guards, who in turn told our monarch."

"Hellfire clubs are not unusual, surely," Monty said.

"I believe this is vastly different, my lord. After they alerted the king, he asked that Ackland be followed," Geraint said. "He followed him to a building, where Ackland entered and went down below the ground. The two guards followed and found a young woman drugged and tied to a table. There were knives and other instruments of torture there."

Monty stayed silent. Geraint would get to the point when he was ready.

"Ackland was interrogated and admitted that he had killed others, but he vowed he was alone in his satanic behaviors. However, papers found in his rooms suggested he was part of a society that gave their allegiance to Satan. Upon a further searching, more communications were discovered. We found a letter with three names on it. All were crossed out and the words *the gods are appeased* were at the bottom. Your father's name was on there."

"I beg your pardon?"

"Your father's name was one of the three on the list. The other two were Lord Peters and Lord Lionel. Both are deceased, so we cannot ask them questions about why the names are there. There was also the sign of Satan on the top right-hand corner."

If Monty wasn't sitting, his legs would likely have given out. His memory flashed back to the night he'd found his parents. In his father's hand had been a small engraved piece of wood with the sign of the devil.

"I hope you are not suggesting my father was in any way involved in some kind of satanic ritual, that—"

"I knew your father, my lord," Geraint interrupted him, "and if I did not, I know his reputation was beyond reproach. He was not involved in devil worshipping or satanic rituals."

Heart thumping, Monty nodded.

"Unfortunately, Ackland was left alone in a cell and hung himself before anyone could get more information out of him. Our monarch is displeased and wants answers as to what the man was part of. He also has no wish for this to reach society's ears."

"What was the symbol on that list of three names?" Monty managed to get out.

"A pentacle."

He had hidden that small wooden carving because he wanted no one to believe his father a devil worshipper, and until now, he'd managed to push it from his thoughts. Monty remained silent, unsure what it all meant.

His father was not a devil worshipper. Monty would never believe otherwise, but he had died with a pentacle in his hand.

"We will investigate these details, but as your father's name is involved, I wanted to tell you personally," Geraint added.

"I want to be kept informed of everything to do with this case," Monty said.

"Of course. We have as yet found nothing more, but if

there is something to find, we will. Our monarch is quite insistent we uncover what is going on."

Could this all relate to his parents' deaths? Considering what his father had been clutching, Monty thought there was a chance, and that finally he may find answers to the night that had changed his life forever.

"Do you believe the deaths of the other two men on that list suspicious?" Monty asked.

"Peters died in France a year after your father, and we know little other than they found his body on a Paris street. I believe he was the victim of a random attack, as the possessions he was carrying were all missing. Lionel was the youngest of the three, and he died seven years after your father at his home in London. His wife found him one morning. Even though they are all associated with Alexius, we did not believe their deaths were connected," Geraint said.

He now had more questions than answers. *Why were those three names on that list and all were now dead?*

"Now, what is it you wished to discuss with me, Lord Montgomery?"

Monty had thought long and hard about what he was about to say, but he had believed the time was right to leave London and never return. However, with the information that had just come to light, he was now not so sure, but he would be honest and tell Geraint that his time as Plunge was drawing to a close.

"I had no longer believed there would be justice for my parents, Geraint. Before you told me what you have, I had grown weary of playing the fool and no longer wished for the charade to continue."

The man he'd known for many years could not mask his surprise.

"It is true that we have not found those who killed your

parents, but it's my hope with this new information we may do just that, Lord Montgomery."

Monty hoped that as well.

"I understand you joined us to seek justice for your family and acknowledge the sacrifice you have made for your king," Geraint added. "It is my hope we can change your mind, as you are an asset to Alexius."

"Thank you. But should this not yield a lead or name for my parents' killers, then I will leave London at the end of the season and not return." Monty did not mince words when the direct approach could just as easily be taken. He may act the fool for society, but he was not that man away from it.

Hard, unfeeling, he'd become the person his parents had vowed he'd never be. Their death had set him on this course, and Monty had finished it.

"We have searched every corner of England for information regarding your parents' killers but found nothing, so it is pleasing to have a new lead."

"Considering the resources and time we've had, it suggests to me there are powerful men behind my parents' murders," Monty said in an emotionless voice.

He fought the image that wanted to fill his head of the blood-spattered walls and bodies of his parents.

"At the time, Alexius was busy dealing with unrest and animosity focused on our monarch due to changes taking place in England. Your father was one of the people involved. I had believed this was the reason for their deaths and yet have never been able to substantiate that," Geraint said.

"We have discussed this over and over and come up with nothing, Geraint. This new lead may yield something, or it may not. I made my decision. I will leave soon, depending on what is uncovered."

"And you will retire from society?"

Monty nodded.

"There will be talk."

"There will," Monty conceded. "I will fall ill and be unable to return."

Geraint nodded. "Very well, if that is your wish."

No more words were needed as far as Monty was concerned, and Geraint knew better than to persuade him to stay. He rose and left. At the door, he turned to face Geraint once more.

"Please keep me apprised as to what is uncovered regarding Ackland. *Veritas scutum tibi erit.*" He bowed and walked out of the church. After closing the door, he exhaled slowly. It was done. Lord Plunge would retire from society one day soon and never be seen again. If no more new information came to light about his parents, it would be sooner rather than later.

Walking down the path, he saw three men standing around his horse.

"May I help you?"

They spun to face him, fanning out before Monty.

"We found this horse, and we're taking it." The man in the middle of the three addressed him. Monty didn't think they were completely down on their luck, as they were dressed well, but he could smell the spirits.

"I don't believe it was lost. In fact, I tied it to the tree while I went to an appointment."

"We're taking it," one said rather unwisely.

"As that's theft, I cannot allow it," Monty said.

"There's three of us," one man bragged. "You'd best run now."

This had the others laughing. Monty stayed where he was. He never went looking for trouble because someone could recognize him, which was unlikely if he was honest. The man he was and the role he played were worlds apart.

"Hand over your money, and we'll take the horse, and you can walk away while you still can," another said. "Your voice tells me you've more than enough money to buy another animal to ferry you from ballroom to ballroom."

"They have fancy carriages for that," another said.

"Is everything well here, my lord?" Monty heard Geraint say as he stepped to his side.

"Yes," Monty said.

"Still two against one." One man stepped closer.

"If you walk away now, we will not harm you. If you stay, I can make no promises," Monty said.

The men laughed. *Idiots.*

He balanced his weight on one leg and lashed out with his foot. The man fell far too quickly. Had he stumbled, then they may have engaged in more fighting.

One of the other men roared and charged him, while Geraint took the third. Monty jabbed with a fist and enjoyed the sting of pain as the blow was returned, connecting with his jaw. He then plowed his fist into the man's stomach and cheek. He fell hard. Fists clenched, Monty turned to look for another to fight.

"It is done, my lord," Geraint said, standing over the man he had clearly just dropped.

It was disappointingly swift and left him frustrated.

"My thanks," Monty snapped, sounding ungrateful. "Really, thank you," he added.

"I'm sure you had no need of my services, Lord Montgomery. I'll bid you good evening." The man bowed and walked away down the street, disappearing into the shadows.

Mounting, Monty rode away as the three men staggered to their feet and fled. He was never so angry he could kill with his bare hands. He'd been that just then, almost as if a red haze had covered his eyes. He needed to leave London and Alexius, but not until he knew if his parents' deaths were at the hands of a devil worshipper.

Not long and this hell will be over.

CHAPTER 3

*W*hen Monty returned to his town house, he went directly to his study and penned a note stating what he needed sent to London from his estate. The estate he'd lived the first thirteen years of his life at and not returned to since.

He then went to his rooms to bathe and dress.

Staring in the mirror an hour later, he watched his valet style his hair in what Zach Deville called "the dog turd look." His hair was swirled into a point in the middle of his head.

"When this is done, I'm cutting all the hair off," Monty muttered.

"But you have magnificent locks. It is simply the style that is wrong," his valet said. He carried a jacket in his hands.

Monty didn't sigh, but the thought was there. "Surely not the lavender silk again, Jensen?" He sounded like a whiny child.

When he'd gone into hiding in plain sight of every member of society, he'd taken household staff with him he'd trusted. One was his valet, Jensen.

Small, efficient, he had the energy of ten men. He, like the

Harvey family, who were also in his employ, knew the game he played and kept his secrets.

"You wore the rose two nights ago. I'm quite sure someone would notice if you did not wear lavender this evening, as it is your favorite color," Jensen said, smiling.

"Very amusing." Monty frowned. "No heels. Just black shoes."

His valet stared at him.

"No one will notice my footwear," Monty said, "and those things pinch."

"But mincing is expected of you."

"And yet, tonight I will wear the black shoes. They have large gold buckles. Surely that will suffice?"

Jensen knew that tone and did not continue the debate, instead retrieving the shoes.

"I shall put powder on your bruised chin and finish your hair," Jensen said.

"It is styled already." Monty sounded testy, something he never was.

Perhaps he should stay home this evening if this was how he was feeling? Stay home and read every book he had on Satan and devil worshippers again. He'd purchased them after what he'd discovered that night his parents were murdered. That carving he'd attempted, and failed to forget.

"I need no powder, thank you, Jensen," he said slowly. "I'll say I fell down the stairs. After all, clumsiness is expected of me, hence my name."

"As you wish," his valet said in a tone that implied it wasn't his wish to let his employer leave the house without heels and sporting a bruised chin.

Monty left the room without glancing in the mirror because he loathed looking at the man he became when he stepped into society. Contrary to what his peers felt about him, Monty was not vain. In fact, when he was here, he would walk about his house in bare feet, trousers, a shirt, and nothing else. When he left society, his hair would never be trimmed, and he'd be unshaved.

He could imagine all the tittering and shocked gasps if anyone saw him dressed any other way but how they thought he should. A fool in lace and satin.

Arriving at his front door, Monty found his butler, Haven. Tall, wide-shouldered, and a man who had the strength of ten. He had been with him for many years, as had Haven's sister, Polly, who was Monty's housekeeper, and her husband, Lenny, his driver.

"Good evening, my lord." Haven bowed, his eyes dropping to Monty's shoes when he rose.

"What?"

"They are not your usual evening footwear."

"I've worn them before," Monty said defensively.

"Then I must have missed that event."

"Very likely. These are comfortable," Monty added, looking at his feet.

His butler's eyes then went to his head.

"What now?" Monty snapped.

"Is all well with you, my lord?"

"It is an off day, Haven."

His butler smiled. "We all have those upon occasion, my lord."

"Please have someone you trust travel to my estate in Wiltshire and hand this to one of the staff. He is to then return with what I requested."

"I will see to it at once, my lord."

"Excellent. How is the foot, Haven?"

"Much improved, thank you, my lord."

As he spent much of his time locked away inside this house so prying eyes could not see him, he was usually found talking to one of his staff. They knew him well as he did them. Some nights they played cards or charades, which he was terrible at, or they sat with him and drank tea, while usually eating something superb that Polly baked.

Once, boredom had made him ask her to teach him to bake scones. They'd been passable, if he said so himself. He now baked when she'd let him in her kitchen.

"A missive has arrived for you, my lord."

He took the paper his butler held out.

"Enjoy your evening, Lord Montgomery."

"Highly unlikely, but thank you for the sentiment, Haven."

"I will have Polly leave a plate of ginger biscuits in your room."

His mouth was already watering. "I would be grateful. Forgive me for my mood."

"Not at all." The butler bowed.

Stepping out his door into the dark night once more, he headed to his carriage.

"Good evening, my lord." His driver stood with the door open.

"Good evening, Lenny."

"I learned a new card game in the stables, my lord. It's my belief you'll enjoy it."

"I'll look forward to you teaching me it tomorrow night then, Lenny."

Monty climbed inside, and the door was shut. His carriage was hideous. The door was embossed in gold with his family crest, and the seats had recently been re-covered in scarlet velvet with gold stitching. He felt ill just looking at them. The scent of lavender made him want to gag.

"Why the hell did I choose that smell to embrace?"

The carriage rolled toward the Raine town house.

Why was he so unsettled with his life now? He'd been living it for years, after all. It wasn't just because he hadn't found his parents' killers. There was more to it than that. He blamed Mary.

Mary Blake had been his only friend outside the walls of his home, as she, too, worked undercover for Alexius. Highly irregular, as she was a woman, but effective. Last year she'd married her love, a Deville brother.

The Deville family, or the men at the least, who were also members of Alexius, had found out he was living a double life. Since then, they'd become friends.

Monty prided himself on not showing emotion; he had learned to be cold and hard. He didn't get close to people, but the Devilles were persistent and had changed that.

Lately, he felt as if a few cracks were forming in his hard shell.

And that will never do. He'd learned what happened when you cared too deeply, and years of reminding himself of that had taken its toll. Monty's heart was encased in ice.

Or it had been.

He must never forget the pain of his childhood.

In the dark recesses of his mind, he knew it was foolish to think every person he cared about would be taken from him, but it was how he felt.

Staring out the window, Monty watched familiar buildings pass, feeling only dread inside him for what he must do again this evening.

Society thought him a bumbling idiot of a man. A fool in lavender and lace who minced about the place waving scented handkerchiefs. He was far from that, and a very talented actor.

Realizing he was still clutching the note Haven handed him, he turned up the lamp and opened it.

I wish only to reiterate your value to Alexius, Lord Montgomery, and acknowledge the sacrifices again that you have made. I believe, with what we have recently learned, we will find justice for your parents. It is my deepest regret we could not do so before now. It was signed Geraint.

He read the words again. Geraint never showed emotion. In fact, he was a great deal like Monty in that. It surprised him the man had taken the time to send him this.

Was what he had learned tonight really going to lead to justice for the two people he'd loved most in the world?

"I am going to ensure it does," he vowed.

Who killed my parents?

CHAPTER 4

*M*onty inhaled and exhaled several times. He then shook his gloved hands. It was a ritual he did most evenings he was to play the part of Lord Plunge.

You can do this. Just until the end of the season or your parents' killers are found.

The carriage rolled to a stop behind others, all lined up to wait their turn to alight outside the house of Lord and Lady Raine.

When the door opened, Monty stepped down with his usual pious expression in place. When he left London, he would never simper or pout again. In fact, he'd stalk about his estate scowling simply because he could.

He'd only taken a few steps when someone spoke behind him.

"Move it along there, Plunge. No need to grandstand and promenade out here. Save that for inside."

Turning, he found Mr. Zachariel Deville smirking, and Mrs. Mary Deville with a smile of welcome for him on her pretty face. *Friends,* he thought. *Something I never wanted.*

Monty bowed deeply, waving his lavender-scented handkerchief before him. "And where is it you wish for me to move along to, my dear Mr. Zachariel Deville?"

Zach was tall, like his brothers. The five Devilles were all handsome according to the women of society and—most especially—their wives. They had the look of each other in different variations. Dark hair, blue or dark brown eyes, and a wicked sense of humor they used on one another and Monty.

"Stride like a man, Plunge, instead of mincing like a lady," Zach said.

"I protest," the woman at his side said. She then elbowed her husband in the ribs hard enough to make him wince.

Monty really liked Mary.

"Hello, Lord Plunge, how wonderful you look this evening," she said, holding out her hand for him to take. "Lavender again?"

A great deal shorter than her husband, Mary was blond and sweet and had been the first friend he had after his childhood friendship with Iris, his neighbor.

The day he realized that like him, she was living two lives, Monty had been in the church talking with Geraint. A knock on the door had alerted them to a caller. Mary arrived to deliver a note from her ill father, also part of Alexius. After forcing herself inside, they'd been working together ever since.

"Thank you, Mrs. Mary Deville, but of course, I always wear lavender. It is a favorite color and scent of mine, you understand." He felt like the words were choking him tonight. They'd come out raspy, like he was forcing them through a sore throat. The news Geraint had given him today had clearly unsettled him.

Perhaps he should just go home?

Zach and Mary moved closer, so they both stood before him, creating a wall.

"Monty, what's wrong?" Mary whispered.

"Nothing. I am well, Mary."

"I don't think you are," Zach said softly, so only they could hear his words. "Now is not the place to talk more, but we will have the reason for that tight look in your eyes, my friend, and why your voice sounds off."

Good God, he felt a sting of tears at the words "my friend." Was he ailing or something? Monty could find no other explanation for what he was feeling. He was cold and hard; he didn't feel.

"Where did you get that bruise?" Mary asked, pointing to his chin.

"I fell down the stairs," Monty said.

"No, you didn't." Zach's eyes narrowed. "But that, too, will be talked about at another time."

"Something is off with you," Mary whispered.

"No, it's not," Monty protested.

"We'll get the truth from him, my love," Zach said to Mary. "On you go, Plunge, and try not to trip over my eldest brother's doorstep. But if you do, lunge to the right and take the painting on the wall down with you," Zach added, his hand gripping Monty's shoulder briefly before giving him a nudge forward.

Monty walked behind the other guests and entered the Raine town house. His eyes went to the painting of a ship in an odd gray-blue sea. He'd heard a great deal about it as the brothers loathed it, except the eldest, who Monty was sure kept it to annoy his siblings.

Monty had once vowed to live out his days in blissful solitude as soon as his parents' killers were found. No friends or wife. Strangely, that thought did not bring him the joy it usually did.

"Is there a reason you have stopped, Plunge?"

"I was taking in the ambience," he said in a credible

Plunge voice. After all, he'd played the man for years. It shouldn't be that hard.

"Ambience away, old chap," Zach said from behind him, "but join the receiving line, or we'll never get to the supper table."

He reached the top of the stairs and joined the line behind the other guests to greet the hosts.

"Ah, how lovely, another Deville," Monty said, bowing and nearly tumbling into Nathanial Deville, who stood with his wife, Beth. The man righted him. "Silly me, I nearly fell," he added. "Mrs. Deville, you look lovely this evening."

This was Deville brother number two. Monty had once played a hand in providing information to help Beth escape a nasty blackmailing plot against her foolish father.

Nathan studied him, frowning. He then shot Zach a look, who shook his head.

Brothers, Monty noted, seemed to communicate without words regularly. He wondered sometimes what his life would have been like had he a sibling. A great deal different, he was sure.

He walked slowly toward the Earl and Countess of Raine with the other guests and put aside what he'd learned today. He had a part to play this evening as he did whenever he entered society.

"What are we waiting for?" a loud voice asked.

"Oh, I don't know, Duchess, perhaps this is the receiving line, and we are awaiting our chance to greet the host, who just happens to be my brother. I assure you there will be no bowing from me."

Turning at Zach's words, he found everyone's favorite crotchety old lady, the Duchess of Yardly. Perhaps everyone's favorite was not quite true, but Monty liked her, as did the Deville family.

The woman had a sharp tongue and often turned it on

him, but for all that, she could also be nice when she thought no one was looking.

"What color is that?" Nathan asked, looking at the duchess's dress. Monty likened it to a slice of moldy bread. Not quite white, or green, or even gray, but a mix of all three.

"Where did your modiste find that material?" Mary asked.

"I'm thinking tucked far away in a cupboard marked, 'nobody has a use for it,'" Zach added.

The duchess wore two necklaces laden with rubies and sapphires around her wrinkled neck. Rings adorned each of her fingers.

"You look exquisite," Monty said, bowing.

"No, she doesn't," Zach said. "What is on your head, Duchess?"

"It's a turban," she snapped. "Which you'd know if you had style, boy!"

"Well, someone hit me over the head with a large piece of wood should I ever have a brush with your style," Zach said.

The duchess tittered as did most of the other guests. The woman could not be insulted, especially by a Deville, who had adopted her as part of their family. Sort of the grandmother you never wanted but had been forced on you, Monty thought. She'd come when Dimity had joined the family.

"I say, you don't have a book on you, do you, Duchess?" Monty said loudly.

"As it happens—"

"No!" Nathan and Zach roared in unison.

Monty bit back a snort that he'd managed to get under their skin. Clearly, they were rubbing off on him. Looking beyond the people closest, Monty scanned the guests, all waiting like him to enter the ballroom after greeting their hosts. That was when he found her.

A woman was standing beside an older man. The man

was Lord Stilton, his childhood friend Iris's uncle. He'd avoided him since he'd entered society as Plunge because he had no wish to see the disappointment in the eyes of the man who had once read to him and asked him what his dreams were. None of which he'd fulfilled.

He looked at the woman again. Her hair was dark, and she wasn't overly tall. The top of her head came to Lord Stilton's ear. Monty could not see all of her, but her dress was the color of his jacket. He studied her again and realized in that moment exactly who she was, just as he knew she was the woman he'd seen in that carriage earlier.

Iris, his childhood friend. Her eyes caught his, and she nodded before turning away. Monty did the same. Two shocks in one day. It was amazing his heart did not give out.

"What?" Zach whispered in his left ear.

"What?"

"You're clutching your chest."

"I'm Lord Plunge. That is expected of me." He looked at Iris again but saw only the back of her head as she had turned to speak with someone.

He moved along the receiving line, wondering why she was here in London now, when she had never entered society with her husband, Lord Challoner, before his death over a year ago.

"I'm not bowing to him," Nathan said, drawing Monty's attention back from Iris. "I will to Dimity, however."

"How rude. Allow me to acknowledge as is correct, my lord," Monty simpered, bowing deep enough to please the king, "how grand you both look this evening, and—"

"Yes, yes, move it along, Plunge. We do not have all night, and a long line of people to meet," Gabe said. He then winked.

"May I compliment you on your beauty this evening, Lady Raine," Monty said, taking Dimity's hand.

"Just tonight?" She allowed him to kiss her fingers.

"Always." He smiled.

"Very well. You may enter the ballroom then." Dimity wore deep emerald, and the color was stunning on her. But then, the countess could wear a sack and look beautiful.

"Nathan, I insist you bow again," Dimity said. "That was not as low as Lord Plunge's."

Nathan muttered something that no one in polite society should hear. Smiling, Monty entered the ballroom.

It was ablaze with color and noise. Guests he knew well chatted and laughed. Music played. It did not impress him. Not much did these days.

CHAPTER 5

*I*ris put her hand on Uncle Robert's arm. He patted it gently.

"There now, nothing to be concerned about."

"I beg to differ, Uncle. I have never entered society and am not acquainted with anyone in it. I'm unsure why I let you and Aunt Margo talk me into this, as it's terrifying."

"You are out of mourning, and it's best for Henry that you enter society before he is old enough to do so, so you understand what one day he will be part of. Plus, you cannot stay hidden in the country forever. You are a beautiful, intelligent young woman. There may be another man in your future."

Absolutely not!

"I will not marry again, but I concede, for Henry's sake, that it will go easier for him if I make the acquaintance of a few noble families before I run back to my hiding place in the country."

He chuckled.

"I would far rather be home with Aunt Margo and Henry, eating cake and playing cards, however."

"Just a few hours, niece." He patted her hand as they shuffled forward in the receiving line.

Those around her were dressed beautifully, with their hair done perfectly and their jewelry sparkling on fingers and around necks and wrists.

"Some of these people are very nice, Iris, I promise you," Uncle Robert said.

She intercepted a few questioning gazes, wondering who she was. A woman appearing in society for the first time was, she was sure, rare.

Her eyes encountered the man dressed in lavender again. He'd nodded to her, and Iris had returned the gesture. His hair was styled oddly compared to those around him, and his lavender silk jacket was again at odds with the other men in more somber colors. She studied his face and then felt everything inside her still.

"It can't be," she whispered.

"What's that, dear?" Uncle Robert leaned in to hear her.

"I—that man, Uncle."

His eyes found who she was looking at. They could see only his side profile now.

Uncle Robert made a tsking sound. "Yes. That's Theodore Montgomery, your old neighbor. Do you remember him, Iris? You two were friends. He was a wonderful young boy, full of life, but I fear he has changed a great deal in the years since you've seen him. No doubt losing his parents played a hand in that," Uncle Robert said.

"Tell me about him, Uncle. How has he changed?"

"Your aunt and I do not frequent society often, but gossip still reaches us, and much of it is about him. He has turned into quite the spectacle, I'm sorry to say, Iris. The butt of many society jokes. They call him Lord Plunge, as he often falls into the water."

Everything inside her rebelled at what her uncle was

saying. Not Theo. Sure-footed, adventurous, and smart. He'd been that and so much more as a child.

Seeing as we are friends, Iris, we will marry, as I could not marry anyone who was silly, he'd once said to her.

"Very well, if you insist" had been her reply.

She could still remember that conversation, as it had taken place two days before Theo's parents, Lord and Lady Montgomery, were murdered. The day Theo's life had been torn apart.

"'Tis sad to see what he has become," her uncle said. "But after what he endured, I understand much changed for the poor boy we once knew. It is not our place to judge."

Iris thought about the letter she had brought with her to London for Theo. It had been the catalyst to her agreeing to enter society. The contents had horrified her, and she felt he should be the only one to read it.

"Dear lord, Theo," she whispered. *What has become of you?*

"Lord Raine, Lady Raine, please allow me to introduce my niece to you. Lady Iris Challoner," her uncle said, drawing her attention back to her surroundings.

The woman before her was stunning, with thick black hair and a face that could only be described as beautiful. She wore a deep emerald dress. The man at her side was her equal. Handsome, intimidating, and noble.

"Hello," the lady said. "How lovely to meet someone new, when usually we are faced with the same people night after night."

The words surprised Iris into a nervous laugh, which she muffled behind her hand.

"Good evening to you." She sank into a curtsy.

"Charming," Lord Raine said. "I hope you are not yet bored with me, my love?"

"No." Lady Raine gave her husband a soft smile. "You I will keep."

"Excellent." He touched her cheek before turning back to face Iris and her uncle. "It is lovely to make your acquaintance, Lady Challoner."

This was a man like her husband. He'd been born into a title and exuded power. But unlike the late Lord Challoner, it seemed he was a great deal nicer and actually liked his wife. Looking at her again, Iris doubted that, unlike her, Lady Raine had ever cowed to anyone a day in her life.

"I shall find you later and introduce you to my family," Lady Raine said. "Then point out the poisonous members of society you need to avoid."

"Thank you," Iris said, unsure what else to add to that as the words had surprised her.

"There, now wasn't that nice. Lady Raine is one of society's leading ladies and highly regarded by many. She was once a companion to that crotchety old Duchess of Yardly. Now, you mark my words, niece, that old virago is someone to avoid."

"Point her out to me, Uncle Robert, so I know what she looks like." Iris would ensure she kept her distance from the woman.

"I'm sure someone will tell you, so you may as well hear it from me," her uncle continued. "Lady Raine was actually French nobility and is now married to an earl."

"You're not serious?" He could be quite the joker when he wanted to be.

"Deadly. If you make friends with her, you will be quite at ease in no time."

"I plan to only go to a handful of events, Uncle. I am not here to make friends."

"But won't that be a pleasant side benefit?" he added.

Uncle Robert, like Aunt Margo, was the only family who had really seen how she suffered. She'd tried to tell her parents what her life was like. After the first night, her husband had struck her for speaking out about something. Her father had said that her husband was the head of the household, therefore, given time, she would adjust. Her mother had said nothing.

She had an elder sister, but at the time, Margaret had just had her first child, so Iris had not talked to her about what was going on behind the closed doors of the Challoner household. Instead, she'd dealt with it her own way, in silence.

Iris allowed her uncle to lead her into a large ballroom. Noise came from all corners of the room. Her aunt had schooled her on what she'd see and how to behave, but it was still intimidating.

"I wish Aunt Margo had come."

"She will be with us for the next one, Iris," Uncle Robert said. "Would you like a glass of champagne to calm your nerves?"

"That would be lovely, thank you."

"I see a footman just a few feet away. I will procure some and return."

"And I will have my eyes on you the entire time," she told her uncle.

He left with a smile and wound through a few guests to where a waiter stood.

"Good evening."

She didn't visibly shudder, but it was there when she turned to face her late husband's brother.

"Mr. Renton." She sank into a curtsy.

"Come, Iris, we are family. No need to be so formal. Call me Loftus." His smile was revolting, just as his brother's had been. Once she had been fooled by it, but no more.

Loftus Renton was her late husband's younger brother and almost identical to look at. Not overly tall, with a solid build, he had brown hair and eyes too close together. She loathed him.

"We are not family," she said slowly. "We are, in fact, nothing to each other. Further to that, I will not let you near me or my son again. Do not try to enter my house again, as it will go worse for you." This man would intimidate her no more. She was freed from his brother's brutal grip. She would never allow a man to control her in such a way again.

His eyes narrowed, and the pleasant facade faded to be replaced by anger.

"I am your brother-in-law. It is my duty to care for you," he hissed so only she could hear. "Your son is young. Therefore, you and he need my guidance until he is old enough to run his affairs."

"Is that what you choose to call what you did to me three weeks after I came out of mourning?" Iris scoffed. "Guidance? You tried to kiss me, and yelled at my son."

"You have no family but two elderly relatives. It is my duty to my brother to step in and care for both you and Henry." His face was red with anger and now inches from hers. She knew the signs. The Renton brothers could easily fly into a rage. But she would be cowed no more.

"You tried to take advantage of me and then hit my son. Now leave before I scream, because let me assure you that I care nothing about what these people think of me, but you, however, do."

Anger snapped and crackled in the air between them as he leaned into her space. She shot a look at her uncle. He would return soon, and she wanted Renton gone by then. Iris would not allow him to insult her Uncle Robert.

"I will get what I want." His words were a growl. "I am the head of this family. It is my right to go through my late brother's things, just as it is my right to guide you and your son."

Iris did not back away. "You will not intimidate me like your brother did. I will care for my son until he is of an age where he can do so himself. I have a family who can help me, but you are not that. Stay away from us."

His hand shot out and wrapped around her wrist, gripping it hard. She would not make a noise or show him her fear. She'd done that with her husband for years.

Sydney Renton had controlled her by threatening to harm her son. It had been effective, and she'd yielded. She no longer had to do so. This man was nothing to her.

"Hello!"

They both turned at the loud greeting, and there stood Theodore Montgomery. Once her best friend, now a stranger.

"Go away, Plunge," Renton said.

CHAPTER 6

"*My* dearest Lady Challoner! It has been so long. I believe I was but thirteen when last we met?"

"Lord Montgomery," Iris said with a forced smile. "Yes, it has been overlong." She tried to shake free of the grip Loftus Renton still had on her wrist but failed.

"And, Mr. Renton, good evening to you as well." Theo's smile was wide and made him look a bit simple if she was being honest.

"Go away, Plunge. My sister-in-law and I have things to discuss," Renton said, his fingers tightening and making her wince. She didn't want a scene. He wouldn't hurt her here. Iris had to remember that.

"Oh, but you would not be so cruel," Theo begged. "It has been many years since I saw my dear childhood friend. We must reacquaint ourselves. Come, my dear lady, walk with me. There is much to discuss. Do you like my jacket? It is the finest Indian silk, you know."

Iris looked at the arm he held out. The material really was rather beautiful, even if the color surprised her. She'd never have thought Theo would wear such a thing, but then time and circumstance changed most people. She placed her fingers on it, eager to get away from Loftus.

"Let her go, Renton, as I wish to show my dear old friend off," Theo said in a voice a great deal deeper than it had been just moments ago. Looking at him, she saw his silly smile was still in place. Had she imagined that?

"Hurry it up, Renton. We have people to meet." Theo looked at the hand that still gripped her wrist. Loftus released her.

"Good evening, Mr. Renton. I hope not to see you again." She leaned in to whisper, "Keep your distance from me and my son in the future."

"I will have what I want," he snarled, reaching for her again. Iris wasn't sure how it happened, but seconds later, Loftus was stumbling back and fell, landing on his rear at the feet of a lady who squawked like a chicken.

"Oh dear, perhaps you have overimbibed, Renton, and so early in the evening," Theo tittered, peering down at the man. "Sir Hugh, would you be so kind as to help Mr. Renton to his feet? I fear I do not have the strength, and this coat is, you know, extremely fitted. I would not want to tear the seams."

Iris watched Theo give the man she now knew was Sir Hugh a simpering smile. He then led her away toward her uncle.

"Thank you, Theo," Iris said, feeling the tight knot of fear inside her ease with distance between her and that nasty man. She loathed the Renton brothers, and it was beneath her, but she was glad one of them was dead. Her husband.

"My name is Lord Plunge."

"No, it's not." She shot him a look. "It's Theo, or Lord Montgomery."

"But here in London, my dear Lady Challoner, it is Lord Plunge," he said in a silly voice.

"I know it is many years since we saw each other, Theo—"

"So very many," he said. "Why, I barely recognized you."

"I recognized you," Iris said, unsure why she was hurt by his words when she'd been ten years old the last time they saw each other. They'd both changed beyond recognition since then. She certainly had.

"I've grown up, and exceptionally well, don't you think, my dear?"

She shot him a look. His face didn't hold a silly grin now. In fact, his jaw was clenched.

"Very well. Are you all right, Theo?"

"Of course. Why would I not be?" he shouted. "Why, I am one of society's brightest lights."

"Well, that's good then," she said, struggling to find anything else suitable to say. They had been friends and now no longer were. In fact, they were strangers. The thought saddened her.

She looked for her uncle and found him making his way toward her and Theo.

"Good evening, Lord Montgomery." Uncle Robert bowed.

"Good evening," Theo said. "I am taking your niece to introduce her to society."

"And does she wish to be introduced?" Her uncle looked at her.

"Yes, I am quite happy. Thank you, I shall return to you shortly."

"I shall follow. I just need to speak with Mr. Christopher," her uncle said. "Take good care of her, my lord."

"But of course," Theo said, adding a silly titter.

She'd known he'd changed. You didn't go through what he had and not. But she'd not expected him to become the man he had.

Iris let Theo lead her through the guests, stopping to

introduce her as his dear childhood friend. He made silly faces and laughed loudly.

What happened to him?

"Theo—"

"I am Lord Plunge," he said.

"Why are you called that silly name?" Surely her uncle had not been right about the reason.

He looked at her; his dark eyes no longer held the empty expression they had seconds ago. In fact, for a moment, his entire face changed, and she wasn't sure what she saw there. Then he blinked, and his expression was silly again.

"Why, because I constantly *plunge* into water," he said.

"You never used to be clumsy."

"We all change over time." His words had a snap to them.

"I will call you Lord Montgomery or Theo."

"We are no longer familiar with each other. I insist you call me Lord Plunge."

"I don't think so." He made a small disapproving noise.

Iris had seen the expressions on the faces of people who saw Theo coming. All had a resigned or annoyed look. Clearly, he was not liked by many. That saddened her more because the boy he'd been was loved by everyone who met him. Even at a young age, he'd been charismatic, like his parents.

They had nothing in common now, and there was discomfort between them, when once they had finished each other's sentences and been like brother and sister.

He stopped before a group of people, and Theo introduced her to everyone. She noted one of the couples was Lord and Lady Raine, who had clearly slipped away from their receiving line.

"Plunge." The earl scowled.

"Good evening, Devilles," Theo shouted. "This is dear

Lady Challoner, an old childhood friend. She is entering society for the first time."

"Well now, you have my sympathies that Plunge was your old friend," the other man introduced as Zachariel Deville said. "One can only imagine the clothing he wore as a boy."

"He was quite normal actually," Iris felt compelled to say, which produced snorts of disbelief in those closest.

"Plunge normal? I'm not sure he knows the meaning of the word."

Theo moved slightly, and then Zachariel Deville was grunting.

"Oh dear, do forgive me, Mr. Zachariel Deville!" Theo cried. "I stood directly on your foot."

"Really? I hadn't noticed," the other man said, wincing.

"Excellent," Theo said loudly before walking away without another word and leaving her with the Deville family.

Iris followed him with her eyes and saw that one of his hands was clenched in a fist. What path had his life taken since she'd last seen him to bring him to the man he was today?

"Come and chat with us, Lady Challoner. You will have intelligent, lively conversation then." Lady Raine took her hand and tugged her into the female circle. Iris turned from watching Theo.

"Harsh but true," her husband said.

Iris was then introduced to the other ladies, and soon they were chatting. They all seemed pleasant, and she felt herself relax.

"I understand you are an old friend of Lord Plunge's?" Mrs. Mary Deville said, moving to Iris's side. Blonde, pretty. She was married to Zachariel Deville.

"I was, yes."

"I should imagine you have seen a change in him, and not just his age?" she said, watching Iris intently.

"We were children when last we met, so yes, he was bound to have changed, as have I."

"He is... he is a good man for all his silliness," Mary Deville said slowly. "Were you close?"

She nodded. "He was my best friend," Iris said softly.

"Well then, perhaps you should pay him a call and see if you can reinstate that friendship," Mary said. She then turned to answer a question someone asked of her.

Iris would not be in London long enough to make friends again with Theo. In fact, she wondered, considering the man he'd become, if that was even possible.

How could the boy she'd admired and, yes, adored with a girlish fervor change so much? Iris thought that she'd like very much to know the answer but doubted she ever would.

CHAPTER 7

*M*onty kept his smile in place and walked. He nodded to people who looked his way. Most ignored him, which he did not mind. He had no wish to converse with anyone as his mood, at best, could be termed feral.

Stepping through the open terrace doors, he turned right and went down the stairs into the Raine gardens.

Iris was here. He'd believed she would never enter society. Her husband had told everyone she had a weak constitution, and London, with all its social events, would be too much for her.

And yet here she is a year after his passing.

Seeing her should not have unsettled him, but in truth, he'd already been off-balance since he'd spoken with Geraint.

"Were I really the type to have vapors, now would be the perfect time," Monty muttered, heading down a path lit with torches. He hoped not many had ventured out here yet. He needed a minute to himself.

Finding a small bench seat at the base of a wall that the

Raine family no doubt sat in to bask in their familial love, he thought a few minutes there would clear his head.

Excellent. Not only was he unsettled, but he was also now bitter and jealous. Dropping onto the seat in a very unPlunge-like manner, he inhaled the London air.

The gardens weren't huge by some standards, but they were big enough to offer him a moment of solitude before he had to start waving his lavender-scented handkerchief about and making a fool of himself.

"You said she'd never enter society."

The words drifted to Monty from behind the wall he sat against.

"Lady Challoner will not be a problem. My brother controlled her, as will I."

They were talking about Iris.

"She did not look like she wished to be controlled when I saw you confront her in the ballroom. It is imperative Challoner's papers are found and handed back to me."

One man was Renton. He'd know that weasel's voice anywhere. The man had been insulting him for years. Monty had a list of people he'd one day like to punch. Renton and his late brother had been near the top.

The bastard had been hurting Iris when Monty had reached her. He'd not overheard the discussion between her and Renton but had noted the body language. Iris had been furious, but there had been fear, too, in her lovely brown eyes.

Monty's leg trip had worked, forcing the man to the floor in humiliation as repayment for hurting his sister-in-law.

"She will be no problem and knows nothing," Renton added. "Nothing will jeopardize what we are."

"Make sure she isn't. We had to go underground once. I have no wish to do so again. You told us you would have access to your late brother's affairs and find those papers. See that you do so at once. Your brother has been gone over a year now."

"They were in mourning, and my brother always kept his study locked. The room will not have been disturbed, and I will find what we need," Renton said. "I have told her I will guide her and Henry from now on, as my late brother would have wished. She will present no problem. I will control her as Sydney did."

"And yet she stopped you and us from entering the house in Sussex."

"They had just come out of mourning. Give them time. I will see it done," Renton said.

"Go to his place in the country now she is no longer in residence," the other man said. "I want those papers found. Challoner kept them bound with a black silk ribbon."

"I will leave soon."

"Deal with this, Renton, or I will. Your brothers will be watching you and your sister-in-law. Ensure she presents no threat to us. I will have no one stopping us now."

The sound of rustling had Monty moving. He hurried back along the path and then slipped behind a tree. Soon Renton appeared with a man at his side, but Monty could not make out his features in the dark as Iris's former brother-in-law shielded him.

Did he know that other voice? There was something that niggled at his memory.

Waiting until the men disappeared back inside, Monty followed. Was Iris in danger? First Renton had threatened her in the ballroom, and now this. The man had mentioned brothers, but Monty knew Renton and Challoner were the only siblings in their family. What had that conversation been about?

"Is there a reason you are lurking out here?"

A shadow before him morphed into Michael Deville. He sat under Nathan in the brother lineup.

"Hardly lurking, just taking air."

"Is there no air inside, then?"

"Amusing."

"Mary actually sent me to find you. She said something is off with you, and she can't send Zach, as he would stop to talk with seven people on the way."

"Only seven?"

"Gabe is doing his host duty, and Nathan is deep in conversation with someone about something, so she was stuck with me as I was standing looking handsome in all my manliness," Michael added.

"I've always thought Gabe the most handsome," Monty said. He was getting the hang of this brothers' teasing thing. Not that he wanted to, he reminded himself. No connections. He was leaving London soon.

The only problem with that if he was honest, if only to himself, was that he would miss these people who only recently entered his life. They'd accepted him without question and even protected and defended him when required. And then, of course, there was Mary. His sister in every way but blood.

He'd tried to keep his distance and failed.

"What's going on, Monty?"

"Nothing."

"That's a lie. I know you have only recently encountered your old friend Lady Challoner, so it cannot be her entirely, but clearly seeing her has unsettled you," Michael said.

"I have no wish to discuss this further, as anyone could chance upon us here." He went for his cold, hard tone.

"That tone doesn't bother me, Monty. You know who my brothers are. They can cut a man to shreds with their tongues. You will need to try a great deal harder than that."

Monty sighed. Insulting a Deville was like holding water in your hands—a fruitless task.

"Two questions, and then we return to the ballroom," Michael added. "One. Are you in any danger?"

"What? No, why would you ask that?" *At least, he didn't think he was in danger.*

"Two, is this mood related to Alexius or Iris Challoner?" Michael added.

"In part, both."

"Which frustratingly just fills my head with more questions. I should have said four questions."

"Perhaps you are not the most intelligent Deville brother after all?" Monty said.

"Now we both know that is untrue. For now, I will leave it, because I know you are not in danger. Let us know when we can visit, and you can tell us everything."

"Perhaps I have no wish to tell you everything."

Michael snorted. "I think we've explained to you how this friendship thing works, Monty. Don't try to avoid us."

"As you wish," Monty said, feeling calmer and knowing that was because the Devilles had yet again shown him they cared, as did he.

He'd tried to convince himself he didn't want to care, but Monty had been alone for so long. Until now, he'd not realized just how lonely he actually was.

He walked back inside with Michael Deville following and entered the ballroom smiling his Plunge smile. Strained and forced.

Searching the room, he first looked for Renton, and then Iris. The conversation he'd overheard filtered back through his head. Why had Renton said he wanted to control her? The entire conversation had left Monty concerned for Iris.

She'd been his childhood friend as he'd been hers. Yes,

that was many years ago, but he still remembered and felt something for the girl she had once been.

He found her dancing. She moved with elegance and grace, a fact her partner, Lord Burton, seemed appreciative of. As did others watching.

"I say, Plunge."

He raised a hand as if Sir Nigel simply wished to acknowledge him.

"Come here, you fool," the man added.

"No need to be rude, Nigel," Mary said. He hadn't noticed her standing next to her mother and sister.

Monty wondered who Phillipa was hunting for as her future husband, now all the Devilles were taken.

"Rude?" Nigel scoffed. "The man wouldn't know rude if he tripped over it in those ridiculous heels he wears. Would you, Plunge?" He scoffed loudly, making those around him laugh.

Mary got a certain look in her eyes when she was angry and about to seek retribution on someone. He saw it pass across her face.

"What is it you want, Sir Nigel?" Monty bowed deeply and schooled his features as the man drew closer.

He was everything Monty loathed about society. Rich, indolent, and obnoxious.

"I have heard you and Lady Challoner are old friends. Hard as that is for any of us to understand, considering—"

"Nigel, was that you yesterday I saw taking a tumble in the park? It appeared to me and my twin sisters that you tripped over your feet," Lord Sinclair said. He was standing with his brother-in-law, the Duke of Raven, and had clearly overheard the conversation.

"What? Not me, Sinclair," Nigel scoffed.

"Well, I wonder who else is called Nigel then and has your face, because the lady you were walking with screamed your name," Lord Sinclair added. "God save us all if there are two of you."

Nigel made a noise a turkey would be proud of, but he did not retreat. Instead, he angled his body slightly, so Lord Sinclair was now behind him. Not a direct snub. The man was not brave enough to do that. Sinclair was connected to some powerful men.

"Introduce me."

"To whom?" Monty asked, wide-eyed.

"Lady Challoner, you fool. Woman's a widow, from what I hear has money—"

The anger was swift and surprised him. It seemed Monty was, in fact, protective of his childhood friend.

"This is our dance, Lord Plunge," Mary said, holding out her hand. Clearly, she had seen his anger. "I must drag you from Sir Nigel's scintillating company."

"As you can imagine," Monty simpered, "I am desolate." He stepped forward, stumbled, and rammed his shoulder into Nigel's chest, sending him backward.

"Oh dear, begging your pardon." While the man's friends rushed to pick him up off the floor, he walked away with Mary.

"What's going on?" Mary said as he swung her into his arms for the first waltz of the evening.

"I thought you had to dance all these with your husband?" Monty said.

"You're the exception."

"As you can imagine, I am flattered," he said.

"Yes, yes, no need for sarcasm. Now talk. What's going on with you, and why do you have flat shoes on your large feet?"

"The heels pinch," he said, sounding like a child again.

"I'm sure they do, but as you've been having them pinch you for years, I'm wondering why the change now?"

A wave of exhaustion swept over Monty. Like he was at

least one hundred years old and had been awake for three weeks.

"Monty, talk to me."

He looked into the face of the woman who had become his friend when he hadn't realized how much he'd needed one. He'd always believed he was a lone wolf, but Mary had made him question that.

"I can't talk here. But there are things afoot, it's true. Things I will tell you. I promise."

"What things?" Her brows rose as she studied him. He knew that powerful brain of hers would be hard at work, forming and dismissing thoughts, trying to work out what he wasn't telling her.

"What part of 'I can't talk here,' did you not understand?" Monty smiled as he muttered the words.

She harrumphed, which she'd perfected by listening to the Duchess of Yardly.

"She's nice, your Iris."

Monty was usually used to Mary's conversational changes, but this one took him a few seconds.

"Lady Challoner is not *my* anything. We were friends as children. I haven't seen her since she was ten years old."

"She told me you were her best friend, but that you were nothing like you are now."

He felt a stab of pain in the region of his heart and ignored it. "I was thirteen when we last saw each other, Mary. Even if I was not playing the idiot I am, I would still be a great deal different."

"You're tense. You're never tense."

"Conversing with you is exhausting," Monty said.

"Why are you tense?"

One thing that had set Mary in good stead to be part of the male-dominated world of Alexius was her tenacity. Usually, he was proud of it. Tonight, he wanted to shake her.

"I have had a few things happen today that, as I have stated, I will not discuss now. Please accept that and shut up." The words were delivered with a smile.

"What things?"

As her husband danced by with his sister-in-law, Lady Raine, Monty stopped beside them.

"Your wife pines for you, my dear sir!" Releasing Mary, he maneuvered her into her husband's arms and took Dimity into his.

"Do you know, Lord Plunge," Dimity said, looking him in the eye, "my husband told me appearances regarding you are not always as they seem."

In a short space of time, Monty's life was suddenly extremely complicated, and each day becoming more so.

"My dear lady, I have no idea what you speak of." He decided denial was his best tactic until he could speak to the Devilles and ask why they were talking about him to their wives.

"Had I bothered to really look at you before now, and past the silly, simpering fool—"

"I do believe that hurt." Monty pouted.

She snorted.

"You look magnificent this evening, my lady. New modiste?" Monty was excellent at directing conversations away from anything he usually had no wish to discuss.

"No. Now, as I was saying. You seem off somehow. Not your usual jolly, empty-headed self."

Correction, he was *usually* good at directing conversations. It was those bloody Devilles again. Everything in his life had changed since he'd let them in.

"I assure you I am as I have always been," he said with a smile that he was sure looked more like a snarl.

"Lady Challoner, or Iris as she asked me to call her, is very nice," Dimity said, and he exhaled at the change in conversation. "I have a feeling she will become friends with the Devilles."

"I wonder if I should warn her to run now," Monty said before he could stop himself.

Dimity laughed softly. "Well, well, well, Lord Plunge. I do believe my husband was correct. There is more to Lord Plunge than we see."

"I assure you there isn't."

"You and I are going to become excellent friends." Monty looked at her smug smile and thought he should either be happy she thought him a friend or run for the hills. The woman could be terrifying.

CHAPTER 8

"*A*llow me to introduce you to Mr. James, niece."

Iris curtsied to the man with thick black hair and a nice smile who her uncle had brought to meet her.

"My lady, would you honor me with a dance?"

She'd known that dancing was likely to happen. Iris had just not wanted to participate, and she most definitely did not want to waltz. The thought of being held by a man made her uneasy.

Some people she'd met were nice, and until this moment, she'd been enjoying herself in conversation with the Deville family. They were loud, funny, and she thought could become her friends. Not that she planned to stay in London long, but while she did, it would be nice to see them again. They'd also said their children would love to meet Henry. As her son had not spent much time with other children, Iris thought she'd like for that to happen too.

"Is your dance card full, niece?"

She looked at the card hanging around her wrist and knew it was, in fact, empty. Iris couldn't exactly say she didn't want to dance with the man without a valid reason.

"No, Uncle, and of course I would love to dance."

Mr. James smiled. "Well then, would now be too soon?" He held out his arm.

"Do you not wish to dance?" Beth Deville leaned in to whisper. "I'll plead a torn hem and that you need to accompany me if you wish it."

"I am well, but thank you, Beth." Iris put the tips of her gloved fingers on the man's arm and allowed him to lead her to the floor. She took her place in the line across from Mr. James, relieved it was not a waltz.

"Are you really a friend of that fool Plunge's?" The words came from a woman to her left.

She was younger than Iris and pretty. Her dress of cream silk was in the latest style, and her deep brown hair was pinned in place with small pearls.

"We were once friends, yes. My name is Lady Challoner."

"Well, let me advise you to sever all ties with the man. He's a bumbling idiot." She gave a delicate shudder. "He offers very little other than he has a lot of money. One day, some woman will look past his ridiculous facade and take him on. However"—she sniffed—"it will not be me."

The music started, so the conversation stopped, and Iris still did not know the woman's name, but her words had left a sour taste in her mouth. She did not like to hear Theo spoken of in such a way, even though they were now strangers.

She found him dancing farther down the line and watched as he tugged the right cuff of his jacket with his left hand twice. He then lowered the hand to his side. Seconds later, he repeated the gesture.

Why is it you do that, Theo? she'd once asked him after seeing the gesture several times in their youth.

He'd been uncomfortable about her question, but as they were always honest with each other, he had answered. "It helps me focus when I am unsure what to say, or of the situation" had been his reply.

Iris remembered being surprised by his words because she'd always thought Theo was confident.

Theo's head turned as if sensing her regard. Their eyes met, and she felt it again. Awareness shot through her. That look had none of the silliness she'd seen from him this evening. It had been hard and searching.

What was going on with that man?

She lost sight of him briefly as they turned to the music.

"Allow me to offer my sympathies for the loss of your husband, Lady Challoner. He was a well-respected member of society," Mr. James said. "I'm sure you feel his loss greatly."

"Thank you," she said with a small fake smile.

"Are you staying for the entire season, my lady?" he asked.

"I am unsure yet."

Some would say he was handsome. Iris would not be one of those. She'd vowed, when she was finally rid of the devil she'd married, never to wed again. Her future was her son, and that was more than enough.

"It's my hope you are, Lady Challoner." His smile showed his interest in her this time.

"I spend all my time with my son," she said. "He, of course, is my focus after losing his beloved father."

The man's face fell. She was lying, of course. Henry loathed his father, just as she had.

When the dance was over, Mr. James escorted her back to her uncle, who still stood with some of the Deville family members who were not dancing.

"Would you allow me to take you to supper, my lady?" Mr. James asked. It seemed she had not done enough to dissuade him.

"It's her first social event, James. Don't overwhelm the

woman," Lord Raine said with a smile to take the sting out of his words.

"Of course." Mr. James bowed, looking disappointed, and walked away.

"Thank you, my lord."

"If anyone bothers you, Iris, let me or one of my family know," he said. "And call me Gabe."

"Thank you, Gabe. That is very kind of you, but I will not be in London long enough to find trouble."

"I'm sure you are right."

"So, you and Plunge," Mr. Zachariel Deville said. "What was he like as a child because I can't imagine him in anything but lavender?"

Yet more questions about Theo. Most people were either horrified that she'd been his childhood friend or interested to know what he was like.

"Lord Montgomery was a good friend. We were just children. I have not seen him since I was ten."

"Well then, you must take the time to become reacquainted."

Some of these Devilles did not seem to pity or dislike Theo like the guests she'd encountered.

"My dear sister-in-law, I insist you dance with me." Loftus Renton placed a hand on her back. She had not seen him approach. It was instinct that had her moving closer to Zachariel Deville. She landed on his foot.

"I beg your pardon."

"No harm done." He smiled gently down at her. "You weigh nothing. Renton." Zachariel Deville then gave her former brother-in-law a curt nod. "Most people ask to dance with a request, not an order. You should try it."

The horrid man laughed, but it did not reach his eyes, which he kept locked on her.

"Iris and I understand each other. Don't we, my dear sister?"

"Former sister-in-law," Iris clarified. Was it her imagination or had the temperature chilled in the last few seconds? Looking from her uncle to Gabe, who he had been chatting with, and lastly to Zachariel, she saw they were all giving openly hostile looks to Loftus. Clearly, she was not the only one who loathed this man.

"Come along, Iris." Loftus Renton held out his hand to her.

"No thank you," she said.

He laughed, as if she'd made a joke. No one else joined him.

"I believe you heard the lady, Renton. She has no wish to dance," Gabriel Deville said.

"My dear Lady Challoner!" Theo called as he arrived. He stumbled into Loftus, sending him lurching backward. "Oh dear, please forgive me, Renton!"

"You idiot!" Loftus Renton roared. Righting himself, he raised his fist at Theo. "That is the second time this evening you've run into me!"

"That will do," Mr. Zachariel Deville said, stepping between Theo and her former brother-in-law. "He did not mean it."

Loftus bared his teeth.

"Yes, it was an accident," Theo said, looking hurt. "I hope you do not believe otherwise, my dear Mr. Renton?"

"Come, Iris," Renton snapped, holding out his hand.

"Oh dear," Theo said loudly.

"What?" Loftus demanded.

"My name is on dear Lady Challoner's dance card. We are childhood friends and have not had a chance to converse for more than a few minutes. I thought a waltz would change that. After all, I'm sure she wishes to bask in the magnificence of what I have become," Theo added.

"Which is why I said no thank you, Mr. Renton," Iris lied. She placed her fingers on Theo's arm, and he led her away.

"Can you waltz?" he asked her loudly.

"I can, yes. Are you hard of hearing, Theo?"

"My name is Lord Plunge." He shot her a look.

"I am not calling you that silly name."

"It is my name."

"No, it is Lord Montgomery."

"You have not walked in society. I have been called Lord Plunge for many years." His tone was haughty, but he didn't look at her, and she could feel the tension in the arm she held.

"So, are you hard of hearing?" Iris asked him again.

"What?" This time he shot her a look. "Why would you ask such a thing?"

"You yell when you speak."

"I do not yell," he said, doing just that.

"Is that you not yelling?"

His lip twitched, but he said nothing. He then swung her into his arms. Iris placed her hand on his shoulder. One of his went to her back. Theo took her hand in his. Large and warm, even through the silk of his evening gloves, his fingers encased hers.

That odd little shiver of awareness traveled through her as she felt the hard planes of his body briefly before she put some distance between them.

"Will you tell me of your life, Lord Montgomery? How was Eton? I thought of you often."

"I have long forgotten my time there, and as you can see, my life is exactly as I wish it to be." Those words did not sound like he was happy. In fact, they were clipped and icy.

"My sister has two children," Iris said when he did not speak again. "Nieces. Ellery and Anna. They are wonderful."

His eyes looked down at her again, then away.

"My parents have passed."

"I know. Allow me to say how sorry I am about their deaths," he said. His jaw muscles were bunched again.

"Thank you. We miss them very much."

She felt like there were more than a few inches between them. In fact, it was the entire channel between England and France. So many years and things had happened to each of them, and she had no idea how to talk to this man who was now a stranger to her.

CHAPTER 9

$\mathcal{M}$onty stared at the ledger before him three days after the ball where he'd seen Iris again. The numbers were a blur. He wondered why now his life had taken another turn. As if all this business with Ackland and his father's name being on that list wasn't unsettling enough, seeing Iris had added to that. She was from his past, and with her came memories of his parents, and a life he'd loved.

Seeing her again had stirred something deep inside Monty that hadn't stirred for a long time. He thought it was possibly longing. The girl she'd been was his friend. She was now a stranger, and he knew that would never change considering the life he now led.

He thought about the bundle of letters he still had in his study. She'd written long stories about her days and funny anecdotes to make him smile when he was at Eton. On the bottom of each, she'd said, "I miss you, Theo. Love, your friend Iris."

He'd never, not once, written back, but he'd read each letter as it arrived and then again and again. She was the one tie to his past he'd never been able to completely sever when he was at Eton.

Renton's behavior to her was aggressive and proprietorial. Monty didn't like it, and after overhearing what he had in the gardens, he was worried for her well-being. How could he ascertain if Iris was safe if he didn't actually talk to her and find out what was going on? But how could he talk to her as Plunge when no one took the man seriously?

Maybe he'd tell the Devilles his fears, and they could watch over her? They would get closer to her than he could.

Thinking of the Devilles reminded him of the conversation he'd had with Dimity. Clearly, she knew who he really was. Complications came with attachment to people, and he'd avoided that because of living two lives. Now it seemed he'd allowed people in, and the floodgates had opened. Was his identity in danger, and did he care? The short answer was no, but the long answer was his life would become extremely complicated if it was ever leaked who he really was... or more importantly, that he'd been living a lie.

His head actually ached from the continual whirl of thoughts.

"My lord, someone has called," Haven said from the doorway.

"I beg your pardon?" Monty was now sucking on one of his new favorite treats while he attempted to tally a column for the fourth time. Nathan Deville had introduced him to peppermint sticks, and he'd been hooked ever since.

"Someone has called to see you, my lord."

"Who? Is it a Deville? Of course it's a Deville. No one else ever calls, and why wouldn't they simply turn up as they usually do?" Monty said.

"It is not a Deville, my lord."

He'd ensured no one ever visited him by declining the

early requests, and because he was so unpopular, no one knocked on his front door.

"Lady Challoner has called, my lord."

Monty's head snapped up so fast, he was sure it made a cracking sound. He stared at his butler. "Send her away," he got out around the tightness in his throat. "At once." He then choked on part of the peppermint stick.

"I tried that, sir. She said she has a matter of grave importance to discuss with you and will wait until you can see her."

Monty looked down at his clothing. He wore a shirt, open at the neck, and trousers. His feet were bare. In his house, he wore as little as possible, seeing as he had to wear all that other clothing when he left it.

"Grave importance," Monty repeated. "What the hell does that mean?"

"I'm not sure, sir, but clearly it's grave."

Monty narrowed his eyes at Haven. The man always spoke in the same tone, but often he was teasing, cutting, or making a joke at a person's expense. One never quite knew what.

"Is she inside the house already?"

"I left her on the doorstep."

"What?"

"She is in the small rose parlor, my lord. You'll forgive my poor attempt at humor."

"I'm going to fire you one day," Monty said. Rising, he grabbed the bag of peppermint sticks and hurried out the door. Reaching his room, he ran inside, startling Jensen who was folding shirts.

"Hurry, I need a jacket and necktie. Shoes as well. Make haste, Jensen, someone has called."

"Here?" his butler squawked, rushing about the room like a chicken.

"Where else would they be, as I am here?"

"No one but those handsome Devilles call, and of course, the lovely Miss Mary."

"Well, now a lady has called. Hurry!"

He shoved his arms into the sleeves of the jacket and let his valet tie his neckcloth. "That is enough folds." Stepping out of Jensen's reach, he jammed his feet into his shoes.

"A lady?" His valet gasped.

"Yes, it's a shock, I know, and yet it is the case. A childhood friend, actually," he said without thinking.

"A childhood friend?" His valet clasped the hairbrush to his chest and sighed. "How lovely."

"That expression is something I would wear. Stop it at once," Monty muttered. "We are no longer friends, and in no way is it lovely."

His valet advanced on him with the brush raised.

"There is no time for hair. I must go." He ran back out of the room. Looking at his feet, he noticed he was once again in the plain black shoes. His jacket, however, was rose. Pushing the bag of sweets into his pocket—he would go for a walk in his garden after and eat them—he sprinted along the hall.

He'd danced with Iris three nights ago and, later that night, had convinced himself he had not felt the flare of attraction as he had inhaled her scent and felt her body brush his during the waltz. Monty couldn't remember the last time he'd reacted to a woman that way.

And it had to be her, the woman who had once known him better than anyone. His childhood friend. Clearly, he needed to keep his distance from her, which would not prove easy as she was, at this very moment, inside his house.

Passing a mirror, he glanced and saw the scowl on his face. He attempted to school his features to a more Plunge-worthy expression.

"Why is this getting harder and harder?" he muttered.

His hair was not in its usual nest on his head but a tousled mess. There was little he could do about that. Iris did not know him or what he'd become—not really. Not all of it anyway, so he told himself she wouldn't notice his changed appearance.

Reaching the parlor, he exhaled slowly and then entered.

She stood with her back to him, looking out the window at the gardens below. This was his haven, the place that kept him sane. Here he could be and do as he wished. He walked in his gardens and let the sun warm his body when it was sunny—this was England, after all, and the weather was notoriously fickle.

Iris was invading his haven, and that worried him a great deal.

"My lady," he said. She turned, and he bowed.

She wasn't overly tall. He'd noticed that last night. Iris had once told him she would be a great height one day. That had not happened. She wore a long mint green coat over an ivory dress. Her bonnet was also mint.

His childhood friend had grown into a beautiful woman, who he told himself he felt nothing for, and never would. There was no jolt of awareness or aching need to get close to her again.

He was lying.

"What has you here, Lady Challoner?"

Her posture was erect, brown eyes cool. Sharp ridges rode her cheekbones, and her nose was a gentle curve. Dark brows and lashes. Monty's eyes skimmed her body, but he could see little beneath the coat. But he'd briefly felt those curves last night.

"Lord Montgomery." She sank into a curtsy.

"Lord Plunge."

"That is not your name," she said slowly as if she was teaching him something he didn't already know.

They'd once been close enough that he knew her favorite color was lemon, and that she loathed jelly of any description. He knew she'd hated it when her father patted her on the head, as she was the shortest member of their family.

"Please allow me to offer you my condolences for the loss of your husband, my lady. I did not do so at the Raine ball." Monty realized he was using his home voice, which was hardly surprising, as that's what he did here, but he needed to be careful. Iris was nobody's fool at ten years of age. He doubted that had changed. He may have fooled society for years, but she would smell a rat if he gave her a reason to.

"Thank you."

"What has you here, my lady?"

"It is a delicate matter, Lord Montgomery."

He nodded for her to continue.

"When my husband died, I was left to go through his things. Henry and I." He watched as she spoke. She didn't move or look away from him. Her hands didn't twist around the strap of the small bag she held. Iris stood statue still.

"I did not do so for a year. When the mourning period was complete, we tried to get into the study, but the door was locked and we could not find the key," she added.

"I understand you were grieving, and to go through his things, even if you had the key, would have been painful," Monty said.

"Yes, of course." That dismissive tone suggested the opposite, and that, in fact, she did not grieve the loss of her husband.

What kind of marriage did she have with Challoner? It was true Monty had loathed both him and Renton, but there were many who had liked the man. He'd always felt it odd that Iris had not entered society, and now more so when clearly, she was in good health, unlike what her husband had told everyone.

"Henry?" Monty asked instead of prying into her marriage. She'd mentioned that name at the ball.

"My son. He is eight years of age."

He'd never considered she had a child, but of course he should have.

"I'm glad you had your son at your side so you could grieve together when your husband passed, my lady," he said.

Something passed across her face and was gone in seconds before Monty could identify it.

"My son is now and always will be my main concern."

That came out sounding like a threat, and he wasn't sure why she'd felt the need to issue it to him, of all people.

"You are to be commended, then. Will you take a seat, my lady?" Monty waved toward one.

His furniture was not what Plunge would have. It was comfortable, not ostentatious, and he'd never had a problem with that until now.

But Iris had not walked in society until last night, so perhaps she'd leave and not mention the inside of his town house to anyone.

She sat with a minimum of fuss and did not mention the fact he'd not offered her tea. He didn't want her to stay any longer than necessary. Monty took the seat across from her.

"What can I help you with, my lady?" he said instead of "How has your life been since we parted? Was your husband good to you?"

"I have something I wish to give to you," she said.

Curious, he watched her open the small bag on her wrist and take out a folded piece of paper.

"Before I do so, I need you to know that I was unaware of anything my husband did when he left our house, or indeed in it. I never sat with his friends when they came over, only on the rare occasion that he entertained. I did not walk in society either. When he was in his study, I was not to disturb him."

"Why did you not enter society? I remember once that was something you were excited about." He'd told himself he wasn't interested, and yet he'd just asked the question that suggested he was.

"My husband thought it best," she said in a cool, clipped tone that Monty guessed was to stop him asking any further questions.

"Why?"

She waved his words aside with an elegant flick of her hand.

"When my mourning period was up, I started receiving callers. My former brother-in-law many times, but I did not let him enter the house. He grew more forceful over time."

What the hell did that mean?

"He was not the only one who called. Several of my husband's friends also, and all wanted to get into his study for various reasons. I had no wish for them to enter, even if I could gain access to the study. It wasn't until later that I found the key."

She spoke in a cool, precise way. No emotion. In fact, she talked like he did when he was here in his house.

"I have no idea what this document pertains to. However, when I found it in a hidden drawer under my husband's desk, I felt you needed to read it. There were other papers there, but after reading this, I could not bring myself to look at the rest."

She was clearly nervous, as her hands were clenched now around the small bag she carried.

"In part, the reason I am in London is to hand deliver this to you. I felt it would not be right to send it to you any other way."

He got out of his seat again to take the piece of paper.

Their fingers brushed, but as she was wearing gloves, it should not have made him react as strongly as he did.

Monty didn't feel things for people. Mary and the Devilles, perhaps, and his staff, but that was his limit. So why did he just feel a bolt of heat lance through him as their fingers touched?

Sitting, he unfolded the paper and read.

Your work on behalf of our brotherhood will be rewarded. Another step toward revenge for our leader has been achieved with the death of Lord Montgomery. We have sacrificed to appease the gods.

Your servant,

Fratres Fidei

Monty's heart started thudding hard inside his chest as he reread the words and studied the symbol in the top right-hand corner of the sheet of paper he was holding. He felt himself slip back there to the day he lost his parents. It all came back, the rage and injustice of losing them.

"Lord Montgomery," Iris added when he didn't speak. "I will leave you," she said when he fell silent again.

"No. Stay."

Because right then, he needed her to. If she was here, the pain would recede, and with it, the memories of the day he'd walked into his parents' rooms and found them murdered in their beds. Memories he'd pushed into the dark recesses of his mind for years. The day he'd found that small wooden symbol in his father's hand.

It would arrive in London soon. The same symbol as the one on this page, and that Ackland had on the paper holding his father's name.

The sign of the devil.

CHAPTER 10

The words Theo had just spoken came out harsh, and nothing like the way he spoke as Plunge.

Iris had watched him walk into the room. She'd seen his jacket, a beautiful shade of rose, and then taken in the rest of him. His chestnut hair was not styled as it had been at the ball but was unbrushed in a tousled mess. Barring the jacket and necktie, he'd looked the man she'd always thought he'd become.

She'd then handed him the note, and the blank facade had changed. Shock, anguish, and finally, anger; Iris saw it all on his face.

"My lord, are you all right?"

He was reading the note again. She guessed he had done so at least three times by now. He lifted his head, and the look in those dark eyes had her releasing a breath. They blazed with emotion.

"And you found this in a secret drawer in your late husband's desk?" Gone was the simpering voice. This was harder and deeper. Demanding.

"I wanted to know why my late husband's friends and

brother were determined to enter his study. Especially Mr. Renton. He was persistent."

So persistent, he broke into her house.

"Why did you not want these people to enter your house, Iris?"

"Because I did not like them and wanted them nowhere near my son."

He nodded but added nothing, so she continued.

"Henry and I searched through my husband's possessions and found the key to his study. It was attached to his watch chain. It was a place, until then, we were forbidden to enter —"

"Forbidden?" The word came out like the crack of a whip.

"It was always locked and remained that way after his death. Neither Henry nor I wished to go in there. But we decided it was time, considering the persistence of the men."

When word reached her that her husband had passed in a riding accident, the elation she'd felt was not a suitable reaction for the late Lord Challoner's recent widow to show. So she'd felt it on the inside as had Henry when she'd told him. Both had played the part of a grieving family on the outside.

"What else was in there?" he demanded.

"My entire married life I was spoken to like that, ordered hither and yon. I will not allow it anymore." Iris felt her own anger rise. "Please adjust your tone."

She'd not been allowed to speak out, raise her voice, or act in any way that her husband did not think his wife should. When he'd passed, she'd vowed to cower to no man again.

Iris watched him inhale and slowly exhale.

"Forgive me, Lady Challoner." The words were still a rasp, however, spoken more softly, but his expression was still hard with anger. "My parents' killers were never found. I have never given up hope that one day I will bring them to justice."

The sick feeling she'd had inside her since the day she found that note increased. Could her husband have had something to do with the deaths of Theo's parents?

She'd spent as much time running over their lands and through their home as she'd spent in hers. Theo's parents had loved each other, and him, deeply. There had seemed to be so much laughter when they were near. She'd been devastated by their deaths.

"I did not read the rest of what I found after reading that one, but there are more. I don't know why my late husband had that letter in his possession signed *Fratres Fidei*, which is Latin for brothers of faith, my lord."

"Do you recognize the handwriting?"

"I do not. I was not party to anything my husband did, nor did I read his correspondence unless it was addressed to me." And there was plenty of that, Iris added silently.

I heard from a staff member you were running through the halls with my son, Iris. It is unseemly, and I will not have them witnessing such a disgraceful act from my wife.

Do not interfere in the education my heir will receive, Iris, or it will not go well for you.

I heard you visited the Burton family. You will not do so again, as they are not fit company for my wife and heir.

The notes she'd received from London, or wherever her husband left for, were constant. He had spies all over the house, watching her every move.

"I don't know why it says what it does, or why it was in my late husband's possessions. But I knew I must give it to you, Lord Montgomery."

"Thank you, Iris. For bringing me this." He regained his feet. "Can I keep it?"

She nodded. "Of course. I have no wish for it in my house,

considering what it says. As I have stated, there are more documents I have not gone through. However, I brought the remaining papers to London, as I know I must."

"You brought them with you?"

"I did. Those men were persistent. I did not want to take a chance of them or my former brother-in-law entering the house when Henry and I left for London."

"And you believed they would?" he asked her.

She nodded.

"Did they threaten you, Iris?"

She knew he had not even realized he'd again used her first name.

"It matters not. What matters is you find out what the letter means and why my husband had it in his possession."

"Could you please give me the names of the men who called to go through your late husband's possessions, other than his brother, who I believe is his only remaining relative?"

"Yes, Mr. Renton came often and demanded to enter the house. Once, he gained entry, but I had locked the study again and hidden the key, so he could not get in there."

"Did he use force on you, Iris?" Theo asked.

"The men who wanted access were Lord Picton, Lord Heather, Mr. Clipper, and Mr. Buford," Iris said instead of answering his question. "They each had a different reason for seeing my late husband's papers."

"What reasons?"

"He owed them money, or they'd purchased something together. Lord Heather said my late husband was running a venture that he had helped fund, and he needed the paper-work to take control of it."

"And you didn't believe them?" Theo asked.

She shook her head. "My late husband's man of affairs, or his lawyer, would hold these documents, surely?"

"Yes, it's my belief they would. Where are they?"

"What?"

"The papers you brought to London," Theo said.

"At the Challoner town house."

"Then we must go there and look through them at once."

"Pardon?" Iris regained her feet, feeling like she needed to be standing suddenly. "I do not have to do anything of the sort."

"Iris, I need to know if there is anything else in your husband's files that relates to this." He waved the papers at her. "They may finally offer me a clue as to who killed my parents."

"Lord Montgomery—"

"Plunge," he cut her off.

"I told you I'm not using that silly name."

His eyes never moved from her face, but it was his mouth that held her attention. Theo's lips twitched.

"It is what society calls me, and yet we digress. I would be grateful if you would allow me to look through those papers, my lady."

"They are my husband's personal things." She may not have liked Sydney very much. Even so, Iris had to consider Henry.

Frustration flashed across his face.

"I will look first and hand you anything I think could be of interest," she added. "I can have them sent here." She couldn't stop him from finding answers. She knew that, even if it incriminated her worthless husband.

Iris didn't want to spend too much time with this man. Already she felt as if they'd both revealed a part of themselves to each other that no one usually saw. She couldn't allow him to see more of her.

"I have no wish to wait," he said slowly. "I need to see if

there is anything in those papers, Iris. This is very important to me."

There was tension in him, which was understandable considering what he'd just read on that piece of paper he still held.

"You can't just enter my house and search it. I won't allow it." She was no longer someone people could walk all over.

"I don't want to search your house. I want to come with you while you do it."

She could feel his desperation. Were their roles reversed, Iris was sure she would feel the same. She'd want justice to avenge her parents if they were murdered as well.

"Very well, I will allow it if you tell me why your voice is different from the one you used in that ballroom the other night."

"We are all playing a part, my lady. Now let's go." His long fingers wrapped around her arm, and he was tugging her toward the door. "Is your carriage outside?"

"That's all you will say? We are all playing a part?"

"It is. Now answer the question."

"I don't like being spoken to like that."

"Is your carriage outside, Lady Challoner? May we use it to go to your house?" The words came out dripping with sweetness. The look on his face, however, was entirely different. His expression was almost fierce.

"Yes, my carriage is outside your front door," she said, instead of asking more questions because she was totally confused.

Iris needed to remember to keep this man at arm's length, just as she was sure he wanted to keep her. He could not intrigue or interest her. No man would ever do that again.

"Excellent, it will save time calling for mine." They stepped from the room. "Haven! Hat and gloves at once!"

"Don't bellow at your staff. It's rude," Iris said, horrified.

"I pay them well."

"Paying someone well is no excuse for bad manners."

The butler who had answered the door appeared. In his hands were a hat and gloves. White satin, she noted.

"Surely those are evening gloves?"

"I like to wear satin," he snapped, stuffing the gloves into his coat pocket.

Stalking through the house, he slapped his hat on his head and headed out the door with Iris behind him. Reaching her carriage, Theo opened the door and lifted her inside before she could take another step.

"Take us to the Challoner town house at once," he then directed her driver.

Iris poked her head out the window and added, "Please, Samuel." After she'd sat, and they were moving, she told him, "You had far better manners as a young boy."

"I had many far better things in my life as a boy."

His eyes were on the window, jaw clenched.

"I don't understand this… you," she said in a quiet voice.

"You don't need to, so don't try."

That definitely put her in her place, so Iris said, "I'll just point out that it is my carriage, which I can have you thrown from. I'm also allowing this because I choose to, so perhaps you can think about that for a minute or two, my lord, and adjust your manners." She'd spat out his title.

He shot her a dark look.

"Why does society think you are a fool? Even my aunt and uncle believe that of you."

"Because I am."

"No, you're not and never were. I have seen two different sides to you already, and I have only been with you briefly—"

"Don't meddle in something you will never understand, Lady Challoner. The only outcome will be a sore head."

Everything that she'd seen of Theo since arriving in

London was confusing. Society saw him dressed in bright colors, simpering and foolish. Today, he was a very different man. Cold and hard, but definitely not foolish.

"My son will be there. Please do not frighten him," she said softly.

His eyes switched to hers briefly. "You think I would?"

"I don't know the man you've become. How do I know what you will be like with Henry?"

His eyes closed briefly. But all he did was nod, which she did not know how to interpret.

She'd gone to give him a letter. Hoped to deliver it, then leave. Now she was in the carriage with the man who had once been her best friend. A man who seemed to be two people, neither of which she understood.

When the carriage stopped a short while later, he climbed down, holding a hand out to assist her. She stared at it. Gloveless, it was large, and she saw a scar from the palm to the middle finger.

"What is the problem?" he demanded.

"Nothing." Taking it, she stepped down and then led him to her town house. Her son's actually, but until he was of age, she would help him control what needed to be controlled.

The town house was white fronted with plenty of windows and a grand entrance of columns and steps. Just as her late husband would have wanted. Everyone needed to know that the Challoners were not only titled but wealthy too. Sydney Challoner had been a pretentious snob.

"Why did you not enter society?" Theo asked her again as they stood outside her front door. "The rumor was you had a weak constitution and could not handle it. I had my doubts then, but equally so now I have seen you."

"It was my husband's wish I remained in the country." And for those months, she could not have been happier, even if he had his minions watching her every move.

"Why?"

"It matters not." She opened the door and entered. "Why do you play the fool when I don't believe you are?"

That had his teeth snapping together.

"My lady." Her butler appeared, and Iris wondered if Theo would recognize him.

"Please bring tea to the upstairs parlor, Norman. Lord Montgomery and I will take it there. Also, have the small crate that is in the corner of my room brought to the parlor. Thank you."

"I have no wish for tea," Theo said, his eyes on Norman.

"Fine. I will take tea," she said, "seeing as you didn't offer me any."

"Which makes me sound childish and petulant. I'm sorry."

She looked over her shoulder as she walked away from him and found him still watching Norman. "Which seems to be your persona, so at least that is in keeping with your character."

"I do believe that hurt." He turned to face her again, a confused look on his face. "Do I know your butler? I have the oddest feeling we've met before."

"Do you remember the Smittens?"

"They lived in the village, and there were about ten of them from memory... good lord. Is that Norman? The young skinny boy we played with?"

"The very one, but no longer skinny," Iris said.

"Good lord," Theo said again.

Iris had arrived in London to find a household of her husband's staff. It had taken her a day to realize that some of them would need to go. They were rude and spoke to both Henry and her dismissively. She fired them on the spot. She'd then, with her aunt's help, contacted an agency to replace them.

Norman came for the position of footman, but he'd told

her he wanted to be a butler. Iris had employed him and been extremely happy about that fact when her former brother-in-law tried to enter the town house a few days after she'd arrived in London, even though she said she was not receiving visitors. Norman had stood in the doorway unmoving until he'd left.

"Yet another who has changed," Monty said softly. Iris did not answer, as it was the truth. All three of the childhood friends who had once run wild in the local village were vastly different adults.

"Come this way, my lord." Iris started up the stairs. She knew he was looking at the decor inside her husband's town house.

"I'd expect this in my house, not yours, my lady."

"It is my husband's town house. Therefore, it is decorated to his tastes, not mine. Did you never come here?"

"Once, to a ball," he said. "Your husband and I were never friends and, in fact, disliked each other very much."

"I didn't like him either." The words were out of her mouth before she could stop them.

CHAPTER 11

*S*eeing those words on that paper Iris handed him had shocked him into letting his Lord Plunge persona slip yet again. It was only now that he could fight his way through the rage to the calm and return to the part he played.

"Why do you play the fool when I don't believe you are?"

How was it Iris was suspicious when he'd only spent a few hours in her company since she arrived in London? Other than the Devilles, no one had questioned who he was. No one had seen through him. He'd played this part for years, but she'd noticed something was off in a day.

Looking around him, Monty thought the interior of this house pretentious. He had been in here once to attend a ball. He remembered that Lady Mary Sutherland had been the stand-in hostess for the evening, as Iris had not been able to attend. There was never any doubt in Monty's mind that Sutherland and Challoner were lovers at the time.

He'd not once questioned why his old friend did not appear in London because Iris brought up memories of his childhood that he'd also locked away in the dark recesses of his head.

His mother playing the piano and he and Iris singing. *No!* Going back there caused pain and could achieve nothing.

Looking at the rigid back in front of him, Monty guessed he was not the only one with secrets. She'd just told him she didn't like her husband. Just how bad had her life been?

Monty told himself he didn't care. She was not his concern. They'd been childhood friends; he owed her little, just as she owed him nothing.

They entered a room that was decorated to show whoever set foot inside that the owner was wealthy.

Monty refocused on the reason he was here. How was Challoner involved in all this? You didn't have a letter in your possession stating, *another step toward revenge for our leader has been achieved with the death of Lord Montgomery*, and not have played a hand in his death.

Could Iris be involved? But if she was, why would she hand him that note?

They sat in a heavy silence with thoughts churning and so much unspoken between them. It was broken by Norman's appearance bearing a tea tray.

The man was nothing like he remembered, except for the red hair and bright blue eyes. Once he'd been a tall, skinny, stick of a boy, and Monty's friend.

"Hello, Norman." He had to say something, but the words felt odd on his tongue. He rose after the man had lowered the tray to the table before Iris. "It is good to see you again."

"Hello, Lord Montgomery." Norman bowed.

He looked like a wrestler. Huge hands and feet. Theo rather liked the idea of this man being in Iris's household. The boy he'd been was kind and compassionate. He would always protect her if protection was required.

Was Renton a threat?

Iris, the warm, open girl he'd once known, was now as emotionless as he. She sat still and controlled. Once, she'd been unable to stand or sit still for more than a minute.

"Mother."

He looked to the door as a young boy entered after Norman had left. Behind him was a woman. Monty's guess was the nanny. The boy was tall, with brown hair. His eyes were like his mother's, but his face was all his father's. He gave Iris a small smile as she held out a hand to him. That fell when he noticed Monty.

He stopped walking and stood still. Nothing moved, not even his eyes. His hands hung at his sides, fists clenched. The tension in him was obvious—and fear, Monty thought. The boy was terrified.

"Henry, this is Lord Montgomery. He is an old friend of mine from when I was your age." Iris had risen and was now beside the boy. "Greet him properly, my love."

Monty rose as the boy bowed in a stilted movement.

"Hello, Henry. Do you mind if I call you that?"

The boy's eyes shot to his mother, who nodded.

"My name is Monty. Lord Montgomery, as I'm also known by, but it is such a mouthful, don't you think?"

He hadn't had much to do with children until he'd met the Deville family. Their offspring were wonderful. He'd come to cherish the sound of their laughter the few times they'd met. As it turned out, he quite liked children; he'd just not had a chance until lately to realize that.

"Do you know, I think"—he dug into his pocket—"yes, I do have a bag of peppermint sticks in my coat pocket. An acquaintance recently introduced me to them. Have you tried them, Henry?"

The boy shook his head, eyes solemn.

"How old are you?" Monty moved closer. The boy

watched warily, as did his mother. Almost as if Henry would flee if Monty moved too fast or made a noise.

What the hell kind of life had they both lived with Challoner?

"Henry is eight."

"Well, Henry, allow me to teach you about the delights of peppermint sticks." He held the bag out to the boy.

He didn't reach for it but again looked at his mother.

"W-well if he's having one, so am I," she said. Her tone was strained.

Monty watched her take one and suck on it. Looking at those plump, soft lips wrapped around that peppermint stick was not entirely comfortable, so he studied the boy.

"Try one, Henry," Monty said.

He did and slowly put it into his mouth and sucked. Unlike the Deville progeny who did everything as loud and rambunctious as the adults around them, Henry sucked it quietly.

"Nice?" Monty asked him. The boy nodded, and he felt like he'd been rewarded with something far greater than just a nod.

"Do you know, Henry? I think peppermint sticks may have to be a weekly staple in our household. What say you to that?" Iris asked.

"Yes, please," he said in an excruciatingly polite voice.

"I have four left in this bag. I will give them to you, and you can eat three and give your mother one." Monty held out the bag.

"That hardly seems fair," Iris protested. Monty transferred his eyes to her and saw she was holding back tears.

"Take the bag, Henry," Monty said. The boy did. He then clutched it to his chest.

"I-I will return to my room," he said. "Thank you, my lord."

Iris kissed her son's head, and then he gave Monty a brief bow.

"Thank you, Robyn," Iris said to the woman who'd arrived with the boy. "Perhaps you could take Henry for a walk in the gardens rather than back to his rooms?"

"That sounds lovely, don't you think, Henry," she said. "And you can share one of those peppermint sticks with me."

The boy gave her a genuine smile, not one of the stilted ones he'd given Monty. It changed his face completely. Suddenly he looked relaxed and happy instead of terrified. He and the woman left the room.

The silence that followed was even louder than the previous one. Iris walked away from him to the window. He guessed she was putting distance between them to collect herself. Monty followed.

"Henry is shy," Iris said, turning to face him. Her eyes widened when she saw he was close.

"I can see that." Monty doubted he was just shy. There was a great deal more going on here, but he didn't want to know what. He couldn't let himself care about any more people, especially with how soon he was leaving London.

They stood there staring at each other. Strangers who both lived behind a facade. Something about this woman reached that cold, hard place inside him that he'd shut and bolted long ago.

"You... we are very different from who we were," she whispered.

In that moment, he wanted to be close to her. Needed it when he'd never sought contact with anyone before. In seconds he was cupping her soft cheek, and Iris did not pull away. It felt so warm under his palm. *When had he last touched a person like this?*

It would have taken ten men to pull him away from her in

that moment. Had she flinched or made a move, he would have released her, but she didn't.

"Theo," she whispered.

"Iris," he rasped, and then Monty was lowering his head and placing his lips on hers. The gesture was soft, yet he felt it thawing him from the inside. Need pulsed through him. *More.* He took her mouth again, soft, seeking. The warmth crept through him as Iris placed a palm on his chest. He couldn't feel the contact—they wore too many clothes—but it branded him.

He raised his head and looked at her.

What the hell was he doing?

Her breathing was erratic, as was his, and Monty's heart pounded inside his chest. He'd just kissed a woman, and not just any woman—his childhood friend. He backed up two steps.

"I have what you asked for, my lady." A footman came in carrying a wooden box.

Monty moved to the seat he'd recently occupied and sat once more.

"Thank you, Bryce," Iris said, her voice shaky. "Please place it on the floor."

The footman did and left, and Monty had to fight with himself not to move to her side and touch her. The warmth she had given him was seeping from his body.

"That won't happen again," she said, her voice cool.

Monty nodded, still reeling from what they'd done. He never reacted without thought. Never did anything impulsively. Yet, in that moment, he'd needed to kiss this woman as much as he needed his next breath.

"I will look through the contents, and then you can leave."

"Iris—"

"We never speak of that again."

"Very well," Monty said. That he was here, in her house,

when clearly, she didn't want him to be, meant he had to tread carefully.

You kissed her. That is not treading carefully.

He tried to rationalize his behavior. It was because he was emotional. Angry after reading that paper. That was why he'd kissed her. He was not himself.

Conflicted and confused, he sat back to watch as Iris started going through the papers. He'd give her space after this. Leave here and never return. Just as he would leave London at the season's end.

Or would he? Now that he had clues as to who killed his parents, he may stay. Looking at the woman seated across from him, he wondered if she remained in London if he'd have another reason.

CHAPTER 12

*M*onty watched as Iris looked at the papers in her hand. He should never have kissed her, because there had been tension between them before, but now it was a great deal worse.

"I will look through them and pass any that I think could be of interest to you, my lord," Iris said. Her voice was cool, but the eyes she shot him and away again were nervous.

"Thank you," Monty said with more calm than he felt.

He had been trained to be cool and collected. To think before taking action. Right in that moment, he felt the exact opposite. Monty's focus should be solely on the fact he could finally be closer to finding his parents' killers. Instead, he couldn't stop thinking about the feel of Iris in his arms.

As she read the paper in her hand, he slowly inhaled and exhaled quietly. He did it again and felt his calm returning. He could do this. What had happened between him and Iris was wrong.

It hadn't felt wrong.

"Are you in need of anything further, my lady?" Norman asked returning.

"How is your family, Norman?" Monty said to ease the heavy silence between him and Iris.

"Well, thank you, my lord. My mother and father have plenty of grandchildren, which they are very happy about."

"What brought you to London?"

"Adventure, my lord. I have always wanted to be a butler, you see. I'd been unsuccessful until Lady Challoner was hiring staff. I applied for the position of footman, and when she realized I aspired to be a butler, she was kind enough to give me a chance."

Monty saw his old friend now in the boyish smile the man gave him.

"I am glad Lady Challoner found you, Norman."

He took the tea handed to him but waved aside the food. His stomach was still churning for all he had control of his emotions. He sipped and watched as her fingers picked up and discarded papers. He saw the frown line down her forehead as she read.

Iris Challoner was a beautiful, disturbing woman.

"I don't want to believe my late husband could have been involved in the deaths of your wonderful parents, and yet..." Iris's words fell away.

"Yet?" Monty prompted her.

"My late husband was not always what he appeared."

What the hell did that mean? *Had Challoner hurt her?* The thought made his stomach clench.

She didn't chew her lip like Mary sometimes did when she was reading something. Or flick her fingers like Zach, or hum like Nathan. Iris just read through each and then placed it beside her. Back straight, eyes down.

"What do you mean, your late husband was not always what he appeared?" he asked.

"He was a hard, cold, controlling man, Lord Montgomery. He could also be cruel. It would not come as a surprise to me if he was involved in something nefarious," she said, raising her eyes from the papers in her lap to look at him. "If he had anything to do with your parents' death, I would rather know."

Had he been cruel to her and Henry?

Monty nodded in acknowledgment of her words. If her late husband was involved, then her son's name would be blackened; they both knew that. But they would cross that bridge when and if they came to it.

He would protect them in any way he could.

"I have gone through the box, and this bundle of papers contains the only ones that I cannot explain. They are signed, but I can't decipher the names," Iris said. "There is a small wooden carving attached to the black ribbon that bound them."

Monty rose, heart pounding to look at what she held out to him.

The wooden carving was, he was sure, like the one in his father's hand Monty had found upon his death. The same symbol, he thought.

What did that mean?

"I believe that is the sign of the devil, my lord."

He nodded and sat before his legs gave out, and while Iris drank her tea, Monty tried to focus on the papers. He was excellent at Latin; his years at Eton had ensured that.

Reading the words, he ignored the small symbol that felt like it was burning a hole through his thigh where he'd rested it.

"That symbol is the same one on the note mentioning your parents, Lord Montgomery," Iris said.

"It is, my lady, but it could just be a symbol used by men in their private club," Monty added.

She nodded but didn't speak, so Monty continued reading.

There were meeting dates and times but no address. He found papers with columns of numbers and another that appeared to be an agenda. A line at the bottom drew his eyes. *We must sacrifice those that betray us to please the gods.* The words were similar to those on the correspondence found in Ackland's possession and the note Iris had brought to his house earlier. It was enough to tell Monty that Iris's husband was indeed involved in something, but was he connected to Ackland, or was that coincidence? And where did his father fit into all this?

He remembered what Geraint had said about what was written beside his parents' names on that list. Written and crossed out alongside others who were dead. *The gods are appeased with their deaths.*

Was it all connected?

His eyes went to Iris again.

"What does it mean, my lord?"

"I don't know yet, but I cannot thank you enough for handing these to me, my lady. I will contact you when I have information."

"Did I live with a murderer? I can almost believe it of him," she whispered, regaining her feet. "Was he really the devil as I always believed?"

He rose and joined her. Instinctively, he moved closer as if he wanted to comfort her, but this time he kept a distance between them. Touching Iris was something he could never do again, as a single touch would not be enough.

"Did he hurt you?" The words came out before he could stop them.

"It matters not. What matters is that if he or any of them were involved in your parents' deaths, then I want them brought to justice. If my husband is guilty, then it must be known."

"I will not have yours or Henry's names darkened because

of your husband's actions," Monty found himself saying. Would he let that stop him when, for years, the only thing he'd wanted was justice for his parents? He wasn't sure of the answer to that question.

Her laugh was harsh and held no humor. "I care nothing for my name. Just as I had no wish to walk in society, and yet my aunt and uncle believe it was for the best for Henry. I care that one day, if he wishes, he can, but if that cannot happen, we will be all right."

"I will do what I can to keep your name out of this." *Whatever this was.*

She nodded.

He held her gaze for long, tense seconds and then retreated, looking around the room before he spoke again. "Just so I have everything clear, my lady. Lord Picton, Lord Heather, Mr. Clipper, Mr. Buford, and your former brother-in-law called to search your husband's things?"

"Yes. Their persistence angered me, and I wanted to know why they were so determined to go through his study. I am no fool, or should I say, never will be again, and I know that being forewarned is forearmed."

"I know you are not a fool, my lady. And it is sensible to do as you have. Many women are left in the dark until creditors knock on the door."

She nodded. Her eyes were cool again. Like him, she was distancing herself, but he could still feel the warmth from her cheek. Her soft lips beneath his.

Monty had not felt a person's touch for many years, until Mary had hugged him. He wanted to feel Iris's hands on his skin again but would not give in to that need.

"Did any of these men threaten you?"

"They were persistent" was all she said. But he was sure he had his answer, especially after the other night. Renton had hurt her when he'd grabbed her.

"Who will you tell about this? Who will help you find out if, in fact, my husband is involved with your parents' deaths?"

"I have people I trust with this information."

"Well then, I wish you good luck, Lord Montgomery. If I find anything more, I shall send word."

She was dismissing him, and he was more than happy to comply with her wishes.

"Thank you again, and Lady Challoner?" he said as he reached the door.

"Yes?"

"Should you need anything, please contact me."

"I won't but thank you." She gave him a cool look.

"If you feel threatened or in danger at any stage—"

"Why would I be?"

"I don't know, and likely you won't, and yet if you do, then contact me."

She studied him once in control. "I assure you that will not be necessary. I have an uncle and aunt."

Monty wanted to say more. Instead, he tucked the papers inside his jacket and made himself bow. Then he walked out the door. Inhaling deeply, he tried to relieve the tightness inside his chest. Iris bothered him; there was no getting around that. When she was close, he reacted to her nearness. Her scent, the lure of her skin and her body, and now he knew what her lips felt like pressed to his.

He wanted his old childhood friend.

Monty had wanted no one—other than for slaking his desire—in years.

"Distance," he muttered, reaching the front door. "I must keep my distance from that woman."

Walking down the front steps, he schooled his expression into Lord Plunge and hoped no one noticed his hair or shoes were different, and he did not have a dozen lavender-scented handkerchiefs on his person. In fact, he hoped no one saw him leaving the house of Lady Challoner.

"Goodbye, my lord."

He found Henry to his right, standing in the middle of a bed of flowers. Face solemn, he was staring at Monty.

"Goodbye, Henry. You let me know if you want any more peppermint sticks, and I'll send you some."

The boy blinked and then nodded. "I will. Are you really my mother's old friend?"

"I am. Did she speak of our childhood?"

"No, but my uncle says he is our friend, and he's not."

And wasn't that a telling statement? He thought about asking him some more questions but decided that wasn't a good idea, as it would likely anger Iris.

"Well, Henry, let me assure you I am indeed your mother's friend, and if you will allow it, I could be yours also?"

He was subjected to another long look. Where the Deville children would have shrieked their answer at him by now, Henry simply watched Monty. Clearly coming to a conclusion, he then nodded, and Monty let the breath out he hadn't known he was holding.

"Yes, we need more friends," the boy said.

"Your mother and I used to do many things together, including climbing trees and running over our parents' estates."

"My father did not like us to run," the boy said seriously.

"Well then, perhaps now you can?" Monty's life might not have been what he'd thought it would be after his parents' death, but he'd had a wonderful childhood.

"Mother sat on the floor with me to take tea yesterday, and we toasted bread in the fire."

"That sounds like fun, Henry. Did you have jam or honey on your toast?"

"Jam," he said with a small smile.

"I have jam usually too," Monty said. Looking at Henry, he saw the lost boy he'd become at twelve. But at least Henry still had a mother who loved him.

"I didn't like my father."

"I'm sorry about that."

"He was horrible to my mother and me."

The thought of Challoner hurting this serious little boy and his lovely mother enraged Monty.

"Henry, I want to promise you something." Monty moved to stand before the boy. "Now we are friends. That means if you ever need anything, then you can come to me. Now I know your mother will always be around, or your aunt and uncle, but for any reason if you need me, then here is my address." He handed over a small white rectangular card with his details on it. "Do you understand?"

The boy looked up at him and then nodded, taking the card.

"Excellent, well, I will bid you good day."

"Goodbye, my lord." Henry left and had soon disappeared around the side of the house, head lowered, walking slowly and not running.

Monty looked up at the window behind him. Iris was not standing in it, but he felt she was watching him from somewhere inside the house.

How had she and Henry suffered at the hands of the late Lord Challoner? And why did he want to know the answer to that question desperately? What was the deal with Renton, and why was he now worried about her when he had enough to worry about in his own life?

Suddenly after years, there was a chance he could find who had killed his parents. For now, he must focus on that.

Walking out to the street, he started toward his town house, waiting for a hackney to appear.

"I say, is that Lord Plunge looking fierce?"

He found an open carriage carrying Mary's mother and sister. Both were looking at him open-mouthed.

Damn, he'd forgotten his hair wasn't styled, and he hadn't worn heels. He schooled his expression into a suitable Plunge look.

"'Tis a beauteous day, dear ladies." He bowed deeply, waving his hand before him.

The ladies acknowledged him, and he saw a speculative look in Phillipa's eyes.

"What has you here, my lord?" Phillipa demanded. She was natured nothing like her sister. Opinionated and spoiled, it was hard to believe she and Mary came from the same family.

"I am taking air," he said when nothing else came to him.

"Were you visiting Lady Challoner?" Phillipa asked.

"Indeed. It is lovely to catch up with a dear old friend."

"Why did you have that fierce look on your face?" Her eyes narrowed as she studied him, like she could see he was not telling her the truth.

"I was squinting. The sun is awfully bright today." Monty could feel himself starting to sweat as she continued to study him.

"Have you styled your hair differently, my lord?" Phillipa then asked.

"My valet, you know, he took ill, and I was forced from the house like this!" Monty put a quiver in his voice.

"Well, I for one like the look," Lady Blake said. "Now we must go, Phillipa, or we will be late. Drive on, Brantley," she then ordered.

Phillipa watched him until they disappeared, and he had a terrible feeling she was seeing him in a different light, and, in fact, his name had just been added to her prospective husband list.

"Not bloody likely," Monty muttered. Looking up and down the street, he searched for a hackney. You couldn't set foot out of your house usually without one approaching. However, not today.

He walked with his head down and hoped no one noticed him or wanted to talk.

"Help!"

The scream came from his left. Monty saw a woman looking to the second floor of the house before her. His heart sank as he saw a boy hanging out of a window.

"My son, he'll fall!" she cried. "I can't go up! I need to catch him!"

Monty ran to where she stood.

"I just left for a minute," she said.

"Go inside and pull him back in. I will stand here in case he falls," Monty said. "Hurry, go now."

The woman ran.

"He'll die if he falls," a man said, coming to stand next to Monty.

Monty shrugged out of his jacket and threw it to the ground. He then moved closer to the house. It was near to the road, but there was a railing and a path on one side, and the road on the other.

"You stay outside, I'll go in," Monty said to the man.

"Right you are then," the man said.

He ran through the gate and looked up. Monty watched as the boy's fingers slipped seconds later, and he was falling. Plummeting toward them at speed, the little body wriggled. Monty adjusted his position and held out his arms.

"He's coming to you!" the man called.

He caught the boy and staggered backward for several steps. There was a brief silence and then a scream from the mother, who was now looking down at Monty and her son.

Applause broke out behind him.

"He's all right," Monty managed to get out.

The boy wriggled, and he lowered him to the ground.

"Are you unhurt?"

Big blue eyes filled with tears looked up at him, and he nodded.

"You're all right, lad," Monty said gruffly.

"Teddy!" The woman burst back out the front door of the house.

"Your mother is going to be angry with you for a while now, Teddy. You take that, and then you never climb out that window again, all right?"

The little boy nodded. He then hugged Monty hard around the legs before releasing him. In seconds, he was in his mother's arms.

He turned to the street again and saw they'd drawn a crowd.

"Well done. You saved him," a woman said.

Monty pulled on his jacket and walked back to the street, hoping no one he knew had seen the incident. It was a faint hope at best.

"Good lord, did you see that? Lord Plunge saved that boy."

The words came from Lady Cagney, one of a group of ladies who were notorious for gossip. Monty ignored her, pretending he'd not heard what she said, and walked away at speed. He needed to get to his town house before anyone else saw him doing anything unPlunge-like.

Finally, a hackney appeared, and he waved it down. Climbing inside, Monty thought that perhaps today he would simply not leave his house again. It was not even midday, and already he was exhausted.

First, Iris had brought him a note that was likely another

clue to finding his parents' killers. Then he'd kissed and held her. And now, he'd just saved a boy in front of one of society's infamous gossips.

"Definitely not leaving the house again today," he muttered.

CHAPTER 13

*I*ris had not slept well again. It was now four days after she'd given Theo that letter and the other papers. She'd been unsettled since. She'd tossed and turned every night, thinking about the conundrum that was Lord Theodore Montgomery and that kiss.

His hand had cupped her cheek, the gesture intimate and gentle. No man had ever treated her with such tenderness. He'd not demanded a response from her, but she'd given it. Felt the warmth of his touch slide through her body like warm honey.

When she'd pressed her hand to his chest, she'd felt the thud of his heartbeat and known that he was as affected as she by what they were doing.

After her late husband passed, Iris had never wanted to be with a man again. But that kiss… it was different. Had made her feel different. She hadn't felt fear having Theo close, and she'd wanted his touch desperately.

Wanted to fall into his arms in that moment. Wanted to let him hold her like she'd once longed to be held.

"Who are you, Theo Montgomery?" Iris wondered.

She'd seen a different side to the man in this very house when he saw what else her husband's papers held. He'd looked fierce and nothing like the primped and pampered lord she'd first met again in that ballroom.

What game was Theo playing, and why? He'd been Lord Plunge for many years now because she'd asked her aunt and uncle about him. But she was certain there was another side to Theo. The side he'd allowed her to briefly see.

Henry rarely talked about anyone who called at their house unless it was her aunt and uncle, whom he loved. But he'd mentioned Lord Montgomery twice now.

Henry told her that Theo had said he was her son's friend.

Iris found she did not mind that. Yes, she did not know what was going on with Theo, but she felt deep inside he was a man they could trust. Surely there was some of the honor his parents had instilled in him in the man she saw today. The boy she'd known had certainly been that and more.

Wandering through the town house, she made her way to where Henry would be, reading in his rooms. Her son had learned early in life to stay small and quiet so he did not attract his father's attention.

Iris had spent a lot of time keeping him safe and away from her late husband, but sometimes he'd gone looking for Henry.

"My heir will not cower in his room. He must learn that to follow in my footsteps. He will be respected." These words had been yelled at her many times.

Iris had wanted to scoff at that. She'd never respected a man less than the late Lord Challoner, but if she challenged him, he would punish Henry.

Opening her son's door, she found him in the window seat reading.

"How would you feel about going for a walk, Henry? We could go to the park and perhaps take tea somewhere?"

He lowered the book slowly and rose.

"I would like that."

She wanted him to jump and run. Wanted him to yell and argue with her. It broke her heart just looking at him. She'd tried and failed to let him be raised as a normal child should. As she and Theo had been. Even though he'd been the heir to his father's title and estates, the late Lord Montgomery had ensured his son still had fun in his life along with the more serious side of learning what he needed to for his future.

"Henry, you know your father is dead now."

"I know that." He took the hand she held out to him.

"And you understand that no one here will yell at you should you choose to speak loudly or run down the hallways. That the staff here are new and handpicked by me."

He nodded.

"Excellent," Iris said, unsure what else she could say to make him see that he no longer needed to be contained and quiet. "So, if you yell or speak loudly, I will not censure you for it," she reiterated.

He nodded again, watching her intently. Time, she thought. He would adjust, given time.

"Let us leave then. I shall not need you, Robyn," she said to his nanny.

"Very well, my lady."

They put on their outer clothing and left the house. Henry let her hold his hand, even though his father had told him repeatedly that it was a childish thing to do.

Iris wasn't sure there was a time in their marriage that she'd liked the man she'd married. She'd certainly never respected him and, in fact, learned to loathe him very early in their life together.

They stepped out the front door and onto the street. The sun was high and felt warm on their shoulders as they walked. Carriages rolled by and horses' hooves clopped along.

"Shall we endeavor to find some peppermint sticks?"

"Yes, please."

Well, that was a quick response. Clearly, Henry had liked Theo's offerings.

They walked for a while, letting the afternoon sun warm them, not exactly chatting, but she asked him questions, which he answered.

"We have yet to examine those shops there." Iris pointed across the road. "Shall we do so now?"

"Yes, please," Henry said politely.

They were about to cross the road when a large, lumbering carriage pulled to a stop before them.

"Where are you going?" the elderly occupant demanded of Iris and Henry.

Searching her memory for the woman's name, she found one—the Duchess of Yardly. The woman her uncle had warned her to stay away from.

"Good day to you, Duchess." Iris dropped into a curtsy.

"Who is that?" She jabbed a walking stick in Henry's direction.

"That is my son, Lord Challoner. Henry, this is the Duchess of Yardly."

Her son bowed.

The woman wore a hideous shade of plum. Iris loved the color normally. But this was more a bruised plum that had been left on the tree too long. The dress was made up of a great quantity of fabric and reached her chin. The sleeves were puffy and nipped in at the elbow. Lace banded the cuff and under the bodice.

It was a total fashion disaster, but Iris found herself liking it simply for the audacity of wearing it in a public setting and clearly not caring what anyone thought.

"Hello, Henry. This is Walter." The duchess jabbed her cane toward the large gray-haired dog seated across from her. "And this is Romulus." She swung the cane to where a small brown dog was sitting beside Walter. The little dog was gazing at him adoringly.

Beside her, Henry rose to his toes to look in the carriage. He loved animals, but his father had forbidden one from entering their household. Iris had thought about getting a dog for him. She'd just not gotten around to it yet.

"Come and greet them, boy," the duchess said.

Much to Iris's surprise, Henry did as she asked. Moving to the carriage, he opened the door.

"They both like to be patted. Walter, especially, loves his ears ruffled," the duchess added. She now had both hands balanced on her cane and a surprisingly gentle look on her face.

"You have two lovely dogs," Iris said, joining her son. She held out a hand, and Walter sniffed it.

"Romulus is mine, but Walter is Dimity's—Lady Raine's—dog. He wanders between houses, as he was raised on the streets. You never know when he will turn up," she said and then cackled, sounding to Iris exactly like a witch would.

"Would you like to join me? I thought to have a drive around the park and see what those fools are up to. I like to hurl out a few insults to keep them on their toes," the duchess added.

"Fools?" Iris asked. Henry was now on his knees inside the carriage patting both dogs. Walter licked his cheek with a long slurp, and Romulus was nuzzling his hand. Her son's smile told her they needed to get a dog. It was genuine and happy.

"Society, gal! Keep up."

"Right, of course. Thank you for your kind offer, but we

are going to find peppermint sticks," Iris said. "I am not dressed for promenading."

"Neither am I." The duchess cackled again. "Very well, I will not force you. After all, society is an acquired taste and takes time to adjust to. But, Henry, I wish for you to come and visit me. You can walk Romulus."

"Really?" Her son sounded excited.

"Really. I will send a note round to your mother's house. Now, if you are not coming with me, then may I suggest you head down that road there to the park. It is less frequented by society. There are some things going on that would interest a lad your age, I'm sure."

Henry stepped back, and as he was about to close the door, Walter jumped out.

"Oh, very well, go with them then, and Romulus and I shall try not to feel abandoned," the duchess said.

The carriage then rolled away, leaving them with the large dog.

"It seems Walter wishes to walk with us, Henry."

"He is a very nice dog," her son said, patting his head. "I should like to walk with him too."

"All right then. Shall we investigate this park the duchess spoke of? Perhaps you could find a sturdy stick there and throw it for Walter."

"How will he know how to get home, Mother?"

"You heard what the duchess said. He likes to wander and was born on these streets, so he knows his way home."

Henry didn't reply to that, so they headed toward the park. Entering a few minutes later, she saw the grass was not as neatly trimmed as at other parks she'd seen around London. A path led them toward some trees. Henry foraged for a stick and found one. He then hurled it as hard as he could, and Walter galloped off to retrieve it.

"What is that?" Iris asked, squinting.

"A velocipede," Henry whispered, awed. "I have read extensively about them. There is to be an exhibition soon in London."

"Then we shall have to attend," Iris said. *She would ensure it was so.*

The contraption was heading their way, and as it drew closer, she noted its rider was Lady Raine. A young boy and girl were running on either side of her.

The woman wore a bonnet with two fat yellow ribbons tied under her chin and a matching yellow dress. She looked like sunshine, and her smile was radiant.

Iris couldn't remember when she'd last smiled like that or felt so carefree. And yet her uncle had told her that the countess had not lived without her struggles also, considering her change in circumstance. Clearly, she had risen above them and chosen to be happy.

"Henry?"

"Yes, Mother?" He dragged his eyes from the approaching people.

"We are going to choose to smile, laugh, and be happy. We will, in fact, be making it a daily mission henceforth."

He studied her in that solemn way he had and then nodded. "Yes, I like that idea." He smiled. It wasn't a large, wide one like the approaching countess had, but it was still a smile.

"Hello!" Lady Raine called as she neared them. "Isn't this wonderful?"

Walter let out a loud woof when he realized who was riding the velocipede.

Lady Raine stopped before them. She was straddling the contraption, with her skirts tucked up and long legs in stockings exposed from the knees down. On her feet were brown leather boots.

"Good day to you, Iris."

"Good day, my lady. Allow me to introduce you to my son, Lord Challoner, Henry," she added.

"My name is Dimity. Hello, Henry, it is lovely to meet you. How is it you came across my dog?" she asked. Her cheeks were flushed, and she looked radiant. Iris thought she would have been a great deal different if she, too, had wed someone other than her husband. Possibly not radiant, but happy.

"We just encountered the Duchess of Yardly. Walter decided he'd rather walk with us than drive in the park," Iris said.

"You can hardly blame him for that," Dimity said. "This is my son, Elliot." She waved a hand at the boy, who looked exactly like her husband with his dark features. "And this is Ella. She is Forrest's—my husband's cousin's—daughter."

The girl looked to be about Henry's age and wore a cream dress with tiny sprigs of lavender all over it. Her sweet face was framed with a straw bonnet, and Iris could see sunset-colored curls.

Both children looked happy out here running about with Lady Raine.

"Have you been on one of these, Henry?" Dimity asked.

"I have not, no," Henry said, studying every inch of the contraption. "It is my fondest wish to do so."

"Well, then." Dimity got off. "Ella, you and Elliot show him how it is done."

"Oh, we have no wish to intrude on your... ah, activities," Iris said, coming up with nothing else.

"No intrusion at all. In fact, I shall enjoy your company." Dimity then put her hand through Iris's arm. "There are just the three of us here. Forrest got the velocipede two weeks ago, and I said I wanted to ride it, so Ella decided today would be that day."

Iris had never had a friend who she could walk with arm

in arm. Her sister and mother once, but that was before she wed. She'd made no friends during the years she'd been married.

"Henry has done nothing like this before," Iris said as nerves leapt into her throat watching her son straddle the velocipede.

"Ella will ensure he is all right. Plus, he cannot fall far to the ground."

Henry listened as Ella instructed him, and Henry nodded. Iris held her breath as he started moving.

"Well, he's picked it up a great deal easier than I did," Dimity said.

"He has not had many friends or, in fact, fun in his life," Iris said. "What I mean is, he's an only child, and we lived a great distance from anyone else."

"We shall have to see about changing that. I did not have a great deal of fun in my life either before I married Gabe. He and his family then set about ensuring I did just that."

"I just told Henry we were making it a daily mission to laugh and have fun."

"What a wonderful mission. And today you are succeeding," Dimity said. "It is hard to let go of the past sometimes." She patted her hand. "But the way to start is small steps, Iris."

She nodded. "Yes, it is time."

It was an oddly intimate conversation to have with a woman she did not know well, and yet it felt surprisingly comfortable, Iris thought.

She'd come to London expecting to step out into society and show her son some sights he'd read about in books. She'd only attended one event but felt like she'd made friends, and now it seemed her son would too.

Iris swallowed down the lump in her throat as she heard Henry laugh.

"Gabe always says to me that change is hard, but to overcome it, you must face it," Dimity said. "He is a very smart man, my husband, but don't tell him I said that."

"I promise to not mention it," Iris said solemnly.

"Perhaps we shall walk to the sweet shop after this and get some more peppermint sticks. I have just run out. Something sweet is good for all situations, don't you think?" Dimity said.

"Lord Montgomery introduced my son to those."

"Yes, I had heard they were a favorite of his. He is also the cause of quite a bit of gossip at the moment."

Surely not because of her?

"Oh?" Iris said.

"Phillipa and Lady Blake saw him without his hair dressed in its usual hideous style. Plus, he was scowling instead of simpering. Then Lady Cagney observed him saving a young boy who was hanging from a window. She even said he appeared quite manly. As you can imagine, it has sent some of society all atwitter," Dimity added.

"The boy and Lord Montgomery are unhurt, I hope?" Iris did not like the sudden sharp jab in her side at the thought of Theo in pain.

"Yes. Apparently, he simply put the boy back on his feet and left, scowling. As you can imagine, Lady Cagney has told everyone, and the ears she couldn't reach others have."

"Yes, I should imagine it would be a shock considering how he regularly conducts himself," Iris said.

"Appearances are not always what they seem, Iris," Dimity said.

She wanted to ask more questions, but Lady Raine decided it was time for peppermint sticks, so she kept the questions to herself. But she would find out what was going on with Theo if it was her last act before leaving London.

CHAPTER 14

*M*onty was rarely irrational. He always had a purpose and never deviated from it. He may appear a brainless fool, and yet the reality was far from that. When he rose, he knew what he was doing that day. If there were no engagements, then he was barefoot in his shirt-sleeves and trousers in the garden or reading with his feet hanging over the end of a chair.

He never just wandered anywhere aimlessly.

When you were constantly on your guard leaving the house, you tended to be the exact opposite in your home. No one visited him unless it was a Deville or Geraint—or now Iris.

Had he not been able to be himself inside these walls, he would likely be in Bedlam by now.

He'd thought a great deal about Iris in the four days since that kiss. He wasn't sure why, but he felt like trouble was circling her.

There was her former brother-in-law's behavior, and this business about friends of her husband demanding to enter her home. Then there was the letter and papers she'd given him. It all added up to something he was not comfortable with.

He read those documents extensively, and each had the mark of the devil. Some had "Brothers of Faith," others, "the gods will be appeased." But there were no names. Only details of land purchases or agendas. Times, dates, and other such accountings.

Monty's instincts rarely let him down, so he was now positive the late Lord Challoner was involved in devil worshipping and his parents' deaths. He just couldn't put all the pieces together.

He would not alert Iris that he was worried about her welfare, and yet he was. She need not know he'd set someone to watch her and Henry. Her aunt and uncle would do so, he knew, but did they understand what her husband had been like, and the threat their niece could now face?

Seated at his breakfast table staring at the newspaper, he wondered what his next step should be to investigating these "Brothers of Faith." This had to be his focus now as it had been for many years. Now that he'd set someone to watching Iris, he could channel his energy into this and try to forget the beautiful Lady Challoner and her soft lips and smooth skin.

She'd asked him why he seemed to play the part of two different people. He now had to set about persuading her he was still the brainless fool he'd first appeared to be.

But he'd be lying if he didn't acknowledge, if only to himself, that he was glad she had seen through him.

"You are a fool," Monty muttered, pushing Iris from his head yet again.

He had sent word three days ago to four men he could trust. One to watch Iris, and the other three to search for any information they could find about the Brothers of Faith and the men who had supposedly been the late Lord Challoner's friends.

No murmurs, names. Nothing had ever surfaced about who killed his parents until now. He'd thought the trail was long cold, but now he had a place to start, and he would not stop until he found whoever was responsible.

Monty had told no one except his four trusted men about the new information, but he would speak to the Devilles and Geraint soon. Lingering in the back of his head was what he'd found that day sixteen years ago and then again in the letters Iris's husband had in his possession.

Geraint believed, as Monty did, his father was not involved in some kind of cult or devil worshipping society, but would others?

"A missive has arrived, my lord."

"Thank you, Haven."

Opening the paper, he recognized the writing as Mary's.

Today we are traveling out of London to attend the Duchess of Yardly's birthday celebrations at Lord and Lady Caruthers's residence. Apparently, the duchess has ordered many entertainments for her birthday. If I have to go, so do you, and don't think I don't know that you received an invitation because I do. If you do not come, it will not go well for you. It was signed *Mary.*

He barked out a laugh. She could always get him to do that. Her and that reprobate husband of hers.

"Was there an invitation for me from the Duchess of Yardly, Haven?"

His butler nodded. "I'll get it for you."

He received a lot of invitations; most he attended, as was expected of Plunge. When Haven returned, Monty read the details on the cream card he was handed.

A celebration of the Duchess of Yardly's life was the first line.

"If I'm being honest, I'm not sure we should celebrate her

life," he said to Haven. "The woman has been abusing and humiliating people for years."

"I'll ready the carriage."

Monty sighed.

"Perhaps a gift would be appropriate also, my lord?"

"Would it?" He looked at his butler. "What could I possibly purchase for a woman who has money and everything she wants?"

"You have just received the latest copy of Captain Broadbent and Lady Nauticus, my lord."

"I haven't read it yet."

"But you could easily get another."

"As could she," he said, sounding testy, which he never was. "But yes"—he sighed—"I can give her that."

Haven left, and Monty sat and sipped his tea.

"I have informed Jensen you will leave in an hour, my lord."

"Will I?"

His butler nodded.

Sighing once more, he got to his feet. He felt a great deal older today than he'd been last week. And dissatisfied. He blamed Iris for that.

After dressing, he left the house with his book, which would no longer be his by the day's end.

"Stop at the sweet shop, please, Lenny."

The duchess was in luck, and the weather had stayed sunny, which meant they could be outside and not crammed inside smelling several scents that were unpleasant when mixed.

Monty thought about the Deville family. They would all be traveling together with their children and likely Walter, their lovely big dog. There would be laughter and chatting on the journey, whereas he was in solitude. Which usually he enjoyed. However, not today.

When the carriage stopped, Monty climbed out, leaving the door open.

"I shall not be long, Lenny. I will simply secure us some taffy for the journey and more peppermint sticks."

"Right you are, my lord."

Stomping toward the sweet shop, his driver stopped him with a loud throat clearing.

"Is there a problem?" Monty turned to look at him.

Lenny made a walking gesture with his fingers, and Monty realized he'd been striding instead of Plunge walking. He gave a curt nod and continued with smaller mincing strides, because you never knew who was watching.

"It's a lovely day for taffy, my lord," Mrs. Veronica, the owner of his favorite sweet shop, said.

"Indeed, it is," he said in his high-pitched voice. He ordered peppermint sticks to be delivered to Iris and Henry and then bought two bags for himself as well as the taffy.

Armed with what he needed for his journey, he returned to the carriage, handed Lenny his taffy, and then stepped in through the open carriage door to find a thin, trembling greyhound had joined him. It was on the floor, and Monty only just managed not to stand on it by stumbling sideways and landing on the seat. Pushing himself upright, he looked at the quivering dog.

"Can I help you with something?" Monty asked.

"Oscar!"

The roar came from outside the window of the carriage. Looking at the brindle-striped dog, he noted it seemed to have shrunk lower and was trembling harder. It didn't make a noise or even look his way. The long snout was buried between its paws.

"You mangy beast. I'll bloody kill you when I get my hands on you!"

The man wasn't tall. Monty had a head on him was his guess, but he had a solid build and carried a whip with him.

Tugging off a glove, Monty bent and ran his hand over the dog's back, feeling the welts. Anger that anyone could treat an animal to such a beating had him stroking its head.

"Stay," he then whispered.

Getting out, he shut the carriage door.

"I shall be but a moment, Lenny."

"Need my assistance, my lord?" As a loud sucking followed this, Monty guessed Lenny was enjoying his taffy.

"No. I have it all under control."

Walking around the carriage to the opposite side, he found the man standing there. One hand was on his hip, and his head was swiveling from side to side, searching.

"Can I assist you, good sir?" Monty used his haughtiest tone.

The man spun on a heel and glared at him. Taking in Monty's clothes, he then bowed. When he rose, his expression was still a scowl.

"I've lost me dog."

"May I inquire what type of dog, as I could have seen it?"

"A greyhound."

"Color?" Monty asked with a raised brow.

"Can you see dozens of greyhounds about the place?" The man's scowl was fierce now. Monty, having faced down more dangerous foes, was not perturbed.

"I asked you a question. Kindly answer it."

"Brindle," the man snapped. "Bleeding thing ran off. Useless, it is. Raced two nights ago and came at the rear! I was teaching it a lesson." As his beefy fingers were clenched around a whip, Monty guessed the direction that lesson was taking.

"What is your name?"

"Cyril Curtis."

"Well, Mr. Curtis, is your lesson to beat your animals?" Monty said with an edge to his voice.

"It's my dog. I train 'em how I see fit!" the man roared at him. "I'm the best, and to be the best, you need to make the dogs understand who is in control."

"Where is it you have come from, sir?"

The man pointed the whip down the road to a set of buildings.

"Just to clarify. You train your dogs to race for you by beating them?" Monty asked calmly.

The man had flappy jowls and bloodshot eyes. Monty wasn't close, but he was close enough to smell the stench emanating from him. He smelled like he'd rolled in a pigsty.

"I'm one of the best trainers in London," he said again, punching a fist into his chest.

"I'm sure you are, but as I have no one to compare you with, I am loath to take your word, considering you are holding a whip," Monty said coolly. "Mistreating animals is not something I will ever condone, so I'd better not catch you doing so."

The man made a loud scoffing sound as he took in Monty's hair and scarlet jacket.

"Like I care what a toff in a jacket like that says." Cyril scoffed again.

The jab came with enough speed that no one, not even the recipient, saw it coming. Monty struck him in the jaw. He fell, and the back of Cyril's head landed in a pile of horse manure.

"I say. This man just fell. Could anyone help him rise? My jacket, you understand, it is of the finest silk!" Monty cried. "I cannot abide any animal effluent touching my person." He then bent to talk to the man.

"I know who you are, and I'm coming to find you, and when I do, I will look at your dogs. If I find any in a bad way because of your mistreatment of them, I will take them with me."

Cyril's eyes widened.

He doubted his words would make a difference, but he knew the man's name and had no doubts he'd find him. Which he would and look over his dogs.

Pulling out a lavender-scented handkerchief, he then minced back to the carriage.

"Nice jab, my lord. Right quick it was. I barely saw it," Lenny said.

"I will explain my actions soon. For now, get us moving, Lenny." Monty opened his carriage door and climbed inside.

The animal still lay shivering on the floor. He'd not owned a dog or cat since he'd walked out of his family home to attend Eton. That didn't mean he was completely cold-hearted toward them. He'd just taught himself to be that way. To close himself off to feelings and emotions.

"'Tis all right now, Oscar." Monty touched a hand softly to the dog's head. It trembled.

Why had he addressed that man about his dog? He never got involved in the business of others unless it directly affected him. More proof that he was not quite himself.

Monty knew he was changing. He just wasn't sure how to stop that happening or how to handle it.

"There now, Oscar," he said, stroking the short hair of the animal's head. "What am I going to do with you?"

It was all very well to make the rash, grand gesture of saving a dog that was clearly distressed enough to leap into his carriage, but what did he do with it now?

Theft was also theft, and that's exactly what he'd done, even if the cause had been an honorable one.

The Duchess of Yardly liked dogs. Perhaps he could leave it with her at the birthday celebrations. He couldn't very well open the door and throw it out. Its situation would be worse than what it was.

"Come now, Oscar. We have left your mean owner behind. Up you get," Monty said, bending to speak to the animal. "Do you like taffy? Or perhaps peppermint sticks? Walter likes those, and I got some for him when I purchased the taffy."

He waved the peppermint stick before the dog's long snout. It twitched.

"That's better," Monty said softly as it rose gingerly on thin legs.

He'd always thought them odd dogs, with their angular faces and long legs. He'd watched them race once. Their speed was astounding. The soft brown eyes that Oscar turned on him were sweet and doe-like.

"Hello. I'm Monty. Would you like this?" He held out the peppermint stick.

His guess was the dog was hungry, but it took the offering gently. It then ate two more. When it had finished, it rose on its hind legs and put its paws on Monty's thighs, staring at him.

"There is no way I can know what you're thinking, Oscar." But he thought maybe he did in that moment as a long tongue came out and licked his cheek. Relief that it had escaped its owner. Relief that someone had cared enough to save it.

No one saved me. Where had that thought come from? Pushing it aside with all the others he was avoiding, Monty watched the dog climb onto the seat beside him. It then lay down, making a sound as if air was being squeezed out of its lungs. Placing its snout on Monty's thigh, Oscar then let out a loud sigh.

"Well now." Monty patted the soft head. "You just make

yourself comfortable on my very expensive upholstery, Oscar."

They traveled that way for the rest of the journey, and Monty found himself chatting to the animal about several things, including Iris. It felt strangely comforting and cathartic. Especially, as unlike Mary or the Devilles, it did not answer back.

CHAPTER 15

$\mathcal{A}$s Iris was outside in the front garden with Henry, she saw the exact moment a large carriage stopped before her town house. The door opened, and Lady Raine stepped down. She then turned and helped Ella from the carriage behind her. Next came Lord Raine, holding a little girl in his arms. Last out was Walter.

Iris felt Henry stiffen and then make a sound like a squeak. Looking down, she noted he was smiling.

"Hello!" Lady Raine waved at her. "I hope you don't mind the intrusion. Walter, do not bound over the flowers!" she then bellowed.

The dog changed direction and trotted to where she and Henry stood. He then plopped down on his bottom and looked at them.

"Hello, Walter, it is nice to see you again," Henry said.

"Shake, Walter," the earl directed as he, too, entered the garden.

The dog raised a large paw, and Henry bent to take it, shaking it slowly.

Iris sank into a curtsy, and releasing Walter's paw, Henry bowed at her side when Lord and Lady Raine reached them.

She'd had a lovely time in the park with Dimity and felt as if they were becoming friends. Was this a social call? Didn't people usually send an invite if they wanted to do that?

"My wife wants to invite you to accompany us today, Lady Challoner," Lord Raine said.

He had a lovely smile. They were a very handsome couple, Iris thought.

"My other daughter is with one of my brothers. You never know whose child you will end up with in this family. Today we have Miss Ella."

"She's Iris, as I have already told you, Gabe. We rode the velocipede together. After that, you do not stand on formality," Dimity said.

"Forgive me," he said gravely. "My wife wished for you to accompany us today, Iris."

"Hello again," Ella said to Henry.

"Hello," Henry said in his quiet voice.

"Do you want to come with us today, Henry? We are going to a fair to celebrate the Duchess of Yardly's birthday. She's very old," Ella said. "But nice."

"I'm not sure nice fits the Duchess of Yardly, Ella."

The little girl squinted up at the earl. "She doesn't like adults, only children and animals."

"Well, there you have it then," Dimity said.

The little girl wiggled in her father's arms and wanted to be put down. Her father obliged, and she then ran to her big cousin.

"This is Patrice. She is my cousin," Ella said.

"The celebrations are being held at Lord and Lady Caruthers's estate about two hours away, so if you'd like to get ready, you can come with us. The children can then become further acquainted."

"I really don't think—"

"She will stand here and talk at you until you agree," the earl said, cutting Iris off. "It's best to just give in and comply with her wishes. It's what the rest of the family does."

The countess smiled. "Indeed, that's exactly what happens. Patrice, don't eat the dirt."

The girl did indeed have a handful and was just about to put it in her mouth.

"It will be fun. Your son can make new friends, as can you, Iris" the earl said. "You've only recently arrived, and I'm sure it would benefit both you and Henry to attend the celebrations."

"My lord, I really don't think—"

"He is Gabriel if you find him too imposing, and if not, Gabe," Dimity added.

"I'm the head of our family, my love. It is important to seem imposing, surely?"

The earl gave his wife a look that was full of love. It made Iris's throat tight with longing. She wasn't sure her husband had ever liked her, or his son, for that matter.

"So what do you say, Iris? Will you come along? We will need to leave soon to reach the duchess's party in time," Dimity said.

"I don't know the Duchess of Yardly well," Iris said, hoping this would put the woman off. "I've, of course, met her a few times, but still, she did not directly invite me, so I wouldn't feel right—"

"Just as well, really. You don't know her as intimately as we do," the earl said. "Woman's terrifying. She's infiltrated my household and there seems little I can do about it."

"It's true she is not the easiest person to warm to. I'll give you that," the countess said. Her husband snorted. "But she was quite wonderful to me when I most needed it."

"She's a dragon."

"Who you adore," the countess said. "Now, hurry it along, Iris. You and Henry will have a lovely time."

"Yes, do come, Henry," Ella said. "We will have so much fun."

Her son smiled again.

"I really don't think it's done to just turn up—"

"Oh please. The duchess has no concept of what is done," Dimity said. "She does exactly as she wishes, and if she allowed you to take Walter that day you saw her in her carriage, then I know she likes you... well, as much as she likes anyone."

Iris looked at her son. "Do you wish to go to a fair, Henry?"

He nodded, his eyes still on Ella and Patrice. The little girl was now rummaging about in the flower bed.

"Do not let her eat the snail shells, Ella."

"I won't, Aunt Dimity."

"Now I hate to be forceful—"

"But why stop now?" her husband added.

"We need to get moving, Iris."

"I will need to change." She looked down at her dress. "We could take our own carriage," Iris said. Then they could leave when they wished.

"Ours is quite large enough to accommodate us all. It really is no imposition," the earl said. He looked a happy man, Iris thought. Content with his life. She tried to remember when she'd felt that way and couldn't. Except maybe when her husband had passed, and they were finally rid of his tyranny.

"I would like to go with them," Henry said softly, which made her swallow the next refusal.

"Very well." How could she say no to him when he rarely asked her for anything?

"Excellent," the earl said as he bent to take a snail out of his daughter's chubby hands.

"Would you like to take tea while you wait for us? We will not be long," Iris asked.

"Thank you, but we shall be quite all right out here. The children can play, and Walter can wander before we need to get back into the carriage," Dimity said.

Iris and Henry hurried inside. Was this odd? Was this the kind of thing people did? Came and collected others to take them on outings? She hadn't walked in society before but thought this was not usual.

"Do you really want to go, Henry?"

"Yes."

"Because you like Ella?"

"I like Dimity too. She said I could call her that," he added quickly.

"Well then, you must call her what she wishes you to."

"They're nice people, Mother."

"Very well then. We must hurry, as we do not want to leave the earl and countess standing in our gardens for too long."

She handed him over to his nanny to change and then rushed to her rooms to do the same. With her maid's help, she dressed quickly. Collecting Henry, she ran back down the stairs.

Am I doing the right thing?

Walking outside, she found the earl and countess running around her front garden, chasing the dog and children. Henry's chuckle was muffled behind his hand, but she heard it.

Yes, I am.

They all climbed inside the carriage, and much to her surprise, there was more than enough room even with the large dog.

"My husband likes to travel in comfort. This is our new carriage. We can fit several children, animals, and adults," Dimity said.

"You never know how many you will travel with as I believe I mentioned. We have a large family," the earl said.

Iris sat with Henry to her side, and Ella beside him. Across from her were the earl and countess and their daughter. Walter leaned on the door, watching them.

"Now, Iris, have you read the Captain Broadbent and Lady Nauticus books?" Dimity asked.

"I haven't, no."

"Well, if you walk in society, that is something you need to do in case you find yourself in the middle of a reading."

"Pardon?"

"Don't confuse her, my love. Iris will want to run and never look back if you tell her everything. Leave her to learn some of it slowly, and then we may have a chance that she wants to remain our friend."

The idea of these wonderful people wanting her as their friend was humbling.

"Very well, I shall say no more," Dimity said.

"I believe you and Lord Plunge were childhood friends," Gabe said.

Theo, she wanted to say. *His name is Theo or Lord Montgomery.*

"His father's land bordered my family's. We were friends growing up." That sounded good. Simple and to the point.

"What was he like as a boy?"

Her hesitation had the earl saying, "A great deal different from who he is today, I'm sure."

"Yes, he was very different, but we have not seen each other since I was ten."

"Did he move away or you?" Dimity asked.

Iris looked at Henry, who was listening intently to something Ella was saying. He had a hand on Walter's head, stroking the soft fur.

Tomorrow she would look for a dog. She was slowly erasing what her late husband had done to them. This would just be something else.

"Theo left to attend Eton," Iris said.

"Theo is Lord Plunge's name?" Dimity asked.

Her eyes went to the earl, who held Patrice on his lap. He was staring at her intently, which suggested to Iris he was very interested in what she was saying. She supposed that was normal, considering the man Theo had become. Simpering and lavender wearing.

"Yes, he left a year after his parents were killed."

Lady Raine shot her husband a look, but the earl kept his eyes on Iris.

"Killed?" the countess asked.

"I should probably not discuss the matter," Iris said quickly. If society did not know how his parents died, then that was likely because Theo wished it that way.

"Some of society are aware they were murdered, Iris, but not all," Lord Raine said.

"Murdered," Lady Raine whispered. "Good lord, poor Plunge."

"Does not one call him Lord Montgomery?"

"Most have forgotten he is Lord Montgomery," the earl said.

Some, but not all, she thought. Iris would never forget the name of her childhood friend.

CHAPTER 16

*L*ord and Lady Caruthers's home was large, as you would expect from peers of wealth and status. A stream rambled beside the drive as the carriage rolled toward the house where the Duchess of Yardly was holding her birthday party.

"What am I to do with you now?" Monty asked the greyhound, who had slept with his chin resting on his thigh the entire journey. He'd be lying to himself if he said it hadn't been nice having the company, even if it was a dog.

Looking out the window, he watched the carriage stop beside several others. One he recognized, as it had the Raine crest on the door. It appeared to also have just arrived as said door was opening, and several people were pouring out.

He saw Gabe and Dimity, and their daughter Patrice, and then Ella, Gabe's cousin Forrest's daughter. As they were now his friends, he knew a great deal about them, because Devilles were not ones for silence. They talked constantly and usually about what and who they loved.

But it was the next person to step from the carriage that surprised him.

Iris Challoner took the earl's hand and climbed out. She then turned to watch Henry join her. He had the same serious expression he'd worn the day Monty had visited the Challoner town house.

Why was she here, and with Dimity and Gabe?

"Hello, Lord Plunge!" Dimity waved to him as he opened the door.

"Hello," he said. "Is it not a beauteous day?" he added in Plunge's voice because he'd forgotten to use it, which was odd when you got right down to it. He rarely slipped out of character when attending a society function.

Gabe walked toward him with his daughter Patrice in his arms. He was frowning.

"What's wrong?" he said softly.

"Nothing."

"You just said hello in a cold, hard voice before remembering the beauteous day part. You're also frowning. Plus, you only have two folds in your necktie, and you're wearing those flat black shoes again."

"No one will notice." Monty waved his words away.

"Oh, I assure you they will, but wait, there is more," Gabe said. "There is that business with the Blake women all atwitter with your appearance the day they saw you outside Iris's town house, and Lady Cagney's story about you rescuing that boy."

"Will you just shut up and listen?" Monty snapped, looking over his shoulder to check the others weren't close. "Yes, isn't my jacket wonderful!" Monty added in his best Plunge voice so those around them wouldn't know they were discussing anything but fashion.

Gabe rolled his eyes. "Never behave like him," he said to his daughter.

"I have something I need help with. Come to my home tomorrow night."

Gabe nodded. "To do with Alexius?"

"Yes, but it is also personal. As yet Geraint does not have all the details."

"Very well. Is there anything else you wanted to tell me?"

Any other Deville would have demanded to know what information, but this one could at least keep quiet when required.

"I have a dog in my carriage. It's a long story, but I need you to take it, or say you found it or something. It wouldn't be right for me to suddenly appear with a dog."

"And it would be right for me to?" Gabe then leaned around Monty to peer in his open carriage door to where Oscar still lay on the seat. "Is that a greyhound?"

"Yes. Of course, I have a lavender-scented handkerchief!" Monty said loudly.

"Slipping in and out of character must be exhausting," Gabe said. "How do you just happen to find a greyhound?"

"Your family and Lady Challoner are approaching," Monty hissed. "Why is she with you? I didn't know Dimity and Iris were friends."

"They apparently rode Forrest's velocipede together in the park, and that was after meeting at the ball. My wife decided your old friend and neighbor needed to be folded into our family, and so here we all are."

"She's not a soufflé, Gabe," Monty snapped.

"One would think by that snippy response she is important to you." Gabe smirked.

"La, 'tis it not an exquisite day for a party!" Monty said, ignoring him.

Gabe rolled his eyes again.

"Do something with the dog," he whispered. "But make sure he goes to a good home," he added. The animal had suffered enough. He deserved some happiness.

"I am, of course, at your service," Gabe drawled.

"You look handsome in lavender," Dimity said when she drew near.

"He always wears lavender," her husband said.

Iris, Monty noted, hung back with her son. She was exquisite in a pale peach dress. Her bonnet and spencer were mint green velvet. She had yet to look at him.

He felt that same reaction he had when she'd called at his town house. An awareness of her that punched him hard in the gut. That had only increased after their kiss.

There had been women in his life, but he'd left London to service his needs. It would not do for anyone to think Lord Plunge had urges that included a sexual appetite.

The burning feeling deep in his gut he felt for Iris differed completely from anything he'd felt before.

"Lady Challoner." He bowed to her, so she had to look at him. She moved forward as he'd acknowledged her, bringing Henry with her.

"I thought you were childhood friends?" Dimity was frowning.

"We were," Monty said.

"Well then, call her Iris."

"We have not been a part of each other's lives for many years, Lady Raine," Monty said in his most pompous voice. "But of course I live to serve you."

"Don't give her ideas," Gabe said.

"Is that a dog, Lord Plunge?" Ella asked, stepping around him and into his carriage.

He turned to watch the little girl. She now sat on the seat next to a quivering Oscar, stroking his head.

"A greyhound I believe," Monty told her.

"Why do you have a dog in your carriage?" Dimity nudged him aside and moved into the doorway.

"Aww, look at his sad eyes," Ella said.

"One hopes he's friendly?" Gabe lowered Patrice to the

floor. The child then tugged on her mother's skirts. Dimity lifted her inside.

"Oscar is an angel," Monty cooed. "He was quite taken with my peppermint sticks." He hoped he was right.

Walter let out a loud woof at the words "peppermint sticks" and nudged his way to the carriage. He then jumped inside with the children.

The greyhound, who was sitting on the seat, stretched down with his long snout and sniffed Walter. They touched noses, and Walter's tail wagged.

"If only it were that simple with people," Gabe said.

"Agreed," Dimity said. "Without the bottom sniffing, of course."

Her husband snorted.

"Will he bite?" Iris asked.

"No," Monty said, hoping again he was right.

"Ella, come out of the carriage, my sweet," Dimity said, removing her daughter. "Walter, you too."

They all climbed out, and lastly, Oscar tentatively joined them. He moved to Monty's side and leaned on his thigh.

"He seems quite taken with you," Gabe said.

"La, I have little time for dogs," Monty said. Was that a touch of panic in his voice?

"Where did you find him?" Ella asked. She was crouched before Oscar. Her pink dress dragged in the dust and dirt as she stroked the greyhound's long snout.

"Well." Monty shot Gabe a look. "Ah, well, he found me actually...." The words trailed off, as he wasn't sure how to continue. Did someone just find a dog and decide to keep it?

The life he'd chosen to live now felt like the wrong fit for him, and suddenly he was struggling to keep up with his story and personas.

"Hello, Oscar."

Henry moved closer. Iris reached for him, but he stepped

away from her and joined Ella. The surprise on her face told him the boy rarely rebelled.

Holding out a hand, he then crouched down in the dirt. Oscar stretched his long snout again and sniffed the hand.

"Hello, Oscar," Henry whispered.

The dog moved from leaning on Monty and sat in front of the boy.

"I believe you said the dog needs a new home, Lord Plunge?" Gabe asked. "Due to the owner being unable to care for him anymore," he added, giving Monty a look.

"Oh indeed, that is exactly what happened."

"So you didn't just find him then?" Ella asked him accusingly. No one could give you the eye quite like a child.

"No, Lord Raine is right. My memory, you know." He waved a hand about. "And of course, I can't have a dog. All that hair everywhere." Monty shuddered and waved a handkerchief about.

"Do you want a dog, Iris?" Dimity asked.

"Pardon?" She looked shocked.

"Yes," Henry said at the same time.

"Oh well... I..." Iris's words fell away as her son turned to look at her. "We had thought to get one, but...." Her words trailed off as she looked at Henry.

"Please, can we take Oscar home with us, Mother?" the boy said. "I'll look after him."

Monty had little experience with children, but the few he had met were exuberant. Even on such a brief acquaintance, he could see Iris's son was not that. She'd been full of life as a child. Was that bastard Challoner responsible for Henry's behavior?

Looking at the tears in her eyes as she studied her boy, he felt the surge of heat that came with rage at the thought that Challoner had hurt her. In some way beaten down the spirit she'd shown as a child.

"Are you sure he needs a home?" Iris asked Monty.

He nodded.

"It all seems a bit odd that we can have him just like that, but if you are sure he is looking for a home, then we could take him," she said, and he could tell she was still stunned by the entire proceedings.

"Well, he seems gentle, and clearly Henry and Oscar have taken to each other," Dimity added.

"Plus, we can all go for walks together!" Ella cried. "Walter and Oscar will be firm friends."

Henry looked at his mother, knowing the final say was hers.

"Very well. We will take him for a trial period," Iris said.

He didn't yell his excitement. The boy simply bent and wrapped the dog in a gentle hug. Oscar placed his chin on Henry's shoulder, quivering.

"I think the trial period is over," Gabe said.

"Is that dog smiling?" Dimity asked.

The corners of Oscar's mouth were definitely tilting, Monty thought. He looked away and straight into the tearful gaze of Henry's mother.

And this was why he did not make friends and collect people, he reminded himself again. They brought emotion with them.

"Well, now that that's all worked out to everyone's delight. Shall we attend the Duchess of Awkward's birthday festivities?" Gabe asked.

He shouldn't walk in with these people. In fact, none of what just happened should have happened in his presence. If society saw him behaving as a normal member and not the snooty, effeminate fool, questions would arise, which they already were after his saving that boy, and then the Blakes seeing him looking different. It was time to get back into character.

"If you'll excuse me, I have people who are awaiting my arrival." Monty managed a forced smile and then bowed.

"What do we do with the dogs?" He heard Iris ask as he walked away.

"They can come. The duchess loves dogs," Ella said with all the confidence of a child.

"But he must be on a leash, surely?" Iris said.

"No need. They can simply run about the place, and Walter will look after Oscar," Ella added.

"He's a dog," Henry said.

"Yes, but Walter is a very special, intelligent dog," Dimity added.

Increasing his pace, Monty left the Devilles and Challoners behind. He walked to where two footmen stood on either side of a path that likely led to the festivities. One held a silver tray with a variety of colored fans spread over it. Taking a lavender one—but of course—he walked on.

"Good lord," Monty whispered when he saw what they had set up for the duchess's birthday party.

Several men and women were walking about on barrels dressed in various costumes. Ship's captains, milkmaids, a cat, complete with whiskers and a tail. There were also jugglers throwing fire and skittles into the air. Two large, long red-and-white tents were serving refreshments.

"Those fans are for the women, Plunge. However, I'm sure they'll make an exception in your case."

Ignoring the voice behind him, Monty unfurled his fan with flair while sweeping his hand in an arc. He struck Lord Laidlaw in the cheek hard enough to have him stumble back, gasping.

"Oh, no!" Monty rushed to console the man. "My apologies, my lord. Let me get you one of my handkerchiefs to revive you."

Monty pulled one out of his pocket and pressed it to the man's face. Laidlaw pushed him aside.

"You bumbling, effeminate fool!" he thundered. "How dare you strike me!"

His face was now red with rage, plus the mark Monty had inflicted on him. He closed the distance between them until they were inches apart.

If only you knew how much I could hurt you.

"But you cannot think I would do such a thing on purpose?" Monty's voice rose to a high-pitched warble.

"I should punch you and do everyone a favor," Laidlaw muttered. His friends, who stood at his back, agreed. "You are a pathetic excuse for a man."

"But, my dear Laidlaw, how can you say such a thing? You wound me. Perhaps if I do something for your cheek, you will not be so scathing about my person." Monty lunged at him and struck him again on the other cheek with the fan.

Howling with rage, the man charged Monty. He pretended to stumble to the left, leaving his foot outstretched. Laidlaw tripped over it and fell onto the shell path, hard.

"That has to hurt," Zachariel Deville said, stepping to Monty's left.

"I would say. Laidlaw might need to have the bits of shell removed from his palms," Mary Deville said from his right.

"And perhaps his cheek," Zach added.

Monty had spent years annoying and playing tricks on members of society who had insulted or belittled him. They, of course, had no idea and thought it was just part of his clumsiness. He'd always done so alone and faced the consequences. He now had people who were there for him. Watched over him. He still wasn't entirely comfortable with that.

"I'm going to kill you!" Laidlaw had regained his feet and was now heading for Monty.

"Stand down, Laidlaw." Michael and Nathanial Deville had arrived and stood beside their brother.

"He struck me. Twice! Then threw me to the ground!"

"Lord Plunge?" Mary scoffed. "I'm not entirely sure he's capable of such an act, Laidlaw. Bested by a man such as he... what will society think?"

Laidlaw stood before him now, fists clenched. Monty wanted to punch him badly. He and his group had tormented Lord Plunge for years. While it normally didn't bother him, today it did.

The rage inside him was burning for a release.

"That will help no one," a deep voice whispered into his ear. Which Deville it was, he could not be sure.

"I say, Laidlaw, I, of course, meant you no harm!" Monty roared instead of hurting the man further. "Why, I would never willingly inflict pain on a fellow peer!"

"Stay away from me!" Laidlaw jabbed a finger at him. "I will take you apart should you come near me again."

"No, you will not," Nathan said in a cold, hard voice.

"I'm not sure why you Devilles are protecting him." Laidlaw pointed at them next. "He's not worthy of anyone's respect."

"I will take anyone's side over yours, Laidlaw." Those words came from Gabe, who had just arrived. He had history with the man that included his treatment of Dimity and Walter.

Laidlaw paled and then turned and walked away with his friends. No doubt to find somewhere to pick shell out of his face.

"Well, I never," Monty whined. "Did you hear that? He threatened me." He pressed a handkerchief to his lips to hide the sneer on his face. "I-I feel quite faint."

"Don't overdo it," Zach whispered. "And one day someone will realize you're deliberately meting out punishment to those who insulted you."

"I need to lie down!" Monty wailed, walking to the left with Mary holding his arm. His eyes found Iris, and she was staring at him. He felt the silly look fall from his face before he could stop it.

CHAPTER 17

*I*ris had seen the entire incident unfold with Theo. She couldn't be sure, but she thought he'd struck that man deliberately. Then he'd appeared to stumble and trip him.

"Oscar is really coming home with us?"

She looked down at her son and then to the solemn-eyed dog. Beside the animal walked Walter. He almost seemed to watch over the greyhound, which, of course, was not true, but to Iris, it seemed he was.

"It appears so," she said, still dazed over the turn her life had taken just this morning. She'd had only one plan when she reached London. Get the note to Theo and survive a few social occasions. But she'd made friends and now acquired a dog. It was enough to send a person back to the country.

"Oscar is happy," Henry said.

"How do you know that?"

"I can feel his happiness," her son said solemnly.

"As it is our mission to be happy, Henry, I think today we have achieved that," she whispered in his ear.

He gave her one of those rare smiles she treasured. "Yes, we have."

His words filled her chest with heat. Finally, she was breaking through some of the trauma her husband had created inside their son.

"Can Henry come with me?"

"Where is it you want to take him, Ella?" she said to the little girl who now stood before them.

"There is an area that the Duchess of Yardly, who likes animals and children but not adults, set aside for us to play in."

Iris followed the little girl's finger and saw several staff members milling about with children. There was a table with food, and a long piece of rope was being used for tug-of-war. Other activities had children crowding around them. Other people who she thought could be nannies were there as well.

Neither she nor the Devilles appeared to have brought a nanny with them.

"Do you want to go, Henry?" It surprised her when her son nodded. "Very well, but if you need me, just ask one of the staff to locate me. I will not wander far and will return to check on you often."

"Yes, but I have Oscar."

"Walter and Oscar can come with us. They will enjoy it too," Ella said. "And I will not leave Henry's side."

Her son nodded solemnly. Ella then grabbed his hand and tugged, and soon Henry was running away from her with the dogs.

"Ella will ensure Henry is all right," a deep voice said from over her shoulder.

Turning, she found a man Iris had not met before. But she knew whose family he was part of. The Deville genes were strong, it seemed.

"I am Forrest Howarth. Ella is my daughter. A force of

nature but exceedingly kindhearted. I assure you, your son will be safe with her."

He was tall like the other Devilles she'd met.

"Thank you, and I know she is a kind, sweet girl. She taught Henry to ride the velocipede the other day."

"Kind, sweet, and mischievous," he said. "It is a wonderful contraption. Ella has mastered it way quicker than any of us."

"Children do that," Iris said. "I am Lady Challoner."

"My family told me I had to call you Iris, so if you don't mind calling me Forrest, we shall do as they directed. After all, they are not the type of people one wishes to cross." His smile told her he was only joking.

"We seem to have acquired a dog from Lord Montgomery," Iris said, her eyes on the children still running away with Walter and Oscar. "Your family convinced me to take him."

"I'm sure you were coerced. However, I do believe greyhounds are very gentle and make wonderful pets," Forrest Howarth said.

"It's my hope you are right."

"One thing you need to know about my family, Iris, is they can be forceful and leave you feeling dazed," he added. "But I assure you, they are the very best of people. However, if you disagree with them, then tell them so, otherwise they will simply walk right over the top of you." He smiled again. "But because of them I learned what happiness was and found my wife."

"Oh... ah, that's nice," Iris said. She wasn't used to people speaking to her so openly. Before her husband's death, the only other people she'd talked to besides him were the household staff and her aunt and uncle when they called and demanded to see her.

"One thing my family has taught me is to be candid. Forgive me if that has upset you, Iris."

"It didn't upset me," she said. "I'm just not used to… well, to conversing actually," she finished lamely. "I lived an isolated life until my husband's passing."

"Exposure to my family will help you with that, I promise you. Will you walk with me to meet my wife? She is with the rest of the family."

He didn't hold out his arm, just waved a hand before him, and with a last look at Henry, who was now playing tug-of-war, she started walking at his side.

"Oh dear."

"What?" She shot him a look. "You sound worried, Forrest."

"The Sinclair and Raven men are at the adults' tug-of-war rope, and my family is joining them. This will go well for no one." The words may have sounded dire, and yet he was laughing. "Come along, Iris, and prepare to be entertained."

"I'm not at all fooled, sir. You are looking forward to the experience."

"Of course I am, but it is not the done thing to show such enthusiasm, surely?" he teased her.

"I have found that society has many rules and social behaviors one must navigate," Iris said.

"Amen."

They reached the Deville women who were all standing around chatting.

"Ruby, my love, allow me to introduce you to Lady Challoner, but we call her Iris," Forrest said. "Her son, Henry, is playing with Ella."

"I have heard a great deal about you from Ella, but more importantly, your son," the woman said. She had beautiful red-gold hair and soft, pale skin.

"Excellent. Now, if you will excuse me, I must join my idiot cousins and offer them my arms," Forrest said.

139

"Good luck." Ruby Howarth blew her husband a kiss before he left.

Love, Iris thought, these Devilles had it with their husbands and wives. Once, she'd believed she could find something similar. In that, Iris had been wrong.

"Now, Iris, stand here with me and watch the men, who are, for the most, intelligent individuals until they are participating in an activity like tug-of-war. They then become idiots. It will be entertaining."

"We could always go for a walk and find more intelligent company," Beth Deville said, joining them with Mary, Dimity, and Freya, who she'd talked with at her first society social engagement.

"But it will be entertaining," a beautiful dark-haired lady who was with them said.

"Lady Challoner, allow me to introduce you to the Duchess of Raven. For the purposes of the tug-of-war, she is, in fact, our enemy," Ruby said.

"Duchess." Iris curtsied.

"We call her Eden, so you may as well," Dimity said. She also did not consult the duchess about Iris using her first name.

"We outnumber you," the duchess said. "So your lot is bringing reinforcements. The Duke of Stratton, Lords Ryder and Levermarch bring the Deville numbers to seven. Then the Hetherington twins total ten."

"What are they arguing over now?" Mary asked.

"Dear lord," the duchess gasped. "Plunge is joining them. He's the Devilles' number eleven to even the numbers."

"That can't go well for anyone," Dimity said.

Iris watched as Lord Raine and Mr. Zachariel Deville talked to Theo. He shook his head. They continued talking.

"I almost wish I could hear what's being said," Mary added.

A crowd was forming around the long rope, all watching what was unfolding eagerly.

"For God's sake, Plunge! This is your chance to be a man," the Duchess of Yardly shrieked at him. "And when you're done, we can commence our literary saloon."

The groan that went around the crowd had Iris looking at the women with her.

"We told you about the books of Captain Broadbent and Lady Nauticus," Dimity said.

She nodded.

"Well, the duchess is something of a connoisseur on the subject, and she is known to call impromptu reading saloons —"

"Literary saloons," the Duchess of Raven added.

"We have all participated in them. Some enjoy it, others don't, but if you are there and selected to read, well, you must read," Dimity said.

"Yes, even the men in our family who have tried to fight against it ended up bowing to pressure. The duchess is quite ruthless. Lord Plunge loves a literary saloon," Mary added.

Iris decided it may be time to find Henry and stay with him. No way would she be reading in public.

"I say, are they forcing Plunge to participate?" someone to Iris's right said.

"It certainly looks that way. They're even attempting to get his lavender silk jacket off him," another said.

"Did you hear that rumor about him saving the boy perpetuated by Lady Cagney?"

"Yes, and the Blakes said he looked quite fierce stalking down the street in long strides in a very uncharacteristic manner."

"Do you think he's perhaps decided to be more manly?"

The conversation was taking place between a gaggle of ladies to their right.

"Have you noticed his shoes?" Beth shouted. "Quite manly."

Everyone within hearing distance dutifully looked at Theo's feet. Shiny black shoes with silver buckles adorned them.

"Are they not his usual footwear?" Iris asked.

"No indeed. He often wears heels, but perhaps as we are outside that selection makes sense," Dimity said.

"Even his hair seems different today," one lady tittered. "Do you think he might be considered handsome? I've never really seen past the silliness before."

There was silence then as they studied Theo.

"Has he always been this way?" Iris had to ask.

"Silly and pompous?" Dimity said.

"Yes."

There was more silence while the women thought about that. Iris watched Theo shake his head again. Clearly, he had no wish to take part in the tug-of-war.

"For as long as I can remember," Mary said. "I have known him no other way."

"Oh!" Dimity cried.

"What?" Iris said, returning her attention to the tug-of-war participants.

"They've wrestled Plunge's jacket off," Dimity said.

"Do you know, I think he's angry," the Duchess of Raven said. "I've never seen him angry."

"How can you tell?" Ruby asked.

"His mouth is in a line."

Iris stared at Theo. Was he angry?

"Yes, you're right. He's usually got some silly smile in place," Beth said. "He has nice shoulders, don't you think? I always thought there was padding in his jackets, but it seems not."

He did have nice shoulders and arms. They were strong

and muscled. Excellent arms to hold a person and make them feel safe.

"I've never really looked at the man before, but he's not flabby at all," the duchess said loudly.

In fact, Theo's stomach was flat under his waistcoat.

"How odd to suddenly see him in a different light," one of the women to their right said.

"Extremely odd," Dimity said.

Looking at her, Iris didn't think it surprised her at all. In fact, none of the Deville women seemed to be shocked.

"However, he is still brainless," Mary added.

She wanted to defend him but knew that it was the truth. He was sometimes very silly. She just hadn't worked out why.

CHAPTER 18

"What the hell are you about?" Monty whispered to Michael Deville after he and Nathan had wrestled his jacket off.

"You'll enjoy it."

"No, I won't. This is not Plunge."

"Maybe it's time to change the perception of people toward you," Forrest said. "We can do that slowly. You've already changed your shoes, and your hair is not quite so... so—"

"Dog poo–like?" Zach asked, smirking.

"Desist!" Monty growled.

"And the other business with the Blakes and you playing hero in front of Lady Cagney will help to let people see another side of you," Michael added.

"I have no wish for another side of me to be seen," Monty hissed.

"I say, Plunge. Is everything all right?"

These words came from Mr. Carlton Hyde, who was the second most foolish man in society after Monty... or Plunge, he corrected silently. Although likely he was the first, as

Monty was playing a part, and Hyde, well, he was just extremely silly and simpleminded.

"No indeed, Mr. Hyde. I fear I am about to expire. They ripped my coat from my person, you know! My coats are extremely valuable!" Monty cried from a mass of Devilles.

Mass? Gaggle? One never really knew what to call a grouping of Devilles.

"Oh my poor Lord Plunge," Hyde moaned.

Monty couldn't help it. He looked down and rolled his eyes.

"You can seek comfort in the fact that you're actually not a simpleton… well, not completely, unlike Hyde," Zach said.

"I will make you pay for that," Monty muttered.

They all stepped back after they'd manhandled him enough.

"La, who has smelling salts?" Monty said in a tone that was more filled with menace than dramatics.

"Clearly the Devilles feel they will beat the Sinclairs and Ravens with the extras they have, so they brought in Plunge to even up the numbers. It would be like having a woman on your team," Lord Hipkiss said loud enough to carry to several women nearby.

"Hipkiss, were the women to compete, you would be left weeping pitifully," Dimity yelled back to him.

"Exactly. In fact—"

"Absolutely not," the Duke of Raven said, cutting his wife off. "That is not happening here, my love."

The duchess looked mutinous, as did the other women in their family, and the Devilles' if he was honest. Phoebe Levermarch did not look pleased either. She was something of a society darling, and terrifying alongside Dimity and the Duchess of Raven. Beauty, brains, and wit—a lethal combination.

Monty thought if he'd actually walked in society as

himself, he would have liked to get to know some of these women properly. Yet another thing he'd not considered until today.

Clearly, he was unraveling like the hideous woolen cap his butler insisted on wearing in the cooler months to ward off headaches. It was mustard and lined with something. His mother had made it for him. Monty had offered a replacement; Haven would not hear of it.

"Plunge, try to stay upright!" someone called.

"Don't break a heel!" another called. "I say, he's not wearing heels," the voice added.

He gritted his teeth. Why did these comments annoy him now? Before he'd thought them hilarious and even played up to them.

"Now, Plunge, you will be at the rear. Hold the rope in both hands," Nathan Deville said, nudging him into line behind Zach. "We will do the work," he added loudly.

Several unflattering comments filled his head. Thankfully, he kept them there.

Mincing to where he was told to stand, Monty tried to look terrified and nervous at the same time. His eyes found Iris not far away standing with the Deville women.

Why did just looking at her make him feel desperate for something he could never have?

"Focus, Plunge, we are beginning," Zach said, interrupting his thoughts.

"I will lower my handkerchief, and the tug-of-war will start," the Duchess of Yardly said.

"I have a spare lavender-scented one. Should you require it, Duchess?" Monty said, tearing his eyes from Iris.

"I do not!" she snapped back.

"Simpering fool," someone muttered.

Monty smiled.

"Gentlemen, pick up your ropes!" the duchess yelled in a

surprisingly strong voice, given she was nearing eighty, or so he believed. Not that anyone would expect anything less. The woman was a harridan, constantly scaring anyone who wronged her, and several who didn't.

"Lovely dress, your grace," the Duchess of Raven said. "What color do you call that, Duchess?"

"Wilted cabbage," Cambridge Sinclair answered. "Rather fetching."

"Are you ready?" the duchess snapped.

"No!" Monty cried pathetically.

"Yes," everyone else replied.

The opposition was comprised of all the male members of the Sinclair and Raven family, which included a duke, lords, gentlemen, businessmen, a captain, an academic, and a pirate; even though he'd told everyone he was a privateer, society had not been convinced. In fact, they quite liked having a pirate among them.

For the most, they had strict rules and guidelines they adhered to and yet could be fickle when they chose to. Like having a pirate walk among them.

Monty had found that the Sinclair and Raven clan could get away with a great deal more than the rest of society. Perhaps because they didn't seem to care overly if anyone liked them or not.

"Now, Plunge," Nathan said in front of him. His face was inches from his.

Monty crossed his eyes. Nathan barked out a laugh. He then looked left and right, but as all the women were looking at the men in their shirtsleeves, and the men who weren't engaged in the activity were wondering how to look like those in their shirtsleeves, no one was looking their way.

"Focus. You are the anchor. We will tie this rope around your waist, and all you need to do is stand there and look prettyish… or at the very least, like a man of sense."

"La, I can do that! I am imminently sensible," Monty cried. "You are all paying for this later," he said under his breath.

"There are more of us than you," Nathan whispered back. "No threat will hold any weight."

A loud woof announced Walter's appearance. With him was Oscar. Clearly, they had come to watch his humiliation.

"Hello, Walter. Are you coming to offer Prissy Plunge some support?" Nathan said.

"Bite," Monty said. To his surprise, Oscar nudged Nathan hard in the leg, sending him back a step.

"Good boy." Monty patted his head.

"Sorry, he was with Henry," Iris said, arriving. "I'll get him out of your way."

"Quite all right, my lady," he said in his best Plunge voice.

She frowned, her eyes narrowing.

"What?"

"I can't work you out," she whispered.

"I am, of course, exactly as you see." He held out a hand theatrically.

"Well, there is a long line of people you'd need to join to understand him," Nathan said.

"Go back to your place, my dear lady, and watch as the men compete," Monty said, struggling to speak as Plunge and not himself. He'd shown her his different side, and he'd also kissed her. It was hardly surprising she was confused.

She gave him a hard look and then, with a click of her fingers, turned away with Oscar and Walter on her heels. "Let's leave these silly men to their games," he heard her say.

"Harsh but true," Nathan said. "I do not know Lady Challoner well but have to say that she seems nice. How long has it been since you saw each other?"

"Many years. I was but thirteen." Monty kept his eyes on her. The sway of her skirts and perfectly straight back.

"Tomorrow night, Monty." Nathan leaned in to say the words. "We will arrive after dark. Ensure there is lots of food."

"I live to serve you." Monty bowed.

The men picked up the rope. Monty had no wish to be tied to anything, even though Nathan had tried, and simply wrapped it around his waist.

"I just cannot see this going well for Plunge," he heard someone say.

"On your marks," the Duchess of Yardly cackled. "Pull!"

Monty couldn't just stand there looking pathetic. He had to at least try. Pull without it looking like he was doing a great deal.

"Oh dear!" he cried. "My gloves will be quite ruined!"

"Shut up and pull, Plunge!" Michael Deville roared at him.

He spread his legs and tried to hold as much weight as he could while looking pathetic and terrified. It was no easy feat. The tug-of-war raged on, with sides drawn by guests. They cheered, and every time he looked at Iris, she was watching him with a frown on her face.

"I will be ravenous after this!" Cambridge Sinclair roared.

"As if you need a reason!" his brother Devonshire Sinclair replied.

Before him, the men strained to gain ascendancy.

"I had thought you Devilles were strong. Clearly, I was misinformed!" Captain Wolf Sinclair gritted out.

"And yet we are a man down and still holding our own!" Gabe called back.

The inference being that Monty was less than a man. Gripping the rope, he gave a hard tug and then squeaked for authenticity.

"Plunge is going to expire!" someone called out, which had loud laughter following.

"The Devilles must have taken pity on him to put him in their team!"

He ignored the taunts, more than used to them.

"You will not lose!" the Duchess of Raven called.

"Yes, thank you for the support, my love!" her husband, the duke, replied.

"On three," Nathan growled.

"What on three?" Monty called in his most feeble Plunge voice.

"We pull."

"I thought we were?"

"Well, pull harder, Plunge!" Zach roared.

CHAPTER 19

"*I* will not tell them this, you understand," Freya said. "But it really is a wonderful sight. Look at those arm muscles," she whispered.

"Oh my." Dimity fanned herself with the large leaf Walter had picked up in his mouth from somewhere and spat at her feet. "I feel all aflutter."

Ruby snorted. "You've never been all aflutter a day in your life. But you ladies will excuse me. I will check on Ella and Henry so Iris can stay and enjoy herself."

"Oh no, really, I can go," Iris protested.

"Stay," Ruby said. "I will just check and be back."

"Very well, thank you, Ruby."

"My husband still makes my heart beat just a little harder even after all these years of marriage," the Duchess of Raven said, her eyes on the men like all the other guests.

"Dear lord, did Plunge just tear a seam under his arm? I'm sure he shrieked."

Iris looked at Theo. His feet were forward, and all his weight was leaning back. The look on his face was one of horror. But she was sure he was pulling hard and trying not

151

to show it. The Devilles were yelling orders at him, and he whimpered after every one.

Iris looked around her. Had no one but she noticed he was not what he seemed.

Mary caught her eye and smiled. Was there a deeper meaning to that smile, or was it just… a smile?

"Pull!" Dimity shrieked.

"Harder!" The Duchess of Raven joined her as their men battled each other.

"We're trying, my love!" the Duke said.

"I will not have you losing to a Deville, Hetherington, or those others," the duchess added.

"I thought you liked us?" Alexander Hetherington called.

"Of course she doesn't!" Cambridge Sinclair gritted out. "My sister just knows how to pretend!"

"Never a truer word!" Lord Sinclair, the Duchess of Raven's brother, gritted out.

"Pull, Plunge. For once in your life, be a man!" the Duchess of Yardly shrieked.

"That's harsh!" Theo whimpered.

"But true!" several of the spectators called.

Theo's thighs bunched in their trousers, and his wide shoulders were back. In shirtsleeves, he was quite something to look at. *How is it the women of society have not noticed?*

"Do you know I've decided Plunge could be considered handsome when he is not speaking?" a woman to Iris's right said as if she'd heard her thoughts.

"I can't believe you said that," another replied.

The battled raged on, and sweat glistened on foreheads as no one gave an inch. They were clearly well matched.

"You do realize that we could still be standing here at midnight, don't you?" Beth said. "They are a stubborn lot, and no way will any of them concede. In fact, were one of them to drop dead, the other would simply roll them aside with a booted foot and carry on."

"All true," Dimity said. "Perhaps we should have brought refreshment?"

"The tent is not far," Beth added. She then sighed. "My husband is rather wonderful."

Iris studied Nathanial. His jaw was gritted, and he had a matching fierce expression on his face.

"My Deville is the handsomest," Freya said.

"I will get the refreshments and see if Henry is all right while you debate," Iris said. "Come, Oscar, you can accompany me."

No one answered, so she walked away. They kept their eyes on the battle.

"Place your bets here!" These words had come from the Duchess of Yardly, who was clearly in need of more entertainment or short on money, which Iris doubted.

She looked to where the children played, her eyes finding Henry, who was now running with Ella in a large circle with several other children.

"Well, Oscar, our boy is happy, as are you." She stroked his soft head. "Welcome to our little family." He made a rumbling noise, which she took as thank you.

Returning to the refreshments tent, Iris looked to the tug-of-war and saw the Devilles seemed to move backward slowly, and then she was being jerked sideways suddenly.

"Struggle and I'll make your son pay."

The angry words came from her former brother-in-law, who was walking and dragging her with him.

"Release me or I will scream."

He turned, gripping her arms and pulling her in close. She knew no one had seen him because they were all watching the tug-of-war.

"Let me go or you will be sorry," Iris gritted out.

"We have things to discuss." The words were growled into her face. "My brother wanted me to oversee your son's tuition and teach him how to be a lord. I must have access to his things to do that."

Iris laughed in his face. "You? What could you possibly teach my son? How to be a man with no moral compass or scruples? How to mistreat a woman?"

His scowl grew more menacing. "You need a firm hand too, and I'm going to see you get it."

"You will never touch me again, and if your brother wished for you to teach my son anything, he would have given you guardianship of Henry. He didn't. In fact, he left no instructions, only that my son inherited everything upon his death."

"He died before he made the stipulation that—"

"Let me go!" Iris tried to pull free, but his hands bit into her shoulders.

"You will yield to me!"

"Stay away from me and my son. You are nothing to us, and never will be!"

"You will be mine," he whispered, pulling her closer. One of his hands moved to her throat, where he squeezed, cutting off her air. "I will not let this go. It is what my brother wanted. I am now head of this family until your son is old enough to do so. You will allow me to enter your home whenever I choose."

Iris jerked her head back, and his nail sank into the skin of her neck.

"If you do not yield to my demands, it will not go well."

"I am no longer scared of your threats, Mr. Renton. You are nothing to me." Iris fought harder to free herself.

"You should be very scared," he growled.

"Why?"

"Why what?" he snapped.

"Why do you and those other men want access to my husband's papers when they do not concern you? What is in there you must have?"

The words had been an impulse, but the look on his face told her she'd been right. There was something in her late husband's things this man wanted. Was it the papers she'd handed Theo? Her guess was yes.

"Why would you ask such a thing?" He shook her. "What have you found?"

"Nothing. Release me!"

"You're lying," he gritted out. "Tell me what you found."

"I burned them," Iris said quickly. "All my husband's papers I did not understand, I burned. The rest his lawyers hold."

A growl from beside her had Iris looking at Oscar. The dog was baring his teeth at Loftus Renton. He kicked out with a foot, and the dog lunged. His teeth sank into the man's calf.

He screamed and released her. Iris ran. "Oscar, come!"

She ran back and straight into the refreshment tent with the dog on her heels. Taking a moment to collect herself, Iris studied the table laden with food.

"Can I help you, my lady?" a servant asked her.

"C-Could you follow me with a tray of champagne and some of those éclairs?" Iris said.

Had what she said put her former brother-in-law off? Would he believe she had destroyed her husband's papers? Looking around her, she saw no sign of him and hoped Oscar had bitten him hard enough to cause him distress.

Composed once more, she walked back to where the Deville women stood. Iris took a glass of champagne and swallowed a large mouthful.

"Éclairs!" the Duchess of Raven shrieked.

"What?" Cambridge Sinclair called. His head turned toward them like a hound scenting something in the air.

"Cam, focus!" his older brother roared.

Sensing weakness, the Deville side tugged.

"Pull!" Theo roared in a very unPlunge voice.

A few people gasped.

They had the advantage, and seconds later, it was done. Lord Plunge ended on his bottom with a pile of men on top of him.

Slowly, they untangled and regained their feet. Theo was last to rise, and Iris saw the smile on his face, which he quickly masked.

"La! I am broken," he cried desperately. "My body is bruised and battered; I shall never recover." Clutching his chest, he staggered to the footman who held his jacket. "Help me!"

Iris noted Mary Deville walked to his side. She then helped him into his jacket and patted his hand.

"Champagne!" he wailed.

"Clearly we were mistaken. Plunge has not changed a jot," the young woman beside her, who had thought there was a possibility that he may be handsome, said.

"Such a shame. I was hopeful for a moment there," another said.

Now back in his jacket, Mary Deville was straightening Theo's necktie.

"So, it seems the Devilles are superior to the Sinclairs and Ravens," Dimity crowed to the Duchess of Raven.

"I am not impressed," the duchess said. She then stomped to where her husband was bent at the waist, sucking in large lungfuls of air with the other men in his family.

"Imagine how upset we are," her eldest brother snarled.

The Deville group was looking happier but no less exhausted.

"I think we women should now take part."

These words came from Dimity. Her husband's head shot up, and he leveled her with a look that should have warned her off pursuing what she'd just said.

"Oh, now that could be fun," Beth said.

"Excellent, I have made a tidy sum and am most happy to make more," the Duchess of Yardly said.

"You bet against us, Duchess. I am wounded," Cambridge Sinclair said.

"She knows weakness when she sees it," Zach answered.

"Women! Competing like men! Why the very thought of it is ridiculous," a man who'd been watching said.

By the flush of color in Dimity's cheeks, he was about to regret those words.

Iris had woken up this morning suspecting her day would be one spent in the garden or walking to the park, and yet here she was at a birthday celebration for a crotchety old duchess, with Henry playing happily. She also now owned a dog. Except for her encounter with her former brother-in-law, who she hoped was now nursing a nasty dog bite that turned septic, she had to say she'd been enjoying herself.

"And you are a splendid boy." She bent to pat Oscar, who was still at her side.

"Women do not do such things!" the man who made the initial comment continued.

"Molden, do you know so little about women?" the Duke of Raven said. "You never forbid them from doing something, or they wish to do it with even more determination than they previously had."

"Some of us have women who understand their place, Raven—"

A shriek came from several women. Most of Raven or Deville origins.

"I suggest you step back, Lady Challoner. This could get

nasty." She hadn't noticed Theo's approach. But he was now at her side, and his words were spoken so only she could hear.

"I want to be just like them one day," Iris said in the same tone.

"You are like them," he replied. "Beautiful and strong." He rested a hand on Oscar's head.

She turned her head, and their gazes locked. Iris felt that surge of need she'd experienced that day at her house when he'd kissed her.

"Thank you for your words, even if they are not true."

His eyes skimmed over her face slowly and down her neck, and then he stilled.

"Who hurt you?" The words were a low growl. "Tell me."

"No one. I-I scratched myself." She lifted a hand to cover it. Theo took it and peeled down her glove. Renton had left a bruise.

"Tell me who did this to you, Iris."

"No one did anything to me," she said. "Have you quite recovered from the tug-of-war, my lord?"

"This conversation is not over."

"Yes, it is, and people are staring at you."

His eyes snapped with anger, but the silly Lord Plunge smile slid back onto his face.

"I doubt I will ever recover," he whimpered, blotting his dry forehead with a handkerchief that wafted the scent of lavender her way. "I will need at least a week in bed!" he exclaimed.

She studied him. "Who are you?"

"Why, I'm Lord Plunge," he said with a silly smile.

"It must be exhausting trying to keep up that facade," Iris said.

His dark eyes studied her intently. "Why do you think it's a facade?"

"I have seen the other side of you a few times now. How is it, I wonder? no one else has?"

She suspected that look on his face was longing, but it was gone so quickly she couldn't be sure.

"You have not been in London long enough to see anything," he scoffed in what she termed his Theo voice. It was low enough so only she could hear.

"I like to stand back and watch," Iris said.

His eyes went left and right, checking to make sure no one was watching them.

"The girl I knew never stood back and watched." This voice was all Theo now.

"I was ten. You can't know who I was then or now."

"Come now, there is really no need for all this!" These words came from Lord Molden, who was now facing the Duchess of Raven, Dimity, and one other she had not met.

"Those three women are remarkably beautiful," Iris said, stepping back from the disturbing man.

"No more so than you, but yes, they are. I don't believe you have met Lady Levermarch. All three are strong-willed leaders in society."

Iris didn't answer, just focused on the argument between the women and Lord Molden. The men in their lives, she noted, were standing back, clearly happy to watch the proceedings. She knew they would step in if required.

"Women should not behave in such an undignified manner!" Lord Molden roared. His face was now puce.

"This could get ugly," Theo whispered.

"Molden, you are an antiquated old fool," the Duchess of Raven said.

"True!" the Duchess of Yardly agreed.

"Hold this. I fear things are about to escalate." Theo handed her his glass of champagne. "Someone needs to save Molden, as the husbands of the women haranguing him seem more than happy to stand by and watch them eviscerate him."

Iris watched Theo walk a few feet away from her. He then pulled a book out of his inside pocket.

"I do believe you promised me a literary saloon, Duchess!" He waved the book above his head. "So it is time to give you my birthday gift."

Several people groaned, mainly men. Others clapped their hands, but Iris noted his action had the desired effect. The argument between Lord Molden and the three women had stopped.

That man must be exhausted when he reached his bed every night. Playing two people could not be easy.

CHAPTER 20

*M*onty enjoyed the light reading offered from the Captain Broadbent and Lady Nauticus books, but contrary to what society thought, he did not like reading passages out loud from a bloody book. However, he and the Duchess of Yardly had made a production out of doing just that.

She'd started it by pulling out a book at random moments and getting people to read, and Plunge had reveled in being part of it.

"I have your gift, Duchess!" he cooed, mincing toward her, which was a great deal harder when not wearing heels. But as he'd had years of practice, he managed it.

As he neared the woman, he saw Renton with two other men. Their eyes were trained on Iris. Had he been the one to put those marks on her? He really needed to have a long talk with that man or get someone else to, as he was Lord Plunge.

Frustration had the breath hissing from his throat. He'd made his choices and, until now, not regretted them. But in that moment, he wanted to throw aside Plunge and grab Renton and beat him senseless.

Monty comforted himself with the fact that he had someone always watching Iris. Even so, he needed to uncover what threat the man was to Iris and Henry.

"My dear duchess, I have your gift!" Monty yelled, even though she was now only a few feet in front of him. Holding it before him, he bowed.

"Is that the latest, Plunge?" the crotchety old woman demanded.

"Indeed, it is, Duchess, and my birthday gift to you."

She harrumphed. "Well, I don't know how you got a copy, but well done." The book was snatched from his hand.

"Run," Gabe drawled. "She has a book."

"It's my birthday, Raine. I can do what I like," the old woman crowed.

"Yes, you can. I, however, do not have to do what you like."

"For that, you can read first," the Duchess of Yardly said. "But you have to stand on one of those rolling barrels."

"You'll forgive me for saying this, I'm sure, seeing as just yesterday you ate the last slice of lemon tart at my table, but no." Gabe had his arms folded, and he was glaring right back at the duchess.

"Bring a barrel!" she shrieked loud enough to make those close wince.

Monty fought the urge to stick his finger in his ear and wiggle it.

"It would be my honor to read first," he made himself say.

"You'll get your turn, Plunge, don't be eager," the duchess said. She then looked him in the eye and winked.

Monty looked at Gabe, who had seen the gesture. The earl shrugged as if to say he had no idea why she'd done it. Was it just an eye twitch, and he'd thought it was a wink?

"Barrel!" the duchess shrieked again.

"Give them a chance to reach you with it, Duchess," Zach

said, moving closer. "You can't just stand there yelling like you're selling pickled whelks from your cart. It's rude, even if it is your birthday."

She raised her cane and whacked him on the ankle.

"Ouch." Zach hopped about for a few seconds, rubbing it.

Monty looked to where he'd left Iris. She was watching them, her lips tilting in amusement. The woman was sweet. Far too sweet. He was drawn to her when he knew she was near. *He wanted her.*

She'd been part of his life before his parents' death. Was that her allure? Studying her face, he thought not. He felt differently about Iris. He had an ache deep inside him that he feared only she could ease.

"I am not barrel walking whilst reading a book," Gabe said.

"He's old, and a great deal weaker than me, Duchess. I'm quite handy at barrel walking," Cambridge Sinclair said. "So I will read first."

The man had a smug look on his face that had Gabe scowling. Monty looked at Iris again.

He was unsettled, and that wasn't a good thing for a man like him. He needed to be alert and focused. She was listening intently to something Mr. James, who had joined her, was saying to her. Her smile was only small, but the man responded with a wide one of his own.

Interest, Monty thought. He could see it in the man, and he hated the stab of what was likely jealousy he experienced.

"For pity's sake, Monty, stop scowling. Plunge doesn't do that," Mary hissed as she passed him.

He wanted to curse or mutter. Instead, he smiled. "My dear Mrs. Mary Deville, there is no need to take on so. No need to feel such distress. I am sure the duchess will allow you to read!"

Mary shot him a look that should set all his lavender-scented handkerchiefs on fire.

"Watch your back," she muttered.

He bowed.

"Right. Now someone will need to steady the barrel for me, but once I'm on, I will be fine. I have wonderful balance, you know. Quite superb," Cambridge Sinclair said.

"All it would take to send him tumbling is a little nudge," his youngest brother, Warwickshire Sinclair, said. "Not much at all, and we could all enjoy him tumbling headfirst to the ground."

"Are we women also allowed to roll whilst reading?" Dimity inquired.

"Absolutely not," her overprotective husband roared. A chorus of agreement from the other husbands followed this.

"Oh, pooh to that," Dimity said. "You'll assist me, won't you, Plunge?"

Monty looked at her and the faces of the Devilles around him. He wasn't popular and never had been. He was accepted and nothing more. Monty had wanted it that way. But lately the Devilles were including him, and he knew that would play a part in how some others saw him. The Devilles were popular, after all.

He didn't want that. He wanted to slip away at the end of the season and everyone to be happy they were finally rid of him. Monty included.

"Why, my dear lady, but of course. As I, too, will be rolling and reading." He tittered. "La, my alliteration is quite something, don't you think?"

"Yes, yes." The duchess waved his words away. "Now get up there, Sinclair."

"Which one?" several voices called.

"That one." She jabbed her cane at Cambridge.

He leapt nimbly onto the barrel that Nathan and Michael Deville were holding still for him.

"Book," he said, holding out his hand.

"Here. Hand it to him, Plunge, while I sit. My elderly bones, you know, they ache."

"What? Did you just admit to a weakness?" Zach asked the woman. "Someone get me a tisane. I feel faint."

Her cane swept in an arc toward his knees but luckily missed.

Monty held out the book for Cambridge.

"Your hair is much better styled that way, Plunge," the man said, looking down at him. "Less… ah less—"

"Animal excrement–like?" someone called.

"Exactly," Cambridge said. "The shoes are better too."

"My valet was ill, and my footman has no style," Monty said.

"My suggestion is, send the valet on a long-extended holiday to recover his health and stick with the footman." Cambridge gave him a steady look.

He was the recipient of a few of them lately, and he was not sure why.

"Release him!" Lord Sinclair roared. "I could do with a laugh."

"First, we need a recap!" someone called.

"Oh, very well," Dimity said, moving to stand below Cambridge.

"Careful he does not roll over you," Gabe said.

"Lady Nauticus, Captain Broadbent, and Cerise are in Faiyum in Egypt, the ancient city of Crocodilopolis."

"I say," Monty said. "Don't the inhabitants worship a sacred crocodile named Pegasus?"

"That's the flying horse, Plunge," the Duke of Raven said. "The crocodile is called Petsuchos."

"Is it really?" Monty said with a wide-eyed look that had several people moaning about how brainless he was.

"If I may continue?" Dimity snapped.

Monty bowed grandly.

"Captain Broadbent was struggling with flagging spirits due to the heat, so Cerise sent Lady Nauticus to get water to revive him," Dimity continued.

"He's really something of a weak-kneed, sniveling individual, don't you think?" Lady Levermarch said.

There were gasps of disapproval, boos, and some agreements to this harsh statement.

"There was also a herd of dorcas gazelle bearing down on them. Plunge was relieved they were not lappet-faced vultures," Dimity said.

Monty waved a handkerchief at the mention of his name.

"We all sang. And then Mary fell into the water," Dimity added.

Monty watched Zach's lips draw into a straight line at the memory of the woman he loved falling into the icy depths. He searched for Iris again and saw her former brother-in-law standing behind her. Clearly, she wasn't aware he was there, as she was smiling.

"I say, dear Lady Challoner, my childhood friend, come closer to immerse yourself in your first literary saloon!" He waved a hand to her, and reluctantly, she did as he asked.

Renton's face twisted into a snarl. He wanted Iris. That much was clear to Monty's mind, but there was something else to the man's behavior. Desperation, he thought. Something isn't right. His bet was that it had to do with the papers he now had in his possession.

"I don't want to stand here," Iris whispered when she reached him.

"Well, my dear, by all means retreat. Your former brother-in-law is waiting for you," Monty said.

Her eyes shot to Renton and then back to Monty.

"I am not your concern," Iris whispered.

"Whose concern are you, then? Your elderly aunt and uncle, perhaps? Henry's?"

"I think I prefer you as that fool, Plunge," she muttered.

"A simple thank-you will do," he said.

Her eyes went to Renton and then away again, but she said nothing further.

"And now we are caught up," Dimity said. "You have the floor, or barrel, Cambridge."

"You people are quite odd," Iris said, watching Cambridge as the Deville brothers released him.

They did not move far. Gabe, Zach, and Forrest joined them, surrounding Cambridge.

"Those bloody Devilles and their protectiveness," the Duke of Raven muttered. "We won't see Cam make a cake of himself now."

"Did someone say cake?" Cam asked. His words caused laughter.

The man's appetite was legendary. Monty watched as he rolled back and forth a few times, getting his balance, and then he stopped, seemingly steady.

"Throw something at him." Monty thought the words may have come from the wife of Lord Sinclair.

That family was an odd one, and coming from him, that said a great deal. There was just something about them he'd never been able to put his finger on.

"Lady Nauticus wandered along the covered parapet deep in thought," Cam read. "The cool morning breeze sent a chill through her thin gown."

"When did they reach a castle?" Nathan asked. "Better yet, where is it?"

"It was chilly in Scotland, and she shivered in her thin muslin dress," Cam continued.

"Why would you walk in the morning in Scotland without a shawl at the very least?" Ruby demanded.

"They had come here to find a place to settle. Their adventures had been many, but Dorothea—"

"One word, Plunge," Gabe thundered.

"I but cleared my throat," he said, sounding wounded. "We all know Lady Levermarch gave the names to our dear Lady Nauticus and Captain Broadbent."

The crowd gasped at his words.

"But you never know and always ask why we are calling them Dorothea and Horatio," someone said.

"I read somewhere once that a person needs to hear something seven times to actually understand it," Mary said.

"There you go then," Cambridge said. "Well done on finally remembering, Plunge."

"I'm sure it's more than seven times," someone called.

"Scotland was to be the place she and her dear Captain Broadbent would wed, Dorothea thought. Finally, they would commit to each other."

"I have a problem with this," the Duchess of Raven interrupted. "Clearly he is a useless individual, and surely she should be questioning his commitment to her by now."

"Perhaps it is she who is the simpleton?" Zach said, which earned him another round of boos from the crowd.

"Is this really happening?" Iris asked Monty.

"Oh, without a doubt, and soon it will be your turn to read."

She looked at him, horror in every line of her pretty face, and in that moment, Monty had a terrible feeling that what he felt for Iris was a great deal deeper than even he realized.

CHAPTER 21

"*N*ext!" the Duchess of Yardly demanded.

"I've only read a few lines!" Cambridge Sinclair looked indignant.

"That man walking behind the barrel while Cambridge Sinclair debates with the duchess is his brother, Lord Devonshire Sinclair," Monty said. "My guess is he's about to do something to toss him off."

Iris turned back to watch the man, Lord Sinclair, nudge the barrel with his booted foot. His brother pitched forward and only just saved himself by leaping clear and running for several steps.

"Agile as a cat."

"That's his youngest brother, Warwickshire Sinclair," Monty added.

"Alexander Hetherington is next!" the duchess called.

"The Hetheringtons are twins and vastly different," Theo whispered. "Where Alex is elegant, his brother, Ben, is the exact opposite.

"Up you go, Alex," Michael Deville said, handing him the book.

"'My dearest Lady Nauticus!'" cried the tall, elegant man now on the barrel. "'Dear lord!' Lady Nauticus cried in shock," Alexander Hetherington continued. "Surely it could not be who she thought standing before her. She'd long since thought him dead, but there he stood, the first man to hold her heart."

The gasps in the crowd were loud and followed by plenty of "Surely nots."

"So the author has carried us along on this journey only to produce another player," Gabe said. "Genius really."

"No, it's not genius!" Beth demanded. "We've gone on this journey expecting a happily-ever-after between Horatio and Dorothea, and now that's not going to happen?"

"Are they seriously outraged over a book?" Iris whispered.

"They are invested, as are we all," Monty said. "I shall send you the entire series, and then you'll understand."

"What are lappet-faced vultures?" she asked him.

"A bird with a pink face that looks perpetually grumpy and old," Theo answered her. "A bit like the Duchess of Yardly, actually."

"Thank you, Lord Montgomery," Iris said.

"Most welcome." He waved his handkerchief in her face.

"I don't like lavender."

"I fear that is your loss," he said.

"Next!" the duchess yelled. "I think we should hear from the newest member among us."

"She doesn't mean me, does she?" Iris whispered, backing into Theo. She then stepped to the side and around him to stand at his back, where she could hide.

"Come along, Lady Challoner, the crowd draws restless!" the duchess called.

"I'll read. As you can see, my dear old friend is shy," Theo said. Iris heard the crowd groan.

"I said Lady Challoner!" The duchess thumped her cane

down hard.

"And yet she has no wish to," Theo said in a stronger voice but still wearing a silly smile.

"Oh, very well, but she cannot hide forever," the duchess said.

"How charitable you are." Theo bowed, and to Iris's ears, his words sounded mocking.

"I think he should stay on the ground," someone said.

"Exactly. He'd fall and injure himself on that barrel, and there is the lake close by as well. We know what he's like near water."

While the discussion of his inability to balance raged on around him, Iris watched Theo step onto the barrel with the help of Michael and Nathan.

He was up there because of her, and he'd protected her from her former brother-in-law too. She needed to thank him. Iris moved closer and took the book from Alexander Hetherington.

"I will hold the book, so you can balance," she then said.

"Thank you, my dear Lady Challoner, but I can hold it, as you can see. I am steady on my feet." He took it from her. "Now step aside so I do not crush you!"

"Dear lord, yes," someone said fervently. "He's a terribly clumsy fellow."

Iris did not retreat; she just moved to stand next to Nathan and looked up at Theo. Why did looking at this man make her feel fluttery inside?

"'Why, Mr. Poddington, what has you here?' Lady Nauticus cried."

"He has the silliest voice," a woman said.

Iris had noted that people insulted Theo and did not care if he overheard them. She thought it rude.

"'I did not disappear like you believe, my dearest love. I was abducted and sent on a boat to America, but I escaped by diving overboard. However, the island I found myself on did not have passing ships. I then sailed on the back of a Dermochelys coriacea to civilization to reach you.'"

"Sea turtle," Nathan whispered.

"Wait, wait!" the Duchess of Raven called. "Do we believe this utter rot? Diving overboard and swimming to a conveniently located uninhabited island. Catching a ride on a sea turtle indeed!"

"Good lord, he's lying!" Dimity cried.

The murmurs suggested to Iris that some agreed and others did not. She wasn't sure without having the background but felt the man's story was not entirely plausible.

"He could eat coconuts," Cambridge said. "Milk and food, after all."

His sister shot him a glare.

"'As I was ravaged by the sea and sun and struggling with weakness due to lack of nourishment, you were always in my head, my darling Lady Nauticus.'"

"He could have caught fish to eat, in fairness," Gabe said.

"'But I am now back and determined to find the scoundrel who sent me from you, my one true love,'" Theo added dramatically.

"I struggle with the turtle business if I'm honest," the Duchess of Yardly said.

"Does anyone else feel he is laying things on a little thick?" Michael Deville asked. More murmurs.

"'No!' Lady Nauticus gasped. 'Who would do such a thing?'"

Theo changed voices as he spoke, slipping effortlessly between them. But then she'd witnessed this for herself. His Plunge and Theo voices were vastly different.

"Old friends are perhaps the best friends," Nathan said.

"Indeed," Iris agreed.

"They knew you before circumstance forced you to

change," he added. "Some would say they knew the real you."

She'd certainly felt that she knew Theo better than anyone as a child.

"'I am your love, not him!' Captain Broadbent declared."

"Where did he come from?" Lord Raine demanded. "No one mentioned he'd entered the scene. Exceedingly shoddy writing from the author."

"It's getting awfully crowded on the covered parapet walk," the Duchess of Yardly added.

"There are three people there. Hardly a crowd, Duchess," Zach said.

"'No! It is me you love, Captain Broadbent,' Cerise cried," Theo said.

"When did she appear?" Michael Deville said.

The crowd booed.

"'Mother!' Lady Nauticus gasped. 'How could you say such a thing?'"

"'I could never love another, Cerise. Your daughter is my one true love,' Captain Broadbent said," Theo cried.

"Let's face it, if we're honest, no one else would have him. He's lazy and not very heroly," Mary said.

"That's not a word, my sweet," Zach added.

"Captain Broadbent hurried to where Lady Nauticus stood and dropped to one knee," Theo continued, not missing a beat even considering the interruptions. "However, there was a stone where he landed, and soon he was howling in pain."

"Take Poddington!" a female voice shouted. "Broadbent is continually injured or being pathetic!"

More booing and hissing followed. Iris was now highly entertained. "I have seen nothing like this before," she said to Nathan.

"I doubt there is anything else like this."

"If I may conduct a quick show of hands. Who is for

Poddington?" Theo asked.

Hands rose.

"Broadbent?"

More hands, and the majority, were raised.

"'Oh, my dear Horatio!' Lady Nauticus dropped to his side," Theo continued with the story.

"'No!' Cerise cried. 'You love Poddington! Captain Broadbent is mine!'"

Iris looked around the crowd. Some had their hands clutched, and others had them pressed to their mouths.

"'I have always loved Captain Broadbent, Mother. My love for Mr. Poddington was that of a young woman. My love now is that of a mature woman. A woman who knows her life will be forever empty without her one true love.'"

"Oh, that's quite beautiful," someone sniffed.

"Oh dear, that can't be good," Dimity said as the barrel started rolling.

"I thought you were holding it!" both Deville brothers said at the same time.

Iris watched in horror as the barrel picked up speed with Theo running on top of it, shrieking.

"I can't watch," Zachariel Deville said, following the barrel at a run now with a hand pressed to his eyes.

"If there is water, he will find it," Mary said.

Iris, heart in her mouth, watched as the book flew out of Theo's hands. At the same time, the barrel hit a stone bench. Theo then seemed to fly high through the air, arms flapping, and came down with a loud splash into the pond.

"While you Devilles get him out, someone finish the reading," a man said.

"That's very rude! Lord Montgomery could be hurt," Iris said, stomping away.

"What is she talking about?" a lady asked. "Plunge always falls in the water."

Iris did not wait to hear more. She did not stop until she reached Theo. He was now out of the water and spluttering.

"Are you all right?"

"I am, yes. Wet through and in imminent danger of a chill. My jacket will be ruined!" he wailed.

"Oh, do shut up, Theo," she snapped, quite out of patience.

"Theo?" Zach asked.

"That's his name, and as someone who has known him as long as you all claim to have, you should bloody well know that."

She took Theo's arm and dragged him toward the house, leaving the guests behind. Those closest were open-mouthed after her outburst.

"Release me. I will get you wet as well." His voice had dropped several octaves.

"My hand is barely touching your arm," Iris snapped.

"I'm all right, Iris."

"Why do you do that? Let them ridicule you and behave as you do?"

"I have no idea what you are talking about?"

"That silly behavior."

"It's who I am."

"Stop lying to me, my lord."

He gritted his teeth, and the muscles in his jaw bunched.

"Where is Henry? You need to go to him."

"Ruby is with him. She said she would come and get me if need be. But I can see Henry, and he is having a wonderful time."

They walked the rest of the way to the house in tense silence. Once inside, she found a servant and asked for some drying cloths for Lord Montgomery.

"I can take it from here," Theo said, sounding testy just as she did now. "I will not be returning to the celebrations."

He walked away from her, following the servant who was directing him to a parlor where he could dry off. Broad back, strides long and determined, he looked nothing like Lord Plunge.

Iris followed and found him in a parlor rubbing a cloth over his wet hair, careless of any style it had been in. If he was as vain as they said, surely, he'd care about something like that.

His jacket had been thrown to the floor and now lay in a sodden heap. Pushing the door closed, she approached him.

"Tell me the truth."

He lowered the drying cloth to look at her.

"Go away, Lady Challoner."

"I want to know why you are who you are, and yet you are not he."

"You do realize that makes little sense." He was trying to use his Plunge voice, but the words came out a deep rasp.

"I was once your friend, Theo. Talk to me."

"We are no longer friends. We know nothing about each other," he gritted out, reaching for her. Even in anger, he would never touch her like Renton did. Gentle hands pulled her closer.

They stared at each other, and Iris felt the moment his anger slid into something else. She knew what passion looked like from her late husband but not from this man. Yet when his eyes darkened, and he pulled her closer still so her breasts brushed the hard planes of his chest, she felt a stirring inside her again.

"I'm sorry," Iris whispered.

"For what?" The word were a rasp.

"For how you've suffered."

"You know nothing of my suffering."

"As you know nothing of mine."

His eyes ran over her face and settled on her mouth.

"How did you suffer?"

"How did you suffer?" she parroted back to him.

"They are my demons, and I don't share." He closed the last few inches between them and kissed her.

Unlike the last one, this was harder. It demanded a response from Iris. Her husband had never kissed her; he'd told her what to do in the bedroom but wanted nothing from her but an heir. She was simply a vessel to carry a babe for him.

Theo's hand went to her head and angled it to take the kiss deeper.

So, this was need.

One of his hands slid to her spine and urged her closer. Even the cool of his clothes did nothing to stop her. She wanted this, to be held close by Theo. His mouth asked her to respond, and she did, arching into him. Everything ceased to exist in that moment but Theo.

"Iris." The words were a plea against her lips.

"Yes," she answered, not understanding what she'd agreed to but knowing she wanted it.

His hand moved, and his large fingers were splayed so close to her breast now. It ached to feel his touch. The sound that came from her lips had the hand moving, and then he was touching the full flesh. Cupping her. Desire spiked through Iris.

The sound of the door shutting had them springing apart. Breathless, they stared at each other. Iris moved first. Turning, she ran for the door. Wrenching it open, she saw Nathan Deville there.

"Good day," Iris said, cheeks flaming.

"Good day, Iris," he said gently.

Had he closed the door? Had he seen Theo and Iris kissing? The thought had the color in her face deepening. Lowering her head, she walked away and did not look back.

CHAPTER 22

*T*hey arrived like they always did, just after darkness had fallen and through the rear of his town house. The Devilles walked in arguing. He could hear them from the floor above.

"And our peace is over," Monty said. His butler smiled, happy to have company.

"Haven!" Zach yelled. "What gastronomic delights await us tonight?"

"Send them up. They will simply storm the place otherwise," Monty said.

He heard voices, and then there they were. All the Devilles and Mary. Monty avoided Nathan's eyes, as the last time they'd spoken he'd been standing outside the door while inside Monty had been kissing Iris again and touching her lovely breast.

That woman was playing hell with his life. The kisses had been bad enough, but now he knew exactly what other parts of her body felt like. For the first time in many years, he was struggling to sleep.

Damn, and here he was thinking of her again.

"Almond pastries and chocolate plum cake." Zach closed his eyes and made a humming sound. "It almost makes it worthwhile seeing you." He nodded to Monty, who had yet to rise and greet them.

"No jacket or waistcoat again?" Gabe tutted. "If only society could see the flamboyant Lord Plunge."

"Yes, imagine how upset that makes me," Monty drawled. "Sit, I have things to tell you. Haven will bring seven trays of food to appease you heathens. All except you of course, sweet Mary."

"I should hope so." She bent to kiss his cheek. Monty got out of his chair and poured glasses of whiskey. After everyone was seated, he paced the floor before them, sorting through his thoughts before he spoke.

"There is talk about you, Monty. Women are saying you could possibly, maybe if the light is right, be considered handsome," Zach said. "And that you have been overheard speaking differently. And all this is after the rescuing of that boy and the Blakes seeing you in all your manliness."

"I don't give a fig about talk," Monty said. "Now shut up and listen while I tell you what news I have."

"The news you should have told us long before now?" Mary said with a smile on her face that was just a bit mean. Monty ignored her.

"I recently met with Geraint and told him I would leave Alexius and London at the season's end."

"What?" Zach roared.

"Zach, please let him finish. I'm sure there will be at least another four reasons to roar before then. But let's leave that until Monty is done, and then I want an explanation too for why he has not spoken of this until now." Mary glared at him now.

Monty threw back the liquid in his glass and let it burn slowly down his throat before he continued.

"I went undercover as Plunge to find my parents' murderers. That has not happened," Monty continued. He then outlined everything that had happened since he'd told Geraint of that decision, right down to his dealings with Iris, and the papers in her husband's things.

"And you're only telling us this now?" Gabe was not happy.

"You're lucky I'm telling you at all," Monty fired back. "I usually work alone, but I knew that if you bloody Devilles found out, there would be trouble. I preempted that."

"Oh really?" Mary glared at him. "And why is that? Are we no longer friends? Do I/we have no more rights to your friendship?"

The anger climbed inside him. It was irrational, hot, and he battled to force it back down.

"You preempted that," Mary snapped. "Well let me tell you —"

"That will do, love. Anger will not keep him safe or get to the bottom of all this," Zach said, placing an arm around Mary's waist and pulling her into his side.

Monty and Mary continued to glare at each other. If he'd had a sister, he'd have wanted one just like her. Fiery, determined, and someone who never backed down. If he wasn't enraged, he'd tell her that.

"Good lord," Gabe said, moving to stand next to his youngest brother and stare at Monty. "He's really angry."

Zach leaned closer and studied Monty. "By Jove, I do believe you're right." He then poked Monty in the neck.

"Ouch!"

"That vein is pulsing," Zach said.

The others all joined them to lean over shoulders and stare at Monty.

"Are you quite finished?" he gritted out. "Back away," he snarled.

"Do you know what I think?" Nathan said.

"No," Monty said as the others said yes. He had a terrible feeling he would not like what Nathan had to say.

"I think Iris Challoner has him off-balance, and as he's never that, or had to deal with pesky things like emotions, he's not sure how to cope. And then there is that—"

"Do not finish that sentence," Monty said.

"Expression he gets when he's looking at her," Nathan said, grinning. "And of course, her defense of you after your impromptu swim is also telling."

She had defended him, and he'd been humbled. It was accepted in society to mock and ridicule Plunge, but not by Iris.

"And I thought you were the rational Deville," Monty snapped.

"Entirely rational," Nathan said. "But also, honest. I know what you were up to in that room with the lovely Lady Challoner. My glimpse was brief. However, I know an embrace when I see one."

"What!" Mary shrieked, which had them all wincing.

"Nathan," Monty warned him with a growl.

"You have more secrets than the entire British spy network, Monty. It is time to reveal a few. It is not healthy to keep so much inside you," Nathan added.

"Utter rot." Monty wouldn't meet anyone's eye. "Just because you lot can't keep a thought inside your head does not mean I have to join you."

"You kissed Iris Challoner? And not only that, you did it at the Duchess of Yardly's birthday party? Where anyone could have seen you?" Mary demanded.

"Shut up," Monty said.

"Well, I never." Gabe whistled. "You never slip out of your disguise, and yet I'm fairly sure you would not kiss a woman as Plunge, therefore you must have done so as Monty—"

"Who are one and the same!" Monty snapped.

"But not in public. How interesting that you let your old childhood friend see a glimpse of your other persona," Zach added.

"Stop smiling. You all look like fools." Monty stomped to the side table where he'd put the papers earlier. Snatching them up, he returned to his guests, who were all smiling at him.

"Well, they say it takes a fool to know a fool," Zach said.

"No one of sense says that. Now read these and shut up." Monty held out the papers. "The subject of Iris Challoner is over and will not be raised again."

"Not over," Mary said, her eyes scanning the first note. "There will be more discussion on said heated embrace."

"Oh, it's over." But the truth was, Monty wanted to be in a heated embrace again with Iris.

"Iris gave me the one that had my father's name on it. She said she found it and immediately knew she must bring it to me personally. The rest she found with it in a secret drawer under her husband's desk."

"How clever of her to bring it directly to you," Forrest said, looking at the paper he was handed.

There was silence while they all read. Monty paced the room and knew his reprieve was a short one. They would be at him again soon. He fingered the two wooden carvings in his pocket.

"Thank God, Haven. I need sustenance after the shocks I've just received," Nathan said when his butler staggered in with two laden trays.

"So, from these"—Gabe pointed to the papers—"Challoner is into something, and from the first note Iris gave you, he could be involved in your parents' deaths?"

"Murder," Monty snapped. "My parents were murdered."

Gabe nodded. "I don't know the details, as it happened many years ago, Monty. Will you tell us now?"

He never spoke of that night. Only he and his staff and uncle knew exactly what had taken place. Not even the members of Alexius he'd dealt with when he first entered knew everything.

"I don't speak of that night." The words came out harshly.

"Completely understandable, but perhaps now it's time," Michael said calmly.

"Talking sometimes helps with trauma," Forrest said. "Speaking to someone who is not involved, I believe, genuinely helps heal the wounds, Monty. You have carried this burden alone for many years is my guess."

Monty wanted to tell him to shut up. He never relived that day unless it was in his nightmares. For the most, he'd locked it away in a dark corner of his brain.

"My late wife was addicted to laudanum," Forrest said, "and I walked into my daughter's room one day to find her placing a pillow over Ella's head. It is a memory that has not lessened given time, but now that I have talked of it with this lot"—he waved a hand to the others in the room—"I can think of it with less pain."

"I'm sorry, that must have been hell," Monty said.

"It was. But my child lived. Your parents did not. If you wish to speak about that time, we will listen and never speak of it again if that is also your wish," Forrest said.

"You have been alone for so long, by choice," Mary said, holding out her hand to him. The anger had now eased from her face to be replaced with worry. "Let us be there for you, Monty."

He took her hand in his and saw the bracelet she wore. The one he'd given her on the day she married Zach. It had been his mother's.

"This cake is delicious," Zach said. "And I will allow you to hold my wife's hand as I know she's comforting you."

The words broke some of the tension in the room, and Monty snorted out a laugh. Releasing Mary after a last squeeze, he waved his guests all into seats but did not take one himself.

"One of our mares was having a foal. I often spent time in the stables when this was happening. Iris had been with me for a while too, until her father sent a groom to take her home."

"You and she were close?" Nathan asked.

"Very. She was my best friend as I was hers. We were young, but still, most days we saw each other."

"Because you were young does not lessen the friendship you obviously shared," Forrest said.

"Have you been reading again?" Zach looked at his cousin. "You seem a great deal more intelligent than normal this evening."

Forrest rolled his eyes.

"My parents said I could stay with the mare as long as I liked. The foal was born in the early hours of the morning. Father had told me to tap on his door when I returned and inform him, no matter the time, as he liked to know I was back in the house."

"Your parents were well respected," Gabe said. "A few people have told me that."

Monty nodded. "They were the best parents a child could ask for. I was an only child, but they always ensured I had cousins or friends around. I loved them very much."

"Losing them must have been hell," Zach said.

"It was. That night, I tapped on the door, but Father did not answer. I turned the handle to go in and whisper to him that I was back, and the foal born. The door handle felt damp."

Monty remembered the icy fear as he'd raised the lamp he carried.

"I held the light closer and saw blood on the wood. Pushing open the door I entered the room and found my father lying across my mother. Both were dead."

"Christ," Gabe whispered.

"I knew they were dead, but I still checked," Monty said in a cold, emotionless voice. "I grabbed my father's hand to move him off Mother, and in it was this." He pulled the carvings from his pocket. "Iris found an identical one on the ribbon tied around her late husband's papers."

Monty handed them to Mary. Why he was telling them now, he had no idea, but when Forrest had said the telling helps, he'd thought he needed that. Help to become warm inside again. Help to be someone different from the cold man he'd made himself into.

Iris slid into his head. She would listen if he talked. The girl he'd known would be inside her still. But Monty also knew that she was dealing with her own trauma. And that whatever her late husband had done to her had left scars that were deep and painful.

"What did you do then?" Michael asked.

Monty made himself look at them. These people he now counted as friends. Possibly the first friends he'd had since Iris. There was sympathy in their gazes, but he saw the anger on his behalf too.

"I ran down the stairs screaming until the staff heard me. Our butler went immediately to my parents' rooms and stopped me from entering again.

"He sounds like a good man," Gabe said.

"The staff looked after me until my uncle arrived," Monty said.

"Was your uncle a good man?" Mary asked.

"He wasn't, but that is another story. I went into

mourning and never left the house until that period passed. I was then sent to Eton."

"Tell me you had more than your uncle to watch over you?" Nathan said.

"He decided it would be him and me for the mourning period. No visitors." And I hated him for it. In small ways, Monty remembered rebelling. Little things that annoyed his uncle and made him feel better.

"Bastard," Zach hissed.

"I was eighteen when I was due to leave Eton. Walters, the man in charge of Alexius before Geraint, was waiting for me at my lodgings the day before I left."

"I remember him well," Gabe said. "Serious fellow, but fair."

Monty nodded. "He told me about Alexius, and that my father had been a member." He recalled the conversation as if it was yesterday because it was the second pivotal moment that changed the direction of his life.

"We talked for hours that day," Monty said. "He was the first man after my father that I truly respected."

"Yes, he was someone who talked, and you listened," Gabe said.

"Walters told me to travel for a while," Monty continued, "and when I returned to London, he wanted me to enter society as the persona we would create for Plunge. I was to go undercover in plain sight. The decision was mine alone to make, he put no pressure on me."

Zach whistled softly.

"It was an excellent disguise because no one takes you seriously, and therefore will speak in front of you?" Forrest said.

"Exactly. I had nothing to lose. The years at Eton had not gained me friends, and I had little but revenge to motivate me. Walters told me that if I did this then between us, we would find who had killed my parents. Unfortunately, that did not happen."

"And nobody found a clue or lead that would direct you to their murder... until now?" Nathan asked.

Monty nodded.

"You have our deepest sympathies," Gabe said, getting out of his seat to walk to Monty. "What you did was a selfless act that has saved many. On behalf of our country, I thank you."

"It was my choice. There is no need to thank me." Monty felt uncomfortable with the words.

"You have lived a lie for many years," Gabe added. "You made the choice to do so as a young man, and that is selfless. But know that we stand with you now. We will also aid you in finding who is responsible for your parents' deaths. We will do whatever it takes to help you achieve justice and peace, Monty."

Gabe extended his hand to Monty. He took it, humbled by Gabe's words.

"Now we need to ask our networks to follow these men who were friends of the late Lord Challoner. Find anything that could lead us to what Challoner was involved in," Nathan added.

"When I first joined Alexius, many years ago, there was a rumor about a group of noblemen who were involved in a secret society," Gabe said. "Names were thrown about, but nothing stuck, and then the rumors died. I'd forgotten about it until now."

"I'm so sorry, Monty." Mary hugged him hard next.

"It's all right." He patted her back.

"No, it's far from all right," Zach said, next to hug him.

"I'm not really someone who likes to be hugged," Monty said.

"Well now, to my way of thinking, it's well past time you were," Nathan said, moving in next.

"These." Michael held the carvings up. "Did you tell anyone about the one you found in your father's hand?"

"No."

"Completely understandable," he added. "As a child, your fear would have been that someone thought your father a devil worshipper."

Monty nodded; his throat felt tight, and there was a burning sensation behind his eyes.

"Right, so now that is all out in the open, I'll tell you that there will be no storming off into the night alone without first notifying us as to where you go," Gabe said. "Even if you get word of something that needs immediate investigation."

"I may not have time to—"

"I'll stop you right there," Zach interrupted him. "You will not deal with this solo. It is too dangerous, and you may need backup. That backup will come in the form of us."

"Understood?" Nathan asked.

Monty muttered something that he hoped was yes.

"Not good enough. Say the words out loud, Monty," Gabe said.

"Oh, very well. I agree to notify you," he said with ill grace.

"Excellent," Michael said.

"And what of Lady Challoner? She said these men— Renton, Lord Picton, Lord Heather, Mr. Clipper, and Mr. Buford—all approached her with the express purposes of going through her husband's things. Do you believe she is in any danger?" Gabe asked.

"Renton intimidated and hurt her," Monty growled. "And more than once is my belief. He sees her as his possession now, and Henry. He also sees her as standing in the way of him searching his late brother's things."

"She told you that?" Mary asked.

"No, not outright, but I overheard Renton threatening her

at your ball, Gabe. There was also a mark on her neck and wrist at the Duchess of Yardly's birthday that I cannot discount he put there."

"Then we need to watch over her also," Forrest said.

"I have someone watching her house, and he will follow her when she leaves," Monty said.

"We will keep an eye out also," Gabe said.

He felt relieved about that. The Devilles were honorable people; they would be true to their word.

They talked then. Plotted and planned. Three hours later, they left, taking all the life out of his house. The house he'd once thought he wanted to be a silent haven for when he was not masquerading as Lord Plunge.

CHAPTER 23

*M*onty didn't retire immediately after the Devilles left. Instead he wandered the halls of his home, restless. He felt on edge. Everything was changing around him, and then there was Iris.

He'd told the Devilles it was possible she was in danger, but he could hardly ask her to open up to him when he would not reciprocate. But he wanted to know her secrets, and then he wanted to keep her safe.

Monty had kept himself apart from people in every way, but his guard had slipped with her.

Why?

"My lord, Jimmy has arrived with a message for you."

He'd been studying a painting of his parents. He always saw them just like this, as they'd died a year after the artist painted their portrait.

"Thank you, Haven. I shall come at once."

Hurrying to his office, he grabbed a coin pouch from his desk drawers, then ran back down the stairs and through the kitchens with blood thundering through his veins. Was Iris all right? Jimmy was watching her and had been for days. He wouldn't be here unless there was trouble.

"What news do you have for me, Jimmy?" he asked, entering the kitchen to find his man standing tall in the doorway talking to Haven and Polly. Jimmy had been a soldier. He'd returned to London with a limp and shadows in his eyes. No one had wanted to employ him. Monty had stumbled across him one day when he'd been wandering down an alley. The man had stepped in when three men were about to rob him. He'd been working for Monty since.

Always immaculate, even when he'd been desperate and penniless, the soldier bowed better than any nobleman.

"My lord, a boy called at Lady Challoner's town house. I intercepted him as he walked to the servant's entrance and paid him money to read the missive he carried. The note stated that if Lady Challoner wished to see her son again, she was to go to the White Swan at midnight."

"Tell me she didn't go?" Monty said.

"Lady Challoner departed the house ten minutes later and called for a hackney. I ran here to tell you."

"The boy, Henry. We need to protect him," Monty said.

"The maid I have paid for information inside the Challoner household told me he left yesterday to stay with his aunt and uncle. One footman was sent to watch over him. Oscar, the dog, also."

"Do you know the location?"

"I don't, but I can find out," Jimmy said.

"Find out and go to the house. It can't be far, as her aunt and uncle have attended social engagements this season. See if the boy has been taken or not." Monty threw him a bag of money. "My thanks again, Jimmy."

"I'll leave as soon as I have an address," Jimmy said.

"Send word as soon as you know to the Challoner town house, as the boy's mother will be terrified. I will bring her back there as soon as I have her." He looked to his butler. "Call for my horse, Haven."

"At once," the butler said.

"Pack Jimmy some food, Polly, please."

Worry gnawed at Monty as he ran to his rooms. Pulling on a plain black jacket, he then stomped his feet into hessians. Wrapping his cloak around his shoulders, he grabbed his hat. Running to his office next, Monty unlocked the drawers. He put a pistol into his waistband and slid a knife into his boot. Last, he grabbed more money.

Looking at his desk, he saw the paper, quill, and ink.

"Christ," he hissed. Bending, he penned a note.

The man I set to watch Iris intercepted a missive telling her to go to the White Swan. I'm unsure yet why, but her son Henry was threatened if she did not turn up. I have sent a man to check on the boy and am following so you don't need to. I will inform you what transpires tomorrow.

Monty.

He folded the paper in half, then left the room. Finding his horse waiting, he handed Haven the note.

"Send this to Mr. Zachariel and Mrs. Mary Deville. Do not have the household woken, just slip the note under the door please."

"At once, sir."

"I'm growing soft," he muttered, mounting his horse. Minutes later, he was galloping through London. There was still traffic about even at the late hour, but he wove through them and headed to the White Swan, a place he had been before in his role with Alexius.

Iris would be safe until he got there. *She had to be.* Whoever had sent that note simply wanted something from her, and the threat to her son had sent her out at night alone. He would have words with her about that.

Why had she gone alone and not taken her big, hulking butler? Norman would have protected her.

Was it Renton, or one of the other men her late husband was involved with that had forced her from her home alone?

The cold air slapped him in the face as he galloped. Fear and panic gnawed at his insides with every minute he drew closer to the White Swan. Was Iris still safe or in the clutches of someone intent on harming her? And what of her solemn-faced son? Had someone harmed his aunt and uncle to take him? Could he even now be terrified?

She will be safe. They just want something from her, he reminded himself. "Stay safe, Iris." His words caught on the wind.

Monty halted near the White Swan. It wasn't the worst street in London but not the best either.

"Need someone to hold your horse?" A boy appeared out of the dark. With him were two more children. Monty passed out coins.

"There will be more when I return."

Raising his hood, he ran down the road to the tavern.

"Care to spend some time with a lady for a few coins?" A woman stepped into his path.

"Not tonight, thank you." Stepping around her, he ran on until he reached his destination. A sign swung above the door. Soot had made the white swan on it a dirty gray. Lamplight filtered in through two narrow windows to the left.

Stay calm, he reminded himself. Emotion would not help this situation. Those words were something a Deville would usually say, not him. Shaking his head, he pushed the old oak door and entered.

Smoke, body odors, and the low rumble of voices greeted him as he moved through the patrons, looking at faces.

Monty saw no sign of Iris. Reaching the bar, he faced the large man standing behind it.

"I'm searching for a woman."

"Now that's something I've not heard before." The barman smirked.

"Upper class, and she came here to meet someone," Monty snapped, handing over some coins. Large beefy fingers scooped them up.

He'd learned early in his duties to Alexius that money made nearly everyone talk. The barman nodded to the stairs.

A man in a dark jacket skirting the edges of the throng caught his eye. He couldn't see his face, but his dress suggested this was not a place he normally frequented.

He took the stairs, and Monty felt the need to follow. The man then disappeared through the second door down the narrow hallway. Moving closer, he pressed his ear to the wood.

"Your son will remain unharmed, Lady Challoner, if you hand over what I want."

Monty didn't recognize the voice. Rage that anyone would threaten Iris coursed through him. He tamped it down. No good would come from storming in there until he needed to; he could get both him and Iris shot.

"Who are you? Why have you brought me here?" she demanded.

"Shut up and listen to him, Lady Challoner." There were two men inside with Iris. That voice was coarser and less refined.

"What do you want?"

"A bundle of papers your husband held. They are wrapped in a black silk ribbon. You're going to get them for me."

"But I have no notion of where I would find them. Tell me where my son is," Iris demanded.

"That's not true!" a voice roared. "His desk was empty, as was the secret cavity."

"What secret cavity? When were you in my husband's house searching through his things? Who are you?" Iris asked, sounding nowhere near as terrified as she should be.

She was pretending to be ignorant to what she knew. It was an excellent ploy, but only if they believed her.

"I know of no such place. My husband forbade me to enter his study."

Monty thought seriously about digging the late Lord Challoner up just to put a bullet through his head. He knew now the man had mistreated his wife and son. Iris. It chafed at him to leave her in there at the mercy of those men, but he needed to hear everything that was said. One hint of danger, and he'd be on the men in a heartbeat.

"Where is my son? Have you kidnapped him? I will not speak again until I have an assurance he is well."

"You are in no position to make demands, my lady. You are at our mercy," the gruff voice said.

"I will not talk until I know he is safe." Her voice held no quaver, but he knew Iris would be terrified. But not for herself, for Henry.

"I will not touch your son as long as you do as we say."

"Where is he?" Iris demanded.

"Still with his aunt and uncle, but my men are watching and will abduct him if you do not do as I say. Now, I had someone check your husband's study. He broke in, and that secret drawer under his desk was empty. I want the contents, and I know only you can have them."

"My husband's office was locked, and we had no key. If anyone took some of my late husband's papers, it would be Mr. Renton."

"Renton?" one man said, and Monty could hear the surprise in his voice.

"Yes. My former brother-in-law called upon me here in London. He told me he had accessed my husband's office, so it is likely he who has anything you want. What would I, a woman who knows little about anything, know of what was in there? My husband told me nothing of his affairs."

The woman was a bloody genius. She'd just told whoever was in that room that Renton may have her late husband's papers. Suggesting he was keeping them to himself.

Monty remembered the night of the Raine ball when he'd been in the gardens. Renton had told whoever he was with that he'd searched his late brother's things and found nothing incriminating.

"Don't play me for a fool, my lady. Renton would not go against me—"

"Why?" Iris demanded. "Who are you?"

"I will give you two days, Lady Challoner, and if they have not been handed to me by then, it will go worse for you and your son."

"I don't know what you want! If you touch my son, I will kill you." The words came out as a low growl from Iris.

"I like a woman with spirit." The more guttural voice laughed.

"Heed my words, or you will not be alive to protect your son, that duty will be left to your brother-in-law."

Monty moved quickly when he heard footsteps after these ominous words. Opening the door to the next room, he slipped in and closed it so there was only a crack. The sound of snoring somewhere behind him told Monty he was not alone.

Pressing an eye to the opening, dull lamplight showed him the man he'd seen earlier but only from the back. There was another with him in the hallway.

"I will speak with Renton. If he's lying, he'll pay, but if not, she will. Show her what we will do if she is not telling the truth. Her husband told me she liked to be disciplined," the man he'd seen earlier said. "But don't be too rough, just enough to make her understand we mean business. She is a noblewoman after all."

He'd kill the bastard for those words, Monty vowed, pulling his hood further forward to disguise his face. When he heard the man's feet on the stairs, he slipped back out of the room and headed for the one Iris was in.

Someone was going to pay for scaring her.

CHAPTER 24

*M*onty opened the door slowly and was relieved when the hinges didn't squeak and alert the man he was there. Iris sat in a chair with her hands bound behind her, and over her head was a sack. A man stood before her.

"You and me, we're going to have a little fun before you go home, my lady. You need to understand there is a price to pay if you don't do what we ask."

"Let me go, or I will have you dealt with by the magistrate," Iris said, still defiant even considering her situation was dire. He'd admire that when he was no longer consumed with rage.

The man laughed. "You are in no position to deal with anyone. You are at my mercy." One large hand reached out and touched Iris's breast.

Monty fought for control as a red mist covered his eyes.

"Unhand me at once!" Iris cried as Monty jammed his pistol into the man's spine.

"Do as she says, or I'll put a bullet between your eyes."

The man quickly removed his hand from Iris's breast.

"Who is there?" Iris whispered.

"You will pay for touching her," Monty growled. "I'd kill you now, but the noise would bring attention. Take off the sack and untie her hands."

"I was doing what he told me."

"Who told you?"

"Don't know his name. He just tells me to do stuff, and I do it."

"Touching a woman while she's bound and gagged means you're a gutless coward. Now do what I told you," Monty said.

He reached forward and took the sack off Iris's head. Her eyes went to Monty, and he pushed back his hood. Shaking his head, he hoped she knew not to mention his name.

"Untie her hands." He nudged the pistol into the man's spine.

"They'll find you, whoever you are, and kill you," the man vowed.

"Excellent. I'm looking forward to that day. But right now, do as I asked you to, or I'll shoot you anyway and deal with attention the sound of my pistol brings."

He untied Iris's hands quickly.

"Release your feet, my lady."

Iris did as Monty directed. She then got out of the chair. Her fisted hand moved so fast, the bastard in front of her didn't see it. Her punch snapped his head right.

Monty was angry, but battling with that was pride. Challoner may have tried to break her, but he'd failed.

"Never touch a woman again without her consent," she hissed into his face.

"Put the sack over his head now, Lady Challoner," Monty directed.

"Gladly."

"I don't like the dark!" the man said after she'd done as he asked.

"Imagine how upset that makes me," Monty growled. "Now sit." He nudged the man into the chair. "Bind his feet, my lady."

She did as he said without comment.

"Stand outside the room now, Lady Challoner."

"Why?"

He gave her a hard look and mouthed the word "move." She didn't move an inch. "I need to interrogate him."

"Well do so," she mouthed back.

Bloody woman.

Pressing his pistol into the man's head, he said, "What other things have you carried out on behalf of the man who was here with you?"

"Yes, tell him," Iris urged.

"Be quiet," Monty gritted out, glaring at her again. "Answer the question," he said to the man.

"He just uses me when he needs someone to intimidate people."

"Who else do you work for?"

"No one."

Monty swung the butt of the gun and hit the man on the head. He grunted.

"Now tell me again what you know. Have you attended any meetings with this man and others?"

"Never. I just work for him!"

"What exactly do you do in your work for him?"

"I intimidate people or hurt them for information," the man said as Monty pressed his pistol into his neck. "I sometimes stand outside the church where they meet, but only to ensure no one comes. He pays me well."

"What church?"

"Don't know the name. It's about an hour out of London. No village, just a few houses and the church set in the trees."

"You don't know the name of the man who pays you, or where you go when you leave London to stand guard at the church? Is sounds to me like you're lying."

"I ain't. I don't ask questions. The last man who did, he worked alongside me. He disappeared for talking. Found him dead in a river."

"Do you see who comes and goes from the church?" Monty asked.

"They wear cloaks and masks and just appear," the man said.

"No one just appears," Iris scoffed.

"Be quiet," Monty snapped at her. She glared at him.

"I don't ask questions, and he pays. I have a family—"

"I'm not interested in your family. If that was indeed true, then how would you feel if your wife had a strange man touch her as you did this lady?" Monty snapped.

Silence followed.

"Did you ever hear a name? Anything?"

"Diaboli."

Devil, Monty translated.

"How do you get your orders?"

"A boy brings me a note. It tells me where to be."

"The man you work for, what does he look like?"

"Tall, thin with a right beaky face."

Large nose, Monty thought.

"How long have you worked for him?"

"A year."

"Someone is coming," Iris whispered as the sound of footsteps reached them.

"If I ever come across you again, I'll make you pay for touching her. I can't do that now, as it will draw attention and I need to get the lady to safety, but know that I am aware of what you look like. Do not cross my path again."

Iris's mouth fell open at his threat. He ignored her and swung his fist; it connected with the man's jaw. He slumped, unconscious. There was no more time to interrogate. He had to get Iris out of here before someone recognized her.

"Stay at my back," he directed her as they walked to the door. Opening it a crack, he stared out but saw no one. "Do not look at anyone and walk as close to my back as you can. Do you understand?"

"They are simple instructions—"

"Iris," he growled.

"Yes, I understand."

He left the room and started down the stairs with her on his heels. Reaching the public bar, he felt her hand grip his cloak. Monty walked a straight line to the door. When someone stepped into his path, he pushed them aside and continued until they reached the exit. Only when they were outside did he pull Iris in front of him.

"Walk to the end of the street."

Thankfully, she did as he directed without comment. Monty kept his pistol at his side, following her. Reaching his horse, he paid the boys, and they disappeared into the night.

"I'm not sure—" Her words ended on a shriek as Monty picked her up and threw her on the back of his horse. He vaulted on behind her. His arm slipped around her waist, and he held her against him.

"Pull the front of your bonnet down," he ordered her.

She did as he said, and soon they were heading to her house. Her body was flush to his, and Monty was aware of everywhere they touched; even through the layers of clothing, he could feel her.

He had no memory of wanting someone like he did Iris.

She was becoming a problem, because with exposure, his need for her was rising.

"If you see a carriage, horse, anyone on the street, lower your eyes, Iris."

She nodded. Just a single jerky movement.

Monty was always in control. Always knew exactly what was to be done in any situation. He worked and lived his life in solitude. He never gave in to urges others did. Passions that made a man do something he shouldn't. Emotion exposed people, and they became weak and vulnerable.

But not him. Never him.

His body was hard as he rode through London with Iris in his arms. He was holding a woman, and he hadn't done that before. Mary had hugged him, but he'd not held a woman as intimately between his thighs on horseback like he was Iris.

Closing the inches between them, he inhaled, and her soft, alluring scent filled his nostrils. She twisted to look over her shoulder, and their eyes met.

"I'm not sure why or how you found me, but thank you."

He was too angry and aroused to answer, so he managed a single nod, and she turned to face the front once more.

How the hell was he supposed to compose himself enough to tell her exactly what he thought of her reckless actions tonight? The Duchess of Yardly. He'd think about her and those hideous dresses she wore; that should cool his ardor.

It didn't work.

CHAPTER 25

Theo had saved her. She still couldn't believe he had appeared in that room when that horrid man had touched her. She'd been a fool to go there alone. Iris knew that now, but she would do it again for Henry.

"I must go to my aunt and uncle's at once," she said to Theo.

"I have sent a man to find out if Henry is there. An answer will come to your town house," he said in a cold, hard voice.

"But if he is not—"

"I will deal with it."

"I will deal with it also. He is my son, and I must be there for my aunt and uncle also," Iris said. "I will start looking for him."

"Where?" The word was barked at her.

"I don't know, but I have to look." Just thinking of her son made Iris nauseous with worry for his well-being. Her beautiful boy had already been through so much.

"We will know soon enough," he said.

"How did you know to find me there?" she asked to keep her mind thinking of something other than Henry.

"The questions can wait until we reach your house. Now I must get you there without being noticed." The voice was clipped and cold.

Iris wanted to demand he answer her, but she knew that right now arriving at her town house undetected was important. That and ensuring Henry was safe.

One strong arm held her around the waist, and her back was pressed to his front. Theo surrounded her. His large, hard body kept her safe.

The man behind her was nothing like Lord Plunge. He was so far from him, they could be two entirely different men. Except they weren't.

She'd thought briefly about going to Theo when that note arrived. But her fear for Henry had her deciding she could not take the time. She'd not told any of her staff, just slipped out of the house and went to the White Swan to meet with whoever had sent that note.

Iris had gone into that room up the stairs like she'd been directed, and that man had been there. The one who touched her breast. He'd bound her hands and feet and lowered the sack over her head. Then the other had arrived.

"My man is here, and he will have news on Henry," Theo said as they reached the Challoner town house.

She watched a tall figure in black walk toward them.

Theo dismounted first and then lifted Iris down.

"What did you find, Jimmy?" Theo said.

"The boy is safe there with his aunt and uncle. I spoke with a footman, and he checked."

"I will have you return there now, Jimmy, and watch over him. Have Jack take a shift, so you can get some sleep," Theo told him.

"I'll see to it at once, my lord." The man bowed and left.

Iris's knees nearly buckled with relief that her son was safe.

"Come. Into the house now," Theo said, taking her arm.

"You can go," she said.

"No, I can't. We need to talk about the risk you took tonight."

"That has no bearing on you." Iris walked away from him and to her front door. "Good evening, my lord." She threw the words over her shoulder.

Opening her large front door, she stepped over the threshold, but before she could shut it behind her, a hand in her back nudged her forward. Theo then shut it.

"I-I thank you again for saving me," she said slowly. "But I wish to retire now."

"Do you have brandy, whiskey, or any spirits here?"

She nodded.

"Then lead the way." He held out a hand, and Iris knew he wasn't leaving until he'd spoken his piece.

They removed their outer clothing, and then Iris directed him to the small parlor. She went straight to the decanter of brandy and poured two glasses. She threw hers back, and the liquid hit her throat, making her cough.

Theo did not suffer the same fate.

"Now, explain to me why you would take such a foolish risk. Especially when I had told you if you needed anything to come to me."

He'd moved back a few steps but not many. He stood there glaring at her.

"My son was threatened. I had no time—"

"That man wanted to hurt you," he gritted out, the muscle in his jaw ticking. "Would have hurt you and possibly done something to you that you would never recover from."

"How did you know I was there?" she asked. Her knees felt suddenly weak, and Iris couldn't be sure if that was from the brandy or the night's events. Likely both.

"Sit." He took her arm and led her to a chair. Nudging her

down, Theo grabbed another and dragged it close. When he sat, their knees were touching.

"How, Theo?"

His eyes held hers as he spoke. "I had someone watching your house. What you told me about Renton's behavior, and what I witnessed myself was enough to have me worried you and Henry were in danger."

"You had someone watching us?"

He nodded.

She didn't know what to say to that. She really should be angry he hadn't told her, and yet she was also humbled that he'd cared enough to have someone watch her. Had he not, her fate at that man's hands tonight could have been dire.

"I don't understand. Why did you do that?"

His eyes never moved from her face. "You may be a link to my parents' death."

"Of course." She'd been silly to believe it was because he was worried about her.

"You do understand that when that man realizes you were lying about Renton, and you do not produce the papers, he will come after you again."

"I could produce the papers," Iris said.

"You could after we copy them," Monty said. "My worry is that he will not be content with that. He may get it in his head that you are a risk to keep alive because you may have read them."

"But if I don't produce them, he will keep asking or searching for them," Iris added. "Do you think it was one of my late husband's friends?"

"Likely, but as I could not see his face, I do not know."

"We will go to the country tomorrow," Iris said quickly.

"And be even more exposed. No, you will stay here in London where I can protect you."

"I am not your concern. I will hire men to protect us, and we have Norman."

"This is not a game, Iris. These men will kill and have killed to protect themselves and what they stand for."

"You think I don't know that? That I am not terrified for my son?" she cried.

"You don't need to be terrified. I will protect you," he said in a steady voice.

"Lord Plunge?" she scoffed.

He eyed her. "I think we both know I am not him."

"Then why do you play the part of him?" Iris asked.

"That is my business, and the answer will get you into trouble should anyone try to pry information out of you again."

"Who are you?" she whispered.

"It matters not. What matters is we are going to talk, and you are going to listen and answer questions."

"What questions?"

"Think back to when your husband was in the house with you and Henry. I need to know exactly who was there. If you overheard anything, Iris. If your husband said anything at all suspicious."

"You have not asked me these questions before."

"You were not lured from your house and your son threatened before. Now concentrate. I need any information you can give me."

"I need more brandy," Iris muttered. He didn't move. "Move, Theo."

His sigh was loud and told her he was annoyed. Well, too bad. She was scared and angry. Her nerves felt like a piece of piano wire about to snap.

She went to pour another brandy. He followed.

"Don't drink too much. Your head will be sore tomorrow."

She spun to glare at him. "You have no right to tell me what to do. My husband did that for years."

"I am not your husband. I am trying to protect you."

"No, you are worried in case I die, and you won't get the information you need about your parents' murderers!" She shrieked the words at him. "That perhaps I will remember something that will lead you to them."

"Calm down, hysteria will not help the situation."

She'd had times in her life when she'd been volatile and spoken without thought. Her husband had cured her of that, but in that moment, she felt the rebellion rise inside her. It choked her, and her hand clenched to stop it from slapping the handsome face before her.

"Hysteria?" she said with barely controlled fury. Her voice wobbled as Iris struggled to keep herself in check. "My son was threatened."

"And yet he is well. Now calm down, and we will sit, and you can try to remember anything that will lead me—"

"You should not be here with me alone." Iris suddenly wanted him gone.

"Possibly but as you should not have left the house alone, it hardly matters. Plus, no one knows I am here. Now, talk."

Her chin rose. "I have nothing to say."

"You won't say or have nothing to say?" he demanded.

"Your Plunge is slipping," she said instead of answering his question.

"Iris, answer the damn question."

"Don't speak to me like that."

"Do you realize what could have happened to you had I not found you?"

"We have already discussed this," Iris snapped back. "I'm not a fool, and I am also not your business. Now I thank you for what you did and how you protected us, but you may leave." She said the words with excruciating politeness.

"I'm not leaving."

"Go away." She looked to the wall where a clock hung. The hour was late. "I want you to leave, because suddenly I feel the need to do something I haven't in many years."

"What?" he questioned her calmly.

"Lose control!" She slipped around him, and then, picking up her skirts, she fled.

It wasn't dignified nor rational, but in that moment, she wanted the sanctuary of her bedroom. There was a lock on the door, and she would turn it.

"Dammit to hell!" She heard his curse, and then the thud of his feet. "Stop, Iris."

She didn't stop; she ran. Up the stairs, along a hall, and down another. He didn't know her home like she did. Iris just prayed her staff were all sleeping soundly and would not hear them.

"Stop!"

She was close now, her room just ahead. Reaching the door, she pushed it and ran inside, shutting it behind her. He had it opened before she could turn the key.

"I am trying to help you!" He slammed the door behind him. "Your son's name will be blackened alongside his father's if what information I have is released to society. He could be kidnapped, again," he added with a bite to his words. "Violated or murdered if I do not catch who is behind this. If we are dealing with the same people who ruthlessly took the lives of my parents too, then I want to know!"

She backed away from him. He was no longer calm; now his anger filled the room. Plunge was a man who could inspire fear in no one, and this man was not he.

"My son is not his father," Iris said slowly. She needed to calm down. This was Theo; he would not hurt her. He'd just rescued her.

"It matters not. The same stench will taint him. I believe

there could be a link that draws all these things together, including the murder of my parents, Iris. I must pursue it for your safety and my sanity."

She studied him, all fight leaving her body at his words.

"Did you suffer, Theo?" Iris whispered.

She'd spent long hours as a young girl wondering what was going on in the large house she could see from her bedroom window. Was he being comforted in his grief?

"It was long ago." He brushed her words aside.

"I tried to get to you. You must know that I tried."

Something shifted in his face. Subtle and small, but she saw it softening.

"You were ten. I doubt you could have changed my uncle's mind."

"My parents tried too, but he turned them away."

His eyes dropped to the floor for the first time.

"I thought of you," she whispered.

CHAPTER 26

*M*onty wanted to tell her to be quiet. He didn't think about those days. Didn't go back there, but this woman had known him before. She was part of his life when he'd still had an innocent hope for a future. If anyone had the right to speak of that time, it was her.

"I am no longer that boy, Iris."

"You had no one, didn't you?" Tears filled her lovely eyes. "No one held you when you cried or helped you grieve."

"I am well," he got out around the lump in his throat. Her tears were for him and rolled silently down her cheeks. They made his chest hurt. "Stop crying." He moved to cup her face, and she flinched.

"What did he do to you?" Theo's words were hoarse as he touched her cheeks.

"Who?"

"Your husband. What did he do to you?"

Her laugh was humorless. "He did not beat me if that's what you mean. Once, he slapped me. I learned after that, and he never had a reason to do so again. But Henry..." Her words broke on a sob. "He hurt my son."

Monty's hand found its way to her back and pulled her closer. He held her as if she was made of fragile spun glass.

"I h-hated him, Theo."

"With good reason, no doubt."

She laid her cheek on his chest, and his chin sat on her head, like they were made to fit together this way. In that moment, they were both defenseless.

"I'm sorry you suffered, Theo."

"As I am sorry you suffered too, Iris." He let his eyes sweep her bedroom. The grand bed with its four posts and gossamer drapes. The deep green velvet cover stitched with her late husband's crest. Everywhere he looked he saw luxury and grandness.

"Tell me you hate this room."

Her laugh made him smile. "I do, but as yet have done nothing about it."

"From memory, you loved peach."

"I did."

"Then decorate it that color."

She sighed. "I want the truth about my husband, Theo. And if that comes with the realization that he had something to do with your parents' deaths, I want to know that too."

"I know." And he did. She wanted justice for him, and for his parents who she had loved. "Iris, I need to let you go now and walk away." Because he wanted this. Wanted to hold her and feel her in his arms. Wanted to give and receive comfort like other people did in their lives.

Not him, however. He'd chosen another path.

"For the first time in a long while, I feel safe," she whispered. "Thank you for coming for me tonight, Theo. I know you had someone watching me because my late husband could be a link to your parents' murders, but—"

"That wasn't the only reason, Iris." He eased her off his

chest. His hand once again cupped her face. "I did it because I… I care that you and Henry are safe."

She looked up at him, her eyes damp with tears, and something inside Monty released. He couldn't fight this anymore.

He moved slowly, so she could pull back if she wanted, and placed his lips on hers. Just a soft brush. Iris tensed but did not pull away.

"You say he didn't hurt you, but—"

"He didn't hurt me, Theo. I promise. I was simply a chattel to him."

Monty ran his thumbs over her cheeks.

"What was your life like, Iris?"

"I was controlled. Even when he left to enter society, he had his spies watch me. I received visits from him often and letters dictating what I must do."

"Bastard. Surely your family—"

"I tried when he first showed his true colors, but my father said things would settle and that my husband was head of the household. My sister was busy with her life. But my aunt and uncle demanded to see me when they called. It was they who kept me sane and showed Henry I was not the only person to love him."

Monty hated her husband was dead, because had he not been, he would relish sending him to his grave.

"Why wouldn't he let you enter society, Iris?"

"Because he wanted to live his life as he chose. Mistresses, parties, and likely a lot more. He told everyone I was a nervous sort and prone to illness, and this stopped me from enjoying the excitement of society."

"I never asked after you, and I should have."

"I think you had other things on your mind, Theo."

He sighed. "I chose the path I took to seek vengeance and find who had killed my parents. Until now, with you handing me that letter and other information that has come to light, I had found no clues."

"You became Plunge for that purpose alone?" Iris asked him.

He still cupped her cheeks, and her skin was so warm beneath his hands.

"All I can tell you is that I've been hiding in plain sight for most of my life, Iris. Trust me when I say it's best you know nothing more, but that it was my choice."

He kissed her again, and his body stirred to life as if waking from a lifetime of slumber.

"Theo, we shouldn't—"

"I'm not sure I can let you go, Iris." He whispered the words against her lips. "I would never hurt you."

"I know that."

He felt the tension slide from her body as he continued to kiss her. Monty told himself it was just kisses. He would leave soon and return to his cold, lonely house. They were in her bedroom in the early hours of the morning. Her staff were downstairs, and he was taking advantage of her.

His hands stroked down her spine.

"Tell me to go, Iris."

"I can't. You make me feel things I never thought to feel, Theo. I've been scared and alone for so long."

"As have I. So cold and empty."

"Yes," she whispered.

Her hands went to his shoulders as his roamed her back through her clothes. He was desperate to feel the warmth of her skin against his.

"I want you, Iris." His words were raw and honest.

"My experience with him... my husband was horrid and painful. I vowed I would never again do that with a man."

"'That' being make love?" Theo asked.

Iris nodded. "It was very wrong of me, but when he died,

215

I rejoiced. I dutifully went through the mourning period, and the entire time I felt like a weight had been lifted from the house Henry and I lived in. That finally we could walk out of the dark and into the light. The scars he left us with will take time to heal."

"I remember your father being a bit stuffy, but he loved you. Surely he knew nothing of Challoner's character, or he would never have allowed the wedding," Theo said.

"No. He courted me with flowers and lovely words. My father, like me, believed him a good man for all there were many years between us. All that changed the day we were married, but as far as my father was concerned, I simply had to put up with my new life."

"I'm sorry that your life was hell." He pressed his lips to hers briefly. "But you and Henry will suffer no more."

"My husband laid with me only to have heirs, and nothing more. He ridiculed me when I did not conceive again after Henry and grew more determined." She shuddered.

"He is gone, Iris, cry no more tears for him." He ran his thumbs under her eyes. "I'm sorry that I left, and we did not marry."

"That was children talking," she whispered.

"If my parents had not been murdered, we would have married one day." Monty believed that.

"He left a stain on my soul—"

"It is time for you to live now, Iris," he cut off her words. "He is gone."

"And what of you. Will you start to live also?"

"I had decided to leave society and Plunge behind at the end of this season. Now I am not so sure due to the fresh evidence about my parents' killers."

"You will never return?"

He shook his head. "Likely not."

She rose to her toes and pressed her lips to his. Her hands

braced on his shoulders, and the gesture was innocent and sweet, and the first time a woman had kissed him.

"Theo?"

"Yes?"

"W-Will you help me to forget him. H-Help me to make new memories." She stepped back from him. "I don't want to remember his touch anymore."

"Iris—"

"I feel like he is imprinted on my body. That I will always close my eyes and feel his weight on me."

"No, it would be wrong of me... us to do that." But Christ how he wanted it. Wanted her and her soft, warm curves in his hands touching his naked flesh.

"Yes. I am a widow, Theo. I am no maiden. Show me what can be between a man and a woman."

"How do you know I can give you that?" The words were raw. He felt like she was opening something he'd kept closed inside him for so long. Exposing the vulnerability he'd fought to keep hidden.

"I see you, Theo. The good man who would never hurt me."

Iris stood there, pale and exhausted. Some of her hair had come free, but the rest was still pinned on her head. To Theo, she was possibly the most beautiful woman he'd ever seen, and she saw him... really saw him.

"Let us bring each other into the light, Theo. Let me touch you as I know you have not been touched."

She may not be a virgin, but Monty knew she was still an innocent. He shook his head, and she stepped back.

"I'm sorry. I should have—"

"No. I shook my head because you are right, no one has touched me in gentleness. No one has caressed me," he whispered. "It terrifies me how much I want you, Iris."

She closed the distance between them once more. Her

hands went to his jacket, and Monty watched as she unbuttoned it and then pushed it from his shoulders so it fell to the floor. Her fingers shook as she did the same with his waistcoat.

Monty was frozen, his eyes watching her. The only person since his parents passed to undress him was his valet. Iris was willingly touching him; the thought was humbling, and it scared him spitless.

"Theo."

"Yes." His voice was a hoarse whisper.

"I-I have never undressed a man. Will you help me?" Her voice was small and nervous.

"We don't have to go any further, Iris." He made himself say it, when inside his body was bracing for her touch. "I have no wish to scare you."

The truth was, they were both innocent. Neither of them had felt the touch of a person who cared. Someone who would want to offer pleasure.

"Let me touch you, please, Theo. I want to try. Take off your shirt," she said.

Iris looked up his body until their eyes met. Monty no longer saw fear, but there were nerves, as there were for him. He'd been with women plenty of times but always in the dark, and when it was done, he left without a word.

This was different. This was Iris, and he believed that what happened between them now would change him in many ways.

"Please, Theo."

His fingers were clumsy as he removed his necktie, and he helped her tug his shirt free of his trousers. She pushed the material up, and he pulled it over his head.

"Iris," he said for no other reason than he didn't know what to say or do, and then she touched him. Monty could do nothing to swallow down the low moan as she laid her hands on his chest.

"So warm," he whispered.

Iris ran her hands slowly down his chest. It was exquisite, leaving a trail of heat wherever they touched.

"Christ, Iris."

"I know," she whispered. "It is wonderful to feel you, Theo. I have never touched another like this. You have a lovely chest."

His laugh sounded strangled.

"I want to touch you too," he got out.

She seemed to think about that as her hands ran up and down his chest creating waves of pleasure. Is this what the Devilles had with their women? It was a wonder they ever left their beds.

She dropped her hands to her sides and turned her back on him.

"I-I need you to help me."

Monty's mouth went dry as he looked at the small buttons running down her spine. He'd been unbuttoning items of clothing for years, yet in that moment, his fingers turned into thumbs.

"They are small—"

"I have it," he said, doubting his ability to have anything. His eyes were drawn to the small pale patch of skin above the back of her dress. Monty pressed his lips there, and she shivered.

When he'd released the last button, he pushed the dress from her shoulders. It bunched at her waist and then fell to the floor with his clothes. She didn't turn, leaving him a view of her chemise. Soft, white material that did nothing to hide the vulnerable line of her vertebrae and the round swells of her buttocks.

Monty removed the pins from her hair, and the heavy

locks tumbled down to her spine. Fisting his hands in the curls, he buried his nose in the satin and inhaled.

"You smell so good."

"Honeysuckle."

"Can I touch you, Iris?"

She nodded.

Monty stroked her shoulders with both hands. One he let travel down her arm until he could take her fingers in his. They gripped him, anchoring them to each other.

His other hand then roamed her body. Running along the band of the chemise's neckline and lower. Feeling her through the fabric. She trembled as he soothed her.

"Iris, are you all right?"

"Your hands on me feel wonderful, Theo. I feel the heat wherever they touch."

He turned her slowly, keeping his eyes on her face and not the tantalizing swell of her breasts.

"If you are scared. If anything we do frightens you, then you must say, Iris."

"And you also," she replied.

She then raised her first finger, and he remembered. Raising his, they linked.

"There must always be truth between friends." They both whispered the long-ago pact.

Iris then pressed her body to his, and Monty forgot everything but the feel of her.

CHAPTER 27

*I*ris didn't think she'd ever forget the moment Theo dropped his guard and let her in. Let her see the vulnerability he'd fought so hard to keep hidden. Both of them had been hiding, but here in her room, she felt stripped bare. Her emotions were there for him to see, as his were for her.

"Your touch is unlike anything I've felt before, Theo."

"And yours warms me, Iris."

She felt his lips in her hair, the gesture so sweet it brought tears to her eyes. Was this what others had? Those that cared, did they share this kind of tenderness?

"You are so beautiful, Iris."

"No."

"Yes." He eased her back from him. "When I first saw you in the Raine ballroom, I felt like I couldn't breathe."

His face was serious as he studied her.

"You have grown into everything I knew you would become." His finger ran down her cheek to her neck. "Strong, intelligent, and so beautiful."

Iris shook her head.

"It will take time, but eventually you will erase him from your life. Erase what he did to you, and here, now, tonight, that begins." His words were a vow, and she almost believed him.

His fingers touched the skin above the neckline of her chemise, and she shivered at the contact.

"Let me make you feel what I see when I look at you, Iris."

"Yes. Oh yes, Theo, I want that." And she wanted to feel something other than resentment and anger. Maybe then she could forget and start living.

His fingers traced the band of cotton and then slid inside to touch the swell of one breast. Closing her eyes, she fought back anything but the wonder of his touch.

This was Theo. He'd never hurt her like her husband had.

"Just feel, Iris."

His fingers teased and stroked the skin until the coil of ice inside her thawed.

"I want to see you," he whispered.

She nodded, and his hands lifted the chemise up and off her body. Iris couldn't look at Theo as she stood before him naked. She'd learned to loathe her body since her husband had told her he owned it.

"You are exquisite, sweet Iris."

His words drew her eyes to his. She saw the desire, and it was for her.

"Every inch of you is perfection."

"No." It was instinctive to deny.

"Yes." He pulled her close. "You are a beautiful woman. But as you don't believe me, I will have to show you."

The feel of his chest against her breasts was wonderful. Skin to skin, his body was so hard and hot.

His kiss was more demanding this time, and she felt the hard ridge of his arousal pressed into her belly. It frightened and thrilled her at the same time. This was Theo, and he would never hurt her. Never belittle her.

His kisses grew more heated, and she felt need pull at her. An unfamiliar ache grew between her thighs, and Iris thought perhaps it was arousal.

Theo kissed her neck and then moved lower, his mouth touching and teasing kisses over her skin. One of his hands stroked her thigh in slow, hot circles.

"You have control. Never forget that, Iris." He looked up at her. "Say it."

"I have control," she repeated.

"Good girl, now you just have to believe it."

His lips moved to her breasts. Long licks of his tongue covered every inch of her flesh, and her body bloomed under his ministrations. She was soon arching into him, needing more. When he took her nipple into his mouth and sucked it gently, she moaned low in her throat.

And then she was in his arms, and he was carrying her to the bed. Laying her on the mattress, Theo joined her and continued to kiss and caress every inch of her body until she was writhing beneath him, feeling emotions she'd never felt before.

She could feel herself spiraling toward something. The tension inside her was almost unbearable.

"Open your legs wider for me, Iris."

In that moment, she would have done anything for him. His hand touched her, trailing down her secret places. His fingers stroked the soft, damp folds between her thighs.

"Just feel," he whispered against her lips as she tensed. "You know I won't hurt you."

"I do, but—"

"We are erasing his memory." He kissed her softly as his thumb touched the small, sensitive bud. She shuddered as he ran his digit back and forth.

"Oh my."

"Oh my indeed," Theo gritted out.

She felt him parting her, and then his fingers were there inside her. His head lowered to lick a breast as he stroked, then retreated. It felt wonderful. She'd never experienced anything like this before.

"Theo!" She called his name as sensation hit her hard. Arching off the bed, she rode out the wave of ecstasy.

"Beautiful," he said, kissing her softly.

"I've never… That was wonderful," Iris whispered. "Thank you."

"You are welcome." He kissed her again. "But now I need to go." She could hear the tension in his words.

He moved back from her and got off the bed.

"Where are you going?"

"It is late. I will return to my town house."

She could see his erection straining against his trousers before he turned away. He'd given her that—the most amazing feeling she'd ever experienced—but had taken nothing for himself. The thought was humbling. Theo was so very different from her husband. Getting off the bed, she moved to where he stood, collecting his clothes.

"Theo."

"Get back to bed, Iris. I know the way to your front door." The words were strained.

"Theo, look at me."

"Please go back to bed," he gritted out.

"Now, Theo."

The clothes fell from his hands as he turned. Jaw clenched, he was looking over her head, not making eye contact. Iris had never understood why any woman would seek a man's attention deliberately, and yet suddenly she did. To have this man's attention focused solely on her was a wonderful thing, and she thought perhaps she would want more.

Was she brave enough to touch him again? Touch him intimately. Memories emerged of dark nights when her husband had told her to raise her nightdress and lie still—no, she would not think about that. There was no place for him in her life anymore.

"I need to go, Iris." His words were no longer gentle but harsh.

"Soon," she replied. Her hand went to his chest, and he flinched, but she didn't stop. Instead, she ran it slowly over his skin. She traced a circle around his nipples, wondering if he would feel as she had when he'd touched hers. The nail she scraped over one tip had him shuddering, and she had her answer.

"You don't have to do this." He spaced each word.

"I know that, Theo. I have control."

He nodded and then closed his eyes as she moved down his body. Her finger traced the line of his waistband while she plucked up the courage to move lower.

"But I want to touch you." She stroked a hand over the hard ridge of his arousal, and he moaned, long and loud. "I want to lie with you," she whispered.

"Be very sure, Iris." His eyes were deep pools of desire. "I can promise you nothing more than this."

"I want nothing more than this." She told herself those words were the truth. There was no room in her life for more than now, tonight.

"Will you take off your clothes, Theo?"

He stumbled back from her. Bending, he wrenched off his boots with so much force, he nearly fell on his bottom. He hopped to right himself, which had her giggling.

"You think that's funny, do you?" His smile was strained.

"A bit." Her smile fell away as he stripped off his trousers. The jut of his erection, so big and hard, drew her eyes. He didn't move as she looked at him. Just stood there like a bloody Roman statue, hard slopes and planes of skin over muscle. So strong, she thought. But also gentle, Iris knew that too now.

She made herself close the distance between them again, and she touched him with the tip of her finger. The head of his arousal was smooth. His breathing was heavy now as Iris moved her fingers up and down his length. Learning, feeling the shape and size of him. When she wrapped her fingers around him, he shuddered.

"God, Iris. Your touch is beyond anything I have felt."

"As your touch was for me."

Her husband had done this to himself, telling her it was the only way he could make love to her. But this was different. This was Theo, and she had the control.

As she stroked him, Iris rose to her toes and kissed him. His hands went to her hair, grabbing handfuls as his mouth devoured her. She felt no fear, only wonder that this man wanted her in such a way. Needed her in this moment as she needed him.

"I cannot take much more, Iris."

She took his hand and walked back to the bed. Looking at the mattress, she remembered what her husband had done to her.

Theo turned her, and it was he who sat on the bed.

"No lying down. Straddle me, Iris. Take me inside you."

She did as he asked, her knees on either side of his thighs.

"Look at me now. You have the control, remember?"

His eyes held hers. They were dark with need, and he seemed to will her to focus on him as his hands settled on her hips.

"Lower down now, Iris."

He guided her, and soon she felt him at her entrance, and

then he was sliding inside her. He was so large and thick, stretching her.

"Are you all right?" His words were strained as he fought for control.

"Yes," she whispered.

"Take me into your body."

She lowered the last few inches until he was deep inside her.

"So good." Theo shuddered.

"Yes," she agreed. And it was the truth. Theo was inside her, and she felt no fear. It was so different from her husband. He touched her in reverence. Touched her as if she was the most precious thing he'd ever held.

"Ride me, Iris," he gritted out.

She rose on her knees and lowered again, and the clench and release of her inner muscles caused the wonderful tension she'd already experienced once tonight to return.

"More," he whispered. "I need more of you, Iris."

She rose again and again. His hands roamed her body as she took him inside her over and over. His breathing was hoarse. Her moans grew louder and louder.

"Let go, my sweet. I will catch you."

"As I will catch you!" She cried the words as she felt her release hit her again. He thrust into her once more and shuddered out a loud groan. His arms banded around her, holding her to him as he found his own release.

Breathless, she slumped into him. Her cheek was on his chest listening to the thud of his heart. Her body felt lax, and she simply wanted to lie on the mattress and sleep.

When he stirred, his lips pressed a kiss to her shoulder.

"I must go now."

"Yes, of course." Iris climbed off him. She sat on her bed, knees raised, and watched as he dressed. Every inch of the man was perfection. Long, muscled legs, broad chest and shoulders. "Thank you, Theo."

He paused in pulling on his boots.

"Don't thank me. What we shared was mutual." His words were cooler now, and Iris could almost see him withdrawing from her.

"Of course." Iris felt herself doing the same. Both were so used to protecting themselves from emotion and pain. "Thank you again for coming to rescue me as well."

"Don't leave the house again if you receive a note but come to me or send word. Jimmy or another will be outside. There is much I must do now to find who is behind all of this."

"I could help."

"Absolutely not. You will stay here and wait until I tell you that the threat is gone. We will decide how best to proceed."

"We?" Iris asked.

He ignored her. "If handing over the documents will keep you safe, then that is what we will do."

"I am not staying inside my house. I will be a prisoner no more, Theo." The words came out with more force than required and had him moving to stand before her.

"I did not say you were to be a prisoner."

"He made me one. I will allow no man to do so again," she said, feeling at a distinct disadvantage. He was dressed and towering over her now.

Grabbing her blanket, she wrapped it around her body.

"I am not your late husband," Theo said in that cold, emotionless voice she hated. Gone was her lover and the man who had treated her with such tenderness. "You will not leave this house alone again. I will have your word on that, Iris. In fact, I think you should stay with your aunt and uncle until this is done with. I will have two men stationed outside their house."

"For how long? Whoever lured me to the White Swan wants those papers, or Henry and I will pay the price. So we give them to them."

"And if they decide it is simply easier to remove you, what then? Henry will be alone!" he snapped.

"I will protect my son." Iris felt her anger rise.

"How? Can you shoot a gun and use a knife?"

"I punched that man tonight!"

"A lucky punch when he wasn't expecting it," Theo scoffed.

"They will not force me from this home—"

"Your home," he said.

"It was never mine."

"Well make it yours."

"Don't tell me what to do."

His teeth snapped together.

"There is danger for you and Henry. Perhaps you should think of him when you decide to do something reckless like leave the house alone. He has lost one parent already."

The words were like a slap in the face.

"Go now," she said.

He stared at her for long, heated minutes but said nothing more. Theo then turned and left the room, taking all the warmth with him.

CHAPTER 28

*I*t was early afternoon when Monty knocked on the front door of the large two-story home, which was situated an hour from London. He'd thought long and hard about doing this, but he had to know. Was the symbol he'd found in his father's hand that day found on either Peters or Lionel?

Peters's family had left London, so it would take longer to track them down, but Lionel was survived by his wife who lived at this address, or so he'd been told.

"Good day." The butler opened the door.

"Good day. My name is Lord Montgomery. I wish to speak with Lady Lionel if possible?"

"I will see if she is at home to callers." He was left to cool his heels on the doorstep.

It was six days after he'd made love to Iris. Six long days of wondering if she was safe and thinking of him as constantly as he thought of her. The minute he'd walked away from her, the cold had returned and slid its unwanted fingers into his soul. *Damn her for making him feel.*

The door opened again. "If you will come this way, Lady Lionel will see you," the butler said.

The hallway was narrow, and they passed under a curved staircase. The room they entered had large doors opening into the gardens, and it was through those they walked.

"Lady Lionel is inside the glasshouse. If you will follow the path, my lord, I will bring tea," the butler said, waving him to the right.

Monty walked down a path past neat rows of flower beds. The entire place was weeded and manicured. Someone took a great deal of time caring for this garden. He found the glasshouse at the end of the path and was hit from all directions with scents as he entered. Earth, greenery, and warmth.

"Over here," a voice called.

He found Lady Lionel with her hands in soil. She was tall, wearing a large hat and thick leather gloves. He had a glimpse of a narrow face but little else as she was looking down.

"My Lady, thank you for seeing me," he said, bowing.

The woman removed her hands from the soil and clapped them together, sending dirt in all directions. She then took off her gloves and laid them on a small bench.

"I don't get a lot of visitors, and it intrigued me why a member of society would call. I haven't been to London for many years."

Thank God for that, Monty thought.

"Come, we will sit, and Chipley will bring tea."

She stalked away from him down a narrow path, the skirts of her deep brown dress swishing aside leaves and debris as she walked. Monty followed.

His mood had been dark and dangerous since leaving Iris. He'd shut himself away from everyone since that night, and yet he saw her everywhere, but mostly inside his head. He saw and felt her soft, lush curves. Her moans filled his head, and his hands could still feel the texture of her skin.

It has to stop, he told himself, exiting the glasshouse on Lady Lionel's heels.

He was a bastard for not contacting Iris, but then she had not called on him either. And then there were the Devilles who had called constantly and sent notes, and he'd been not letting them into his house and avoiding them. In fact, he'd told everyone he had a chest inflammation.

"Sit, my lord," Lady Lionel said, waving to a seat under a large jacaranda tree, which had a stunning display of purple-blue, trumpet-shaped flowers. Its subtle scent filled the air, and if he wasn't in a foul mood, Monty thought this would be the idyllic place to sit and drink tea.

"Thank you," he said, taking the seat opposite her. A flower dropped into his lap.

"That will bring you good fortune," Lady Lionel said.

"Excellent, that will be welcome," Monty said.

She smiled, and the lines on her face deepened. She had weathered features, which he thought was from hours spent outside maintaining her gardens.

"What brings you here, Lord Montgomery? If I was to guess, I would say it has something to do with my husband or your father."

"You knew my father?"

"I met him a few times. He and my husband were friends. He was a good man and extremely proud of his son." Her smile was gentle. "I'm so very sorry that he and your mother passed when you were young, my lord."

More emotion, Monty thought. He felt like it was choking him.

"Thank you, and you are right. I am here to ask you questions about your husband, and I am sorry if they upset you." Monty picked up the bloom that had fallen in his lap and ran the flower back and forth between his thumb and forefinger.

"I love my husband and have mourned him since his death, but I like to speak about him to keep his memory strong," she said.

"My parents were murdered, my lady."

"Oh, my dear, I'm sorry. That must have been horrible for you."

"It was, and I don't think I've ever really recovered." Why had he told her that? Monty blamed Iris. She'd made him feel and had opened something inside him he didn't seem able to close again.

"Grief is a terrible thing. But even worse when those taken from us so swiftly were loved deeply," she said.

Monty nodded. He had loved his parents deeply.

"Those who murdered my father and mother were never caught. I have not given up hope that one day they will be held accountable."

"I understand your need for justice, my lord."

"Would you call me Monty?" he asked her.

She smiled. "I would like that, and my name is Marion."

The tea tray arrived, and on it were four cherry buns that looked mouthwatering. It surprised him he was hungry. He hadn't been since he'd left Iris.

"We will pour. Thank you, Chipley."

"Very good, ma'am." The butler disappeared again.

"Now, Monty, it is understandable that you want justice, but to let it consume you would not make your parents happy. They would also want happiness and a life for you."

"How do you know that I don't have a life?" He stared at her.

"Do you have a wife and children and lots of friends?"

He shook his head.

"Well there you have it then, but it is not too late. Now get

233

back to your questions," Marion said, picking up a bun and taking a large bite.

"My father had a small carving of the pentacle symbol clutched in his hand when I found his body." He shouldn't have just come right out with it, but there had been no easy way.

Marion lowered the bun back to the plate and took a sip of her tea. She then rose. Monty went to do the same, but she waved him back to his seat.

"Stay. I shall return shortly."

He watched her until she disappeared behind the glasshouse. *Where had she gone?*

Deciding he would find out soon enough, he picked up a bun and ate.

It was peaceful here, away from the bustle of London. If he was honest, there hadn't been a lot of peace in his life since his parents died. It was time for change. Monty just wasn't sure now in what form that would come. But what he knew was that he could not contemplate it until he saw this investigation through to its conclusion.

He was on his second bun when Marion returned.

"Is this what you found?" She placed a small carving onto the table in front of him.

His heartbeat once again increased as he picked up the item.

"Yes, that's the same as the one my father had in his palm. Will you tell me about the day your husband passed, Marion?"

She took a fortifying sip of her tea. "I was away from our house visiting my sister, and when I returned early one morning, I was informed by our staff that my husband was still sleeping. I entered the room and knew instantly something wasn't right. Opening the drapes, I approached Charles. He was cold, and I knew he was dead. We believed he'd died in his sleep. I found that carving in his palm, and because I knew that was the devil's symbol, I hid it so the doctor who came to pronounce him dead did not see it."

"I did the same thing when I found it in my father's hand. Did you believe your husband could worship the devil, Marion?"

"Absolutely not. My husband was strong in his religious beliefs and would never waver. But I could find no answer as to why it was there in his hand." She was frowning now, and he knew she was back to the morning she'd found the man she loved dead. Just as Monty often went back to the scene in his parents' bedroom.

"Do you doubt your husband died in his sleep, Marion?"

She hesitated.

"I will not speak of this with anyone if that is your wish," Monty said.

"My husband's pillow was lying half over his face. He could have reached for it in his sleep and put it there—"

"But you were suspicious?"

"I was distraught, so I perhaps was not seeing things clearly, but there was bleeding under his nose, and it looked crooked," Marion said.

Which could suggest someone had pressed the pillow into it to suffocate him, Monty thought.

"The doctor said the bleeding happens in death."

He'd never heard of that.

"Do you believe there is a chance that Charles died at the hands of another?"

She took another sip of her tea, and for some reason, Monty held his breath.

"As the years passed, my grief has eased, and I have thought often about that morning I came home and found the man I had loved for so long dead."

He thought of Iris then and the warm weight in his chest

he experienced when she was close. He would be devastated if anything happened to her.

"I'm sorry you lost your husband, Marion."

"He was more than my husband, Monty. Quite simply, he was my life."

It hit him then, hard. Iris could be that for him. They'd not spent much time together, and yet he knew deep in his soul he now carried Iris in his heart. The thought terrified him.

He'd never believed that he would love as Marion did... not until now.

"Do you believe my husband was murdered, Monty?"

He couldn't look away from her intense gaze, and he would not lie to her. "I do, Marion."

"Do you think that whoever killed Charles may have been responsible for your parents' deaths?"

He nodded again.

She exhaled slowly and then said, "If that is indeed the case, then I want you to find who did this and get justice for my husband and your parents, Monty."

"I will ensure those we love are avenged," he vowed.

She reached across the table to lay her hand on his. Monty found himself gripping her fingers.

"I know you will. But what I also wish is for you to find happiness and let the past no longer define you when this is over."

"How do you know I let the past define me?" He looked into her faded blue eyes.

"You are here, many years after your parents were murdered, still looking for answers. You have told me you have no family."

"You're astute."

"Start your life. Your parents would wish it, Monty."

He then sat there with Marion Lionel in her lovely garden

and took tea, and in that moment, he felt like they'd been friends for years. An hour later, he was back on his horse heading to London, to the church, after telling her he would call again soon.

Last night he'd received a summons to meet with Geraint.

CHAPTER 29

The ride to London was spent thinking about his parents and Iris. Marion had told him to start living his life. Could he do that if his parents' killer wasn't found?

Could he start a life with Iris and Henry?

Putting those thoughts aside for later when he was lying alone again in his bed, he pulled the hood of the cloak he'd donned for the return journey over his head. The steady drizzle of rain had started as he'd entered London.

Running to the church, he banged a fist on the old wooden door four times and then entered. His wet booted feet squelched on the stone floor. He'd only taken a few steps, and Monty stopped.

The Devilles were here. When the note had arrived that he was to meet Geraint, he'd thought it would be just him.

"*Veritas scutum tibi erit*," Geraint said.

"*Veritas scutum tibi erit*," he replied, still looking at the wall of Devilles. He could feel their anger.

Theo had been out every night since he'd made love to Iris searching for any information he could find as to what was behind Iris's kidnapping and his parents' murders. He'd not told anyone what he was doing, and by the looks on the faces before him, he was about to hear how annoyed they were with him about that.

"Well now, what a pleasant surprise," Zach said from the depths of his hood. Gabe sat, and his brothers lined his back. Mary was seated to his right, Zach behind her, and Geraint was in his customary place at the head of the table.

"Why are you all here?" Monty asked.

"Aren't we often here when you are?" Michael asked pleasantly.

"Perhaps he still has that chest inflammation and is under the weather?" Nathan asked.

His eyes shot to Mary; she was firing daggers at him.

"Yes, after all, we called to see him many times. Especially after the note he sent us," Forrest said.

"Oh right, yes. The one where he went to the White Swan to find Iris," Zach said.

Monty looked to Geraint, who was watching what was playing out before him with keen interest.

"There is no need to discuss this here," Monty said. "Or at all," he added.

"Oh, there is a need," Mary said. She then bared her teeth at him.

He didn't take his usual position at the table with his hands folded, showing his ring, as Gabe was. If they were honest, he and Gabe just did it to annoy Zach.

Monty stayed where he was, standing, with a few feet separating him and a pack of angry Devilles. Monty was still not used to taking other people's feelings into consideration, so it came as a shock they were annoyed with him.

"If we could focus on the matters at hand," Geraint said.

All hostile gazes turned from Monty to look at Geraint, and he could breathe easier.

"Information has been uncovered about a group called *Fratres Fidei*, Brothers of Faith," Geraint said. "Which is also the name on the correspondence Lady Challoner handed to Lord Montgomery."

All eyes turned back to him and were still decidedly frosty.

"It was also on the correspondence found in the king's advisor's papers," Geraint added. "We have found a link that, until now, we had not been aware of."

"What link?" Monty demanded.

"I think he's about to tell us that, or do you think he'll keep it to himself so we can't assist him with finding out—"

"Shut up, Zach," Monty snapped.

"Yes, well, as I was saying," Geraint said. "A small book was found in the pocket of a jacket of the advisor. An entry mentioned a man called Diaboli."

"Devil," Zach translated.

"We believe this refers to Ernest Silverton. He was the third son of Lord and Lady Silverton. On the surface, a man who kept to himself and everyone liked."

"It's funny how people seem a certain way but aren't."

"Will you shut up!" Monty snapped, knowing Zach was getting at him.

"I'm guessing that wasn't the case," Gabe said to Geraint after he'd elbowed his youngest brother in the ribs.

"It wasn't. He was a devil worshipper, and we now believe the original leader of the Brothers of Faith."

"I wonder why we have not heard about this club until now," Michael said. "There are rumors about most things."

"There is more, and this involves your father, Lord Montgomery," Geraint said.

Monty braced for what Geraint was about to say.

"Two young women went missing in the village near where the Silverton estate was. They were both found dead, but each had the same marks on their bodies, as if they had performed some ritual on them. Marks on the neck, and the mark of the devil on their palm."

Monty twitched.

"What?" Nathan demanded. Monty shook his head.

"One woman was the Duke of Talbot's niece, who had been visiting him. He was close with the king and of course distraught. The king asked Alexius to look into it," Geraint continued.

Monty felt the tension inside him climb, and not simply because of the daggers the Deville party were hurling his way through their eyes. He felt like all the threads were drawing together, and he would have the answers he sought soon.

"Three of our members found evidence that Silverton could be responsible. They tracked him down to an old building on his father's lands, and it was then they saw what he was truly about. He'd been performing rituals and sacrifices on animals and people. The two women were not the first."

"What happened to him?" Mary demanded.

"He died in the fight to capture him."

"Who were the three men?" Zach demanded.

"My father, Lord Peters, and Lord Lionel," Monty said softly.

"Yes," Geraint said.

"I spoke with Lady Lionel today. She said she found her husband dead when she arrived home one morning after visiting her sister. His nose was swollen and there was bleeding from it. The doctor said his heart had stopped while he slept," Monty said. "She found the same small carving of a pentacle in Lord Lionel's hand that my father held the night I found him murdered."

Nathan swore.

"We have three men who caught what we suspect to be

the leader of a club, cult, or whatever they called themselves. Silverton died during this capture," Gabe said. "Now all three men are dead. Two, that we know of, had wooden carvings of pentacles in their hands, and we suspect both were murdered."

"Lady Challoner brought a letter to London that indicated her husband was in some way involved in the deaths of Lord and Lady Montgomery," Nathan continued.

"Her former brother-in-law, Renton, Lord Picton, Lord Heather, Mr. Clipper, and Mr. Buford all tried to get inside her late husband's house to go through his papers," Michael said. "Which to me suggests that they are scared there is evidence of what they are up to, and that they aren't just meeting to drink and participate in revelry under the cover of darkness."

"A satanic cult? Devil worship club? Or are they disciples of the late Ernest Silverton and carrying on his traditions, which likely included virgin sacrifices?" Mary asked.

"The king wants this matter resolved before his fete," Geraint said. "So far no whispers of what Ackland has done have left the court, but—"

"Courtiers are notorious gossips, so it is only a matter of time," Gabe said.

Geraint neither agreed nor disagreed.

"One more thing before you leave," Geraint said, his face grave. "A young woman was found dead behind a church in Saint Pancras two nights ago. She had the same mark carved into her palm as the two women murdered by Silverton."

Zach swore, and the others looked grim.

"We must find these Brothers of Faith. If they have killed and are followers of the late Silverton, then they will strike again," Geraint said. "I will alert the others. *Veritas scutum tibi erit.*" He dismissed them.

"*Veritas scutum tibi erit,*" the rest of the occupants in the church said.

They all left in single file, and Monty was first. He kept walking to where he'd left his horse.

"We are going to eat pies, and you are coming with us." A large hand landed on his shoulder. "Run, and we will follow," Gabe said. "You have things we need to hear, just as we have things to tell you."

"I do not run," Monty scoffed, ignoring the fact he'd been about to do just that. "And I have never been out dressed as I am to eat pies." In fact, he'd never been out to eat pies at all. He didn't go anywhere as Monty, only as Plunge.

"Well maybe it's time."

They mounted and rode toward the Speckled Hen. They put him in the middle and surrounded him with their horses.

"Is this completely necessary?" Monty demanded, and they ignored him. After they reached the tavern, he was escorted inside.

The interior was dark, and he hoped the food was good, as there was little to no ambience. Monty was nudged into a booth beside Zach and Mary, who had yet to speak to him. Forrest sat beside him. Opposite were the other Deville brothers.

"Hello, Hetty," Zach said with a smile that had once lured many a young lady to his side. His wife would castrate him were he to try that now.

"Well now, look at all these fine men in my tavern." She smiled, and Monty noticed one of her front teeth was missing. "And you've brought a friend."

"Yes, this is Mr. Cyril Plumbottom. He is visiting from the country," Zach added.

Everyone kept a straight face, and Monty thought he was going to kill Zach when they got out of here.

"We want ale and pies please, Hetty," the youngest Deville added. "A variety for us. We don't mind what."

"I mind what. I want peas and kidney," Michael said.

"I'll bring you food and drink shortly." Hetty winked at Zach before leaving.

"She responds to the most handsome among us, which just happens to be me," Zach said. Mary rolled her eyes.

"Now, I think we need to explain a few things to you, Cyril," Gabe said.

"Very amusing, and I'm sorry," he said quickly.

Mary punched Monty hard in the arm.

"Ouch! What was that for?"

"You have been avoiding us. You send that letter stating you'd inform us on what transpires tomorrow. We woke up to that, and then when we call at your town house, you will not speak to us!"

"He can hear you, my sweet, as he's only a matter of inches from you. No need to shriek," Zach said, placing a kiss on his wife's cheek.

"I am not one to share my every move with others," Monty defended himself.

"We are not others," Mary hissed. "We are your friends. You and I—"

"I'm sorry," Monty said again, quickly. "I…" How did he tell them why? That he'd made love to Iris, and it had unsettled him. That, and all the other things relating to his parents' deaths. He was falling apart, and he couldn't put himself back together, as the pieces no longer seemed to fit.

"I have dealt with everything since the age of thirteen alone. I don't have strong emotions in my life and have avoided them."

"You should live my life for a day or two. That would cure you of an aversion to strong emotions," Nathan said.

"I visited Iris to see if she was all right—"

"You saw her?" Monty cut Mary off. "Is she all right?"

"Zach and I did. You would not speak with us, and we wanted to make sure she and Henry were well. We of course did not mention why we were visiting. She was as you are. Cool and closed off from us. She would also not mention your name."

Monty wanted to rub the stab of pain in his chest Mary's words made him feel.

"Who did she meet at the White Swan?" Zach asked. "As clearly you went and got her home safely."

"Two men were in the room. One was a hired thug, and the other from our world if I had to guess. I could not see his face. The man questioning her wanted Iris to give them access to her husband's papers and, more specifically, some bound in a black ribbon. The ones she gave me. He knew of some secret drawer in Challoner's desk. She threw them off by stating Renton had gone through everything, and they should ask him."

"Very smart thing to say," Zach said.

"Very. The man threatened her son and left, saying he wanted those papers, and she did not have long to get them to him. We talked about handing them over, but even then, I'm not sure that will help. I think they will see Iris as a loose end."

"I agree," Gabe said. "We need to find who these Brothers of Faith are. This is the connection. The symbols all align, and your parents, and the other deaths too."

"It's all connected," Monty added.

"So, if Silverton was into sacrificing innocent women, did the Brothers of Faith find another Diablo who is leading them now, and they have continued on with his nefarious ways?" Michael said. "And was Ackland part of it?"

"Yes," Mary said. "It all ties together. We need to find this group before they take more innocent women, and if we find them, we may find Monty's parents' killer."

The pies and ale arrived. Monty took a large bite; it seemed his appetite had indeed returned.

"Where have you been for the last six days, Monty? You did not enter society," Michael asked.

"Looking for answers."

"And hiding," Gabe said. "And not just from us is my guess."

"I want justice for Marion too now. She is sure there was something very wrong with her husband's death."

"Marion?" Mary asked.

"Lady Lionel. She is very nice. We took tea together."

"You took tea with Lady Lionel when you always keep your distance from everyone for fear of them realizing you're not the foolish fop Lord Plunge?" Nathan asked.

"I wanted to know if there was anything that could connect Mr. Lionel's death to my parents'."

"Monty, I understand how your life has always been. Your parents were murdered, and a relative cared for you, then put you in Eton. We have slowly been filling in the missing pieces of your life story—"

"Must you?" Monty sighed.

"It's likely whoever became your guardian had the empathy of a week-old piece of fruit bun," Zach continued. "Am I correct?"

Monty bit into the pie that was placed before him. The filling was exquisite.

"We will simply wait you out," Zach added.

"You cannot remain isolated forever, Monty," Mary said, wiping the back of her mouth on her hand. "It is not healthy for your mind to close yourself off from everyone."

"My wife." Zach smiled. "Isn't she wonderful?"

Everyone rolled their eyes.

"She's right," Forrest said. "I've tried that. It is extremely unhealthy."

"I live my life how I feel it needs to be lived. Added to that was the necessity to keep to myself as I was living a lie," Monty defended himself.

"But it is time for change, and I think we have already started changing people's perception of you," Gabe said.

"Oh goody," Monty muttered with his mouth full.

"But right now, our focus is to ensure you and Iris are safe. To do that, we need to get to the bottom of who is part of this Brothers of Faith."

"I am not in danger. Iris is. I need to see her," Monty said, picking up his ale and taking a sip.

"Do you love her?"

Michael's words had him choking and only just managing to keep the mouthful from spraying those seated opposite.

"By that reaction, my guess is yes," Michael said.

"What? You can't know that," Monty spluttered.

"He's not denying it." Mary looked smug.

"What is wrong with you people?" Monty demanded. "Not enough going on in your own lives?"

"Plenty, but we're meddlesome, especially when it comes to people we care about," Mary said.

He didn't know how to answer that because he was one of the people they cared about, which humbled him, so he stayed silent and thought about Iris. Was this love? He had a feeling it was, and strangely it didn't scare him as much as it should.

CHAPTER 30

*I*ris woke to a hand closing over her mouth. She tried to scream, but it pressed her down into the pillow. She swung with her fists, but the man simply laid his body over hers, forcing the air from her lungs.

"This time there will be no escaping me, Iris. This time you will be mine. And when I'm done with you, it will be Henry who is under my control." The words were rasped into her ear.

She fought her former brother-in-law with everything she had, but he was too strong for Iris. Someone else bound her hands and feet. When Renton's hand lifted off her mouth, she screamed.

"Shut her up," someone hissed.

Something was jammed in her mouth, making her gag. Iris was then lifted off the bed and thrown over Renton's shoulder.

"Check the hall."

"It's clear. Let's go. Hurry."

She bobbed up and down as he ran with her draped over

his shoulder. Lifting her head as they reached the stairs, icy fear gripped her as she saw Henry crouched beside a large vase. He often came to her if he had a nightmare. He rose, but she shook her head, and he eased back into the shadows.

Henry would rouse Norman, and her old friend would look after him. Her boy would be terrified, but at least he was safe.

Only when they were outside did she slump against the shoulder that held her. No one had followed them.

And then she remembered. Theo had a man watching her house. Was he still here? Pushing her bound hands into the man's back, she looked around her. *Are you out there?*

Lord, she hoped he was and alerted Theo. But how would they find her? No one would know where they were going.

Henry. Who would look after her son if she did not return? She had to return; he needed her.

A carriage rolled close, and the door was opened, and he threw her inside. A sack was lowered over her head again, and she was dropped on the cold floor.

The carriage then started moving at speed. The horses galloped through the dark streets of London. Iris had no idea in which direction.

Who else was in here with Renton? Lord Picton, Lord Heather, Mr. Clipper, or Mr. Buford? She had received no further direction from them about her husband's papers. Had they decided simply to kill her so she was no longer an obstruction and her former brother-in-law could control Henry?

Thoughts whirled in her head as she struggled not to throw up. She felt dizzy, and her stomach roiled as she was thrown from side to side with the carriage's movement.

Theo slipped into her head, and she clung to his image and fought back the fear.

She had not seen him again since they'd made love. That magical night where everything had changed between them —well, at least for her. Once, she'd worshipped him with the fervor of a ten-year-old, but what she felt for him now was a great deal more complex.

Did she love Lord Theodore Montgomery? Iris believed the answer to that was yes. She also knew that what happened between them had terrified him as much as it had her.

"He'll be happy it went so easily," Renton said from above her.

"You convinced him that her death was the best plan," another voice said. "If she's out of the way, you can control the son and find anything relating to us. It's the best action to take."

"She knows too much, and after someone rescued her at the White Swan, he doesn't want any further risk of exposure. If only she'd done what I wanted." A booted foot nudged Iris. "This could have been avoided."

"She's not innocent, but she'll do," the other man in the carriage said. "The gods will be appeased."

Ice filled her veins. Those words were on the note she'd given to Monty. What did they mean?

Iris wasn't sure how long she lay on the floor of that carriage, but when it slowed, she wished they would keep moving longer, because now she was to meet her fate... whatever that fate may be.

The road beneath them became more rutted, and she was jostled again before they stopped.

"Out you get, my dear sister-in-law," Renton said. She was then thrown over his shoulder again.

They walked up stairs, and she was sure they entered a building, as the floor sounded different, more solid. Soon they were walking down what she guessed were steps. The air was colder now, and Iris shivered. She was in her night-dress and nothing more. She heard a door creak.

"Did you have any trouble?" a voice she didn't know asked.

"None. The boy and staff all slumbered, so there was no need to subdue either," someone said.

Iris shuddered at the thought of anyone subduing her son. He was safe, for now, but she had to get back to him. To do that, she had to keep her wits about her, as no one would know besides Henry that she'd been taken. There was no help coming. She had to find a way to escape herself.

She was lowered to sit on something. The sack was removed, and she stared into her former brother-in-law's evil eyes.

"Well now, Iris, I warned you to yield to me, but you didn't. Now I'm going to ask you some questions, and if you want to see your son again, you will answer them."

She didn't respond.

"Who saved you at the White Swan?"

Iris stayed silent.

"You found my brother's papers, didn't you? The ones with information about the Brothers of Faith. Where are they?" Renton bent so his face was inches from hers.

"I gave them to someone who will find every one of you and make you pay for your crimes," Iris hissed back at him.

"What crimes? We are but a group of men who—"

"Partake in nefarious deeds," Iris said. "And you wouldn't have shown your face to me if you weren't going to kill me, Loftus, so why would I tell you anything?"

"You always were too intelligent for your own good, but my brother just never saw it." He ran a finger down her cheek. Her hands were bound in front of her, so she raised them fast and got him under the chin.

His curse was loud and vulgar.

"Where are my brother's papers?" he demanded.

"I gave them to the magistrate," Iris lied.

His face turned the color of a ripe plum. "You lie!"

"Do I? You'll never know what I found in my late husband's things. The papers I handed over to the magistrate had an interesting letter about the late Lord and Lady Montgomery. There was also a bundle of papers tied with a black ribbon, which was what whoever was in that room in the White Swan asked me to find and hand over. It had an interesting wooden symbol attached to it." Iris watched the color now drain from Loftus Renton's face with every word she uttered.

"I don't believe you. You're not brave enough to hand those over and thereby sully your son's future heritage," Renton said, but she saw he wasn't so sure of himself now.

"Really? Well, you'll just have to wait and see who comes knocking on your front door," Iris said with far more confidence than she had.

"Liar!" He moved so fast she couldn't stop him. His hand clenched around her throat and squeezed. "Tell me the truth!"

Iris felt her vision waver as she struggled to make a sound.

"She can hardly speak if you have your hand around her neck, Renton. Release her at once."

They pulled him off her, and Iris sucked air into her mouth. She looked at the other man who had just arrived. It was Lord Picton, one of her husband's friends and one man who had been insistent about searching his study.

"Forgive him, Lady Challoner." He smiled at her, and the evil in his eyes made her shiver. His thin lips formed a sneer as he gave her a mocking bow. "Now I want you to tell me. Who rescued you in the White Swan?"

"It was you that night!"

"How clever of you to recognize my voice. Now tell me who rescued you."

She clamped her lips together. They were clearly going to kill her anyway; she was not telling them the name of the man she loved. Theo would look out for Henry alongside her aunt and uncle after they had killed her; she was sure of it.

Iris swallowed down the pain of not seeing those she loved again. Not watching her son grow into a man.

"She said she took the papers to the magistrate," Renton snarled.

"Did she now?" Picton looked at her, his gaze mocking now. "Well, as two of our worshippers are magistrates, I'm sure that will not be a problem."

"People know about you," Iris said. "Lots of people."

Picton laughed. "No, my dear, they do not and won't. We are too powerful and too well hidden, and you are nothing and a nobody with a title. Your husband ensured you never stepped into society and made friends."

"Did you kill Lord and Lady Montgomery?" It had been a hunch, but the surprise on Picton's face told her she was right.

"He killed our leader, and as such, revenge was needed. The gods needed to be appeased."

"You do realize how ridiculous that sounds, don't you? What do you worship? Surely not the devil, or is that Satan?" She scoffed. If Iris was to die this day, she'd go down fighting. Besides, she'd vowed never to be weak before a man again.

The hand came out fast and slapped her. "You are insolent and need disciplining!" Picton roared. "Never speak such filth in our presence again."

Her lips stung, and she tasted blood, but Iris did not look away.

"It is a strong man who hits a woman who cannot fight back."

His face went as red as Renton's had.

"You are nothing more than a pathetic little man who gets his excitement in a silly group with a silly name vowing allegiance to a fallen angel."

He hit her again, hard, and this time darkness followed.

CHAPTER 31

*M*onty left the Speckled Hen with the Devilles. They were no longer angry with him but had lectured him repeatedly over what they saw as his bad behavior. From now on, they would watch him, and he must account for his actions.

He realized their concern was making him smile, so he frowned. Sitting there in that tavern with the Devilles, he realized one thing. He no longer wanted to live his life alone as Plunge.

"Tomorrow you can tell Iris you love her, and we will deal with how to make Lord Plunge less simpering and foppish so you can wed her and still be part of society," Michael said.

"Do I get any say in this?" Monty asked mildly because everything Michael said was what he wanted. He did love Iris and needed to tell her so.

He watched Zach throw Mary up into her sidesaddle and then mount his horse beside her. They were all like that, these Devilles. Protective of one another. Women and men who cared deeply for their mates and those in their inner circle.

He wanted that kind of closeness with Iris and Henry. Monty no longer wanted to be alone in the dark, and her touch brought him into the light.

Soon they were riding through the dark streets of London. It was late now, and people would be attending society balls and events.

"Why are you lot not at the Beldon musical?" he asked, running mentally through his weekly list of invites.

"Because Geraint called," Gabe said, "and we were concerned about you."

He wanted to rub his chest as it burned again.

Monty had no idea what his life would look like from now on. He just knew he wanted Iris, Henry, and these people to be part of that. Tomorrow he would talk to her. If he was honest, he didn't excel at talking in the way he would need to with her, but then he didn't think she was a great deal better having lived with that bastard Challoner.

"Someone is in a hurry," Zach said suddenly, nudging Mary's horse with his to the left as the sound of a speeding carriage reached them. Turning in his saddle, he noted it was a hackney and, yes, it was going fast, but it slowed when the driver saw them before him in the road.

"Move!" he bellowed.

A head appeared out the window.

"Jimmy!" Monty called. "Stop this hackney!" he roared at the driver.

When the hackney had stopped, the door flew open, and his man appeared in the doorway.

"What are you about, Monty?" Gabe demanded.

"That's the man I had watching Iris."

Jimmy jumped down and behind him was Norman, Iris's butler.

"Norman, what is going on?" Monty demanded. "Why are you both here? Where are Iris and Henry?"

"Who the hell is Norman?" Nathan demanded.

"Lady Challoner was kidnapped from her bed, my lord," Jimmy said. "I brought the butler and the young Lord Challoner with me in the hackney to reach you. The lad was insistent we come to you immediately."

The fear that gripped him almost bent Monty double.

"Breathe easy, friend. We will get her back," Forrest said, gripping his shoulder.

"The boy saw it all, my lord," Norman said. He was dressed with his nightshirt tucked into trousers and a jacket buttoned up over the top. "He woke up the staff, and by the time we had roused, Jimmy was inside."

Monty stepped into the hackney and saw the boy huddled into the corner with his arms around Oscar.

"Come, Henry. You know me. We are friends, so there is no need to be afraid." Monty held out his hand to the boy. He needed to find her, Iris, but to do that, he had to know who had taken her and where to. Henry could hold the key to that. He was crying; the lamplight showed him his damp cheeks. "Let me help you, Henry. That is what friends do. Take my hand and know I will find your mother and keep you safe." *Always,* he vowed silently.

The boy got off the seat and took his hand. His fingers were so small, Monty thought, closing his around them. He was trembling.

Norman was standing just outside the door when they stepped out, and all the Devilles had dismounted and were gathered a few feet away.

"Hello, Oscar," Gabe said as the dog came to greet him.

"Tell them what you told me, my lord," Jimmy urged the boy. "I will then explain what I saw."

Henry looked around the Devilles and back to him. Monty saw the fear.

"Hello, Henry, I am Ella's father. You remember me, don't

you?" Forrest said. "I'm sorry you are going through this, but know that we"—he waved a hand to his cousins and Mary—"will do what is needed to return your mother to you."

"They are good people, Henry. Talk freely," Monty said as he battled down the fear clawing at his throat.

Where was Iris?

Henry stepped closer to Monty, still clutching his hand.

"You said that if ever I needed you, I could go to the address on the card," Henry said.

"I did."

"I saw them, two men. They came into the house and took my mother."

"Did you recognize the men, Henry?" Monty asked.

"One was my uncle," the boy whispered.

"Mr. Renton, Henry?" The boy nodded to Monty.

"I had only just arrived to take over from Jack when I saw Lady Challoner being carried out of the house over the shoulder of a man," Jimmy said. "Before I could get close, a carriage had pulled up, and she was put inside. I tried to climb on the back, but it took off so fast I couldn't catch it."

"I know you would have tried, Jimmy," Monty said. "I would ask you to take Henry and Oscar—"

"To Dimity," Gabe interrupted him. "She will care for them and keep them safe there until we return with Iris. It is for the best."

He was humbled at the offer and knew Dimity would take care of the boy until they returned.

"I will come for you as soon as I have your mother, Henry." He turned to the boy. "Go with Jimmy, Norman, and Oscar. They will take you to Lady Raine, who will care for you."

"Henry, you rode the velocipede with Lady Raine—Dimity," Forrest said. "She is a lovely lady."

The boy nodded. Monty grabbed his shoulders, making

him look at him. "I will be back with her, Henry. Trust me. Trust us to bring your mother back." He then pulled the boy close and hugged him hard. "Go now." He nudged him at Norman and Jimmy, who were receiving instruction from Gabe on what to say to Dimity.

Monty watched the hackney roll away seconds later.

"Where do we start?" Michael asked, grim-faced.

"Picton, Heather, Clipper, and Buford," Nathan said. "We start with them. All are in London."

They reached the Heather residence first.

"You cannot go in, Monty, in case you are recognized," Zach said.

"I don't care about that," he snapped.

"Very well, but do not speak and keep your hood up. Stand behind us, and for God's sake, do nothing to draw anyone's attention," Gabe added.

Mary stayed outside with her hood up with Zach and Forrest when they reached the Heather residence. The man of the house was not home. They knew this because they entered without permission even though a butler and footman had tried to stop them. When his wife was roused at the noise, she was more than happy to say her husband had gone to visit Lord Picton in the country and wanted to know if any of them would like to stay and entertain her. They were in no doubt what form that entertainment would be and made a hasty exit.

Clipper was visiting Picton as well. Buford, however, was at home when they reached his town house. By now, Monty was desperate for anything that would lead them to Iris. He felt like time was running out. That if he didn't reach her soon, he'd never find her again.

Losing his parents had nearly destroyed him, but losing Iris would finish the job.

"I am Lord Raine, and I demand you rouse Mr. Buford at

once as the matter is of grave and national importance," Gabe said in his haughtiest voice. "I am here as a servant of our king."

They had clearly roused the Buford butler from his bed, but unlike Norman, he was fully dressed and immaculate in all but his hair, which stood off his head.

"Mr. Buford is unwell and has not left his bed in many days," the butler said in his snootiest voice.

"Did you not hear what I said?" Gabe demanded. Monty was sure he'd used that voice on his brothers many times. "You are obstructing an investigation on behalf of your king."

The butler swallowed. Monty had had enough. He pushed the man back a step and entered the house.

"Rouse Mr. Buford at once or I will," he growled. "You have ten minutes and not a minute more."

The butler ran for the stairs. Monty walked around the entrance seeing nothing but Iris, the woman he loved, hurting and in danger. If someone touched her, he would spend his life hunting them down.

"Keep your head, Monty," Nathan said.

The butler appeared. "He will see you now but cannot leave his bed."

"Lead the way. We have no problem speaking to your master from his bed," Gabe said.

They ran up the stairs behind him and were soon entering a large room. A pale-looking Buford occupied the bed. Monty knew the man of course, but they had rarely spoken, because no one talked to Plunge or took him seriously. *And that is changing.*

"What is the meaning of this, Raine?" Buford asked and then coughed several times.

He was pale and sweating in his nightshirt.

"Scranton said it was of utmost importance."

The butler stood to one side watching over them.

"Get him to leave," Monty said, nodding to the butler. Nathan glared at him to shut up.

"Who are you?" Buford wheezed, looking at Monty.

"He is Plumbottom, one of the king's guards," Michael said quickly.

Buford nodded, and he dismissed Monty as a nobody. He then sent the butler from the room.

"We have reason to believe you are part of a group of men who worship the devil, Mr. Buford," Gabe said.

The man coughed loudly and clutched his chest. "Wh-What?"

"We also believe Lord Picton, Lord Heather, Mr. Clipper, and Mr. Renton are some of your fellow worshippers," Gabe continued. "*Fratres Fidei*, Brothers of Faith."

Monty kept his eyes on the man lying in the bed. He'd started shaking, and it was not solely due to his illness.

"Does the name Ernest Silverton mean anything to you, Buford?" Nathan asked.

The man made a strangled sound now.

"How about Sir Stephen Ackland?" Michael asked.

The man was gobbling like a turkey. Monty stepped forward. Gabe blocked him by stepping in front of him. Nathan joined him, and they presented a solid wall. Frustrated, he stepped back again.

He could feel the panic sending its icy tendrils through his body. Iris needed him, and he had to reach her soon.

"Lady Challoner has been kidnapped, Buford. Where is she?"

"H-How would I know where she is?" The man looked ready to faint now.

"We don't have time to bandy words with you, Buford. I know you are part of this Brothers of Faith, and we believe Renton has taken Lady Challoner somewhere to silence her," Gabe said. "Because her late husband had documents on your little organization. On the innocents and animals you have sacrificed to appease the devil."

"S-Sacrifice? S-Silence her?" Buford wheezed.

"I've seen the letters that belonged to her late husband," Gabe said. "Letters incriminating him and you to the murders of Lord and Lady Montgomery, Lord Lionel, and Lord Peters. All had the small carved symbol of the devil in their hands when they were found."

Buford was gasping for air now, and what little color he'd had in his face had drained away.

"Now you will tell us where you meet, or I let the king's guard, who was given explicit instructions to do what he must to find details about who and what Ackland was involved in, punch the information out of you," Gabe said.

Monty pulled out his pistol when the man didn't speak fast enough. He then parted the brothers with an arm and pointed it at the man lying in the bed.

"Speak."

He did, telling them where they would find Iris and who was involved in the Brothers of Faith.

"W-We are but a harmless club," he whispered.

"Do not play us for fools, Buford, and now I want to know who killed Lord Lionel and Lord and Lady Montgomery," Monty said in a hard voice.

The man's eyes shot from Monty to Gabe and back again.

"Lord Plunge?" he whispered.

"Answer the question, Buford, or I will put a bullet through you." Monty stepped closer.

"Picton and the late Lord Challoner! Silverton was to be avenged!"

Revenge for his parents was close, Monty could feel it, but first he would find his love.

CHAPTER 32

*T*he church was down a rutted track. The block walls were covered in overgrown vines, and if you didn't know what you were looking for, it would never be found. Monty and the Devilles knew exactly what they wanted because Buford had sung like a canary and told them everything.

They'd ridden hard from London. Zach had of course tried to leave Mary behind; she'd punched him in the belly, winding him, which had made everyone but Monty snort.

Buford had told them, with Monty's gun pressed to his forehead, that Challoner had been their leader, known as Diablo. He'd taken over when Silverton had died. Picton was now in control.

There would be more to uncover, but after getting the church's location out of him, they'd sent word to Geraint to have someone guard Buford and left.

Monty pulled them to a halt beside the old stone building that had once been a mill.

"We'll walk in from here. Buford said it is up the next drive," Monty said.

They dismounted and tethered their horses. Keeping to the shadows, they walked toward the church. The small stone building they found was almost hidden behind a wall of trees. It wasn't large and was clearly no longer in use, which they knew was the case from Buford's information.

"In through the front door and then down the aisle," Forrest whispered. "There are stairs through a door behind the altar. I will wait out here and keep watch."

Pistols raised, they climbed the church's front steps and opened the door. When no one appeared, they entered. Pews sat on either side of the aisle, unused and dusty. Reaching the altar, Monty walked behind and found a door. Easing it open, he winced at the creaky hinge and hoped whoever was below had not heard.

The steps down were narrow, but lamplight lit the way. So far there was no noise to suggest anyone was here, just as they'd found no carriages or horses outside.

Had Buford tricked them? Had he sent them to another location? Would Iris not be here?

"She will be here," Gabe whispered in his ear. "Keep moving."

She will be here, he repeated silently.

Reaching the bottom, he found a narrow walkway with two doors. One had a sturdy lock outside and was empty save for a cot. Pushing open the next, he heard the hum of chanting coming from somewhere up ahead. Monty pressed his back to the wall, and the others did the same behind him.

They were in some kind of chamber that smelled of a musky scent. He crept forward slowly and slipped behind a screen, and the others slid in with him.

Monty looked around the edge at the scene playing out before him. Two large candles were raised on an altar, and before that stood a man wearing scarlet robes. His face was covered with a hideous mask. Buford had told them that

Picton was now the head of the Brothers of Faith, so this was likely him. Others all dressed in black stood in a circle. He could see between two to the woman lying on the table.

Iris.

She was in her nightdress, her head turned away from him. A tap on his shoulder had him moving slightly, and he let the others look.

"The gods must be appeased!" the man who Monty guessed was Picton yelled. The others all cheered their agreement. "We can let no one challenge our brotherhood!" Again, more cheers.

"Take what you wish from her, and then she will be sacrificed."

"She's of noble birth," someone said. "And not a virgin as the others were."

"I'll take her if you are too scared." A man stepped forward who Monty knew was Renton. He opened his cloak and then reached for his trousers. Monty roared.

Charging out from behind the screen, he ran at the men closest, shoving them out of his way. He dove over Iris and hit Renton hard in the chest, sending him to the floor.

Behind him were shouts of outrage that turned to howls of pain as the Devilles did what they did best.

"No! I will not let you ruin everything!" Renton cried at him. "She is mine."

Monty wrenched off his mask and followed that up with a fist to the face, snapping his head to the side. Leaping off him, Monty reached for Iris. She was struggling to get free.

"I have you, Iris. Let me cut you free."

"Theo?"

"Yes. Stay still now, my love."

While the Devilles fought on, Monty pulled his knife from his boot and sliced through the binds on her hands and feet. He then lifted Iris off the table and lowered her to the ground.

"Find somewhere to hide!" he told her.

Someone hit him hard from behind, and he staggered, taking her down with him. Monty rolled and took the impact on his side.

"Run, Iris!"

He rolled and regained his feet. Out the corner of his eye, he watched her crawl away.

"She's mine!" Renton growled.

"Iris belongs to no man, "Monty said. "I'm killing you for laying your hands on her, Renton, and for tormenting her and your nephew."

He swung a fist and got Renton on the jaw again. "You are a greedy, sniveling bastard!"

Renton blocked his next punch and hit Monty in the cheek. The blow was hard, and he stumbled but didn't retreat.

"She's a woman and therefore nothing." Renton spat the words at him. "The brat stood between me and what I deserved. I will have what my brother had!"

Monty kicked out with a booted foot and caught him in the stomach. Renton bent in half, and Monty followed it up with another kick to the jaw, sending him backward.

Before he could stop her, Iris sprinted by him in her nightdress.

"Bastard!" She kicked Renton hard in the side. Monty wrapped a hand around her waist on the fourth kick and lifted her away.

"That will do, my sweet. He will not hurt you or Henry again." He carried her to a corner away from the fighting. "Put on my cloak and stay here." He shrugged out of it and handed it to her.

"I don't want to stay here." Her eyes were unfocused, and

she was blinking constantly. Had they drugged her? More anger fueled his need for revenge.

"Hello, Iris."

"M-Mary?" Iris tried to focus on his friend's face.

"Indeed, it is, and I'm pleased to see you are unhurt. The lip looks sore however."

"M-Mary?" Iris blinked again.

"My guess is they drugged her," Monty said. "Get her into that cloak, Mary."

He moved back to join the others, but the Brothers of Faith were all subdued now and being bound hand and foot with various things from neckties to rope someone had found.

Renton had regained consciousness and was now leaning against a stone wall looking pale. Monty stalked closer; he had the urge to inflict more pain.

"You drugged her and hit her!"

"Don't kill him. We want him to suffer. It will inflict more pain if he is humiliated and all his sins are laid bare for everyone to see," Gabe said.

"You have nothing," Renton hissed.

Monty bent at the waist and told him exactly what he had on the man. When he was done, Renton was weeping pitifully. Picton, however, was roaring like a boar.

"You will pay for this! All of you."

Monty moved to stand in front of the man who had played a hand in destroying his life. He then raised his pistol.

"It will be over quickly if you do that, and he will not suffer as you have either," Gabe said to Monty.

"I will ensure you hang for killing Lord and Lady Montgomery, Lord Lionel, and likely Lord Peters," Monty snarled. "You will be nothing by the time I am finished with you, and your family will carry your shame for years to come!"

"You have nothing on me." Picton would not be cowed.

"We have just spoken extensively to Buford," Nathan said. The man flinched at the mention of his friend. "Ackland was also one of you, and it's fair to say our monarch is not happy about what his advisor has been up to. He wants this nasty business dealt with before his fete, so I think it will, in fact, be you who pays for parading about in a red dress—"

"Robe!" Picton roared.

"With the mask of a pig on your face," Zach added.

"Goat!" Picton yelled.

"Was it really? Well, I never. It definitely looks more piggy."

Gabe barked out a laugh. There was absolutely nothing humorous in this situation, but he heard a giggle behind him and found Iris. She wore his cloak, hair loose and hanging in a tangled mess to her waist. Her lips were bruised and swollen, but she was giggling.

"Who did that?" Monty growled as he pointed at her lip.

She shook her head, which told him nothing.

"Move them into the room next door. We'll lock them in, and Geraint can deal with them," Gabe said.

"I am a peer of the realm!" Picton cried. He was the only one still making a noise. The others were silent, understanding their fate. Renton, Monty was pleased to see, was still weeping; clearly, unlike his leader, he knew the game was up.

They dragged them all into the room. Monty counted twelve men. They'd removed their masks, and all were noblemen. He used Picton's face to open the door, hard enough so he would be seeing stars for a while.

"Who are you?" Picton asked Monty after he'd thrown him to the floor.

"One of the king's guards," Zach said.

"Alexius." Picton spat out a mouthful of blood. "The king's puppets. We know about you."

As one, they all bowed, except Mary, who dropped into a curtsy. These men were of noble birth and now knew exactly what the Devilles did. However, Monty doubted they'd ever have the chance to tell anyone.

"He looks like Plunge and yet less silly," one of the men whispered.

Stepping out and slamming the door, Monty lowered the bar and turned the key in the large, sturdy lock.

"Your parents will be avenged now," Michael said.

He nodded and then reached for Iris. She'd stayed outside the room and was leaning on the wall, clearly exhausted and still battling to rid her head of the drug they'd given her.

"Come." He lifted her into his arms and started up the stairs. Her feet were bare, and she was still shivering.

"Henry. He saw me—"

"He alerted Norman, who then spoke with the man I had watching your house. I intercepted them on their way to see me. Norman and Henry are now with Dimity."

"Thank God," she whispered.

They left the church and made for their horses. Once there, he put Iris up in front of him and climbed on behind. They then rode for London.

She turned and laid her legs over his thighs. Her arms went around his waist. When she pressed her head to his chest, Monty kissed the top.

"I care about you, Iris," he whispered into her hair.

"I care about you too."

And for now, that was enough.

CHAPTER 33

$\mathcal{I}$ris woke in a strange bed in Theo's house. He'd insisted on bringing them here and didn't care about the impropriety of the act. They'd collected Henry from Dimity, and Theo had sent Norman back to the Challoner town house, stating that Iris would return tomorrow.

She'd slept in his arms on the way to London and remembered very little of the trip, only that she and Henry were now safe.

Iris looked to the door as it opened and watched Theo enter. In his arms was a tray. He wore only his shirt and trousers, and his feet were bare.

"Where are your shoes?" was the only thing she could find to say.

"I don't wear them here unless it's really cold." He gave her a boyish smile that reminded her of the younger Theo she'd once known. "How do you feel?"

"Sore but well. I am rested now, thank you, and there are no lingering effects from whatever they gave me. Where is Henry?"

"Having a wonderful time with my staff. They are spoiling

him and Oscar in the kitchens, and my cook is letting him help her bake biscuits."

"I need to go to him." Iris looked down at her borrowed nightdress from Dimity. All she remembered was hugging Henry, and then she'd washed and fallen into the large, soft bed when they'd arrived at Monty's town house.

"Soon. Right now, you need to eat."

"Thank you for finding me, Theo."

"You're welcome." He moved to the side of the bed and lowered the tray over her legs.

"This looks wonderful."

He drew a chair closer and sat.

"I have so many questions," Iris said as she picked up a crumpet slathered in jam.

"I know, and I will try to answer them." His eyes were steady on her face.

"I was so scared." She looked at the crumpet. "I thought I would not see Henry, you, or anyone I care for again."

"I will always find you, Iris." The words came out as a vow.

"You can't say that. We…" Her words fell away as he took the crumpet and lowered it to the tray. He then removed it and placed it on the floor. Then he was there, hands braced on either side of her, face now inches from hers.

"I can say that. I will always find you because you are going to be my wife. I will allow no one to hurt you again."

"I—ah, wife?"

He nodded.

"I had planned never to marry again, Theo."

"But seeing as you love me, you will do so."

"Do I? Love you, I mean," Iris whispered.

She saw the flash of uncertainty then. Like her, he had lived without love for so long.

"I do love you, Theo." She touched his cheek.

His eyes closed. "I have never been loved by a woman in such a way before. I'd believed I never would."

"As I never believed a man would love me."

"Iris, my childhood friend, the woman I want to live out my days with, please marry me. Bring me into the light and make me warm with your touch."

"Oh, Theo."

"Oh, Theo, yes?"

"Yes," Iris whispered. "Yes. I love you and want to spend the rest of my life with you."

He kissed her then, long and deep. When he pulled back, they were both breathing hard.

"I know this seems fast, my sweet, and yet we have known each other forever."

"We have." She smiled. "But what about Henry?"

"I would be honored to be his father when he is ready for me to do so. Until then, I will be his friend."

"Thank you," she whispered as the tears started to fall.

"No crying. Now eat your food while I attempt to explain the path my life took."

She ate, and listened, and marveled at what he'd done. At the life he'd chosen to avenge his parents that had turned into so much more.

"You lived the life as Lord Plunge for so long. I doubt I could have carried it off."

He smiled. "Society saw what I wanted them to, but it all changed when Mary became part of Alexius. With her came the Devilles, and they are a forceful lot who broke through my carefully erected barricades."

"They are." He took the second half of her muffin and ate it in three bites. "Do you want to stay in society, Theo?"

"Not especially, but I should miss people if I left completely. Plus, I think you could enjoy parts of it, and Henry has friends to make."

"Then that is what we shall do." He caught her hand as she raised it to her mouth to lick the jam off her fingers and drew her thumb into his mouth.

"Oh," she managed to get out.

"We will be married soon," he whispered. Iris could only nod as he continued to lick each of her fingers with great care.

...

Two weeks later, Iris arrived at the king's fete at Carlton House with Zach and Mary. Theo was to meet her here.

"I'm nervous," she whispered. "I have no idea what is about to happen, only that something is, and Theo is involved."

"All will go well," Zach said, patting the hand she had clenched on his sleeve. "Monty will carry it off like he does everything. The man has been living a lie for years, after all. That takes intelligence and courage."

"Well said, my love," Mary said from his other side.

"It also takes an intelligent man to know one." He smirked.

"You know what is going to happen, don't you?" Iris asked.

"I have no idea what you speak of," Zach said, not meeting her eyes.

Dark had fallen, but the sky was lit with hundreds of torches. One huge tent seemed to cover a great deal of ground outside.

"Prepare to be amazed," Zach said.

And it was certainly that. Grand on every scale, and so much so that Mary and Iris walked about with their mouths open. Opulence was everywhere they looked. Exotic treats to eat and performers to watch.

She looked for Theo, but as yet there was no sign.

"What do you think is about to happen?" Iris asked. "Theo said very little to me yesterday when last I saw him."

He'd called and spent the day with her, Henry, and Oscar, who was now firmly settled in their household and loved by the staff, at the small park near her home. Theo had brought a kite, and her staff had packed a picnic. It had been wonderful, and she'd felt so much hope for the future, especially when Henry had told her that night how much he liked Theo.

"You look nervous," Dimity said when they reached the rest of the Devilles.

"I don't know what I'm nervous about," Iris said.

"Step aside. Make room."

"Duchess, how wonderful of you to join us, and dressed in your drapery," Zach said.

Iris bit her lip to stop from commenting. The dress was a thick brocade in dark gray. She looked like a dormouse in it, except for the array of feathers and small woodland creatures attached to her hair.

"Ah, you look lovely, Duchess," Iris said.

"Thank you. At least someone has taste," she snapped. She then jabbed Zach in the ankle when he snorted.

They wandered with the other guests for a while, and Iris kept looking for Theo. Surely, he would be here soon. With every passing minute, Iris's nerves climbed.

"It is time," Gabe said.

"For what?" Iris asked.

"Come along, I believe we have somewhere to be," the Duchess of Yardly said to her. "Escort me, gal."

She held out her arm because she may be stronger now, but there was no way she would ever refuse this woman. Gloved fingers settled on her arm, and they followed the Devilles. The room they entered was grand as they all were at Carlton House. Iris found herself being nudged forward by Zach and Mary, who had somehow made their way behind her.

No furniture save for the king's throne graced the room, and only a handful of other guests were present. Most were men. Gold-trimmed red velvet drapes were at the windows, and the carpet was a large matching rug. Gilded pedestals lined the walls every few feet, and the ceiling was painted in a delicate pastel scene and framed in gold.

"It's very grand," she found herself saying to the duchess.

"Our monarch puts his breeches on a leg at a time like all men, gal," the duchess said, making her giggle. "Never forget that if you feel intimidated. Now, we will stand right here at the front." The duchess stopped with the Devilles and kept hold of her hand. "I think what is about to transpire will be most entertaining."

"But what is to happen?" Iris asked.

"You shall see. I may be old, gal, but I am in no way unaware. My husband was a close friend of the current monarch's father. We talked a great deal."

"Good lord." Iris found Gabe standing before her. His eyes were on the duchess's chest.

Iris looked and found a necklace. On it was a ring like the one Theo also wore on a chain around his neck.

He'd told her the ring was forged from William the Conqueror's goblet and given to ten men who pledged their allegiance to the queen. She now knew about Alexius, and the man called Geraint who they reported to, because Theo wanted no secrets between them.

"My husband kept no secrets from me, Deville, and his nephew still calls to visit with me upon occasion."

"Who is his nephew?" Nathan demanded, now standing beside his brother, his eyes also on the ring hanging from the necklace. "Actually, I'm not sure I want to know."

"My nephew goes by the name of Geraint."

"I don't know what to say to you right now," Gabe muttered.

"Well, there is always a first time for everything," the duchess fired back, and Iris thought that was almost a smile on her face.

"We should have known," Zach whispered. "I mean, if anyone knew about us, it would have been her."

"True," Michael said, still looking shocked. "And as she has no son, the ring was not passed on."

"Good lord" was all Forrest said.

"Who are they?" Iris whispered, looking at the other men in the room.

"Members of Alexius is my guess," Michael whispered. "I recognize a few we've had dealings with over the years."

"Theo told me the identities of other members were not widely known. Why are they here if secrecy is important to Alexius?"

"Clearly, our monarch wished it to be so."

They all fell silent as a trumpet was sounded. Iris then watched the king walk down the carpeted aisle as the nerves in her belly fluttered. Where was Theo?

CHAPTER 34

*M*onty would rather face a pack of lappet-faced vultures than what he was about to do. But his king had decided to acknowledge him after Geraint told him Monty wished to leave society. He had no idea what he'd find on the other side of those doors, only that when it was done, he could find Iris and touch her. Hold her hand and feel that wonderful warmth. With her, he knew what it was to be loved.

He could feel himself changing because of her and Henry. The boy who had smiled when he'd arrived at his home two days ago. It had been like the sun peeking out from behind a cloud.

They would marry soon, and he could not wait. He could then see her whenever he wanted. Go to bed with her in his arms and wake her with kisses.

Zach and Mary had brought her tonight as he'd had an appointment that he could not cancel.

"If you will go in now, my lord, they are waiting for you," a footman said. He then opened the door, and Monty entered the room and stopped.

The room held Devilles and other men from society. Some he knew were part of Alexius, and others he did not.

"If you'll walk down now, my lord, your king awaits you," the footman said from behind him.

He walked down the carpet. The men bowed as he neared, as did the Devilles. Mary sank into a curtsy alongside his beautiful Iris when he reached them. With her was the Duchess of Yardly, which he thought odd, at least until he saw the ring hanging from the gold chain around her neck.

"Good God," he whispered because he was in the presence of the king.

"Exactly," Mary whispered. "Now walk up to the king. He does not like to be kept waiting."

He dragged his eyes from the ring, managed a smile for Iris, and then walked to his monarch.

"Lord Montgomery, I owe you much and am aware of the sacrifice you have made to keep your king and country safe."

"It was an honor, Your Majesty," Monty said, bowing deeply.

"I have a gift for your services to your king." He handed Monty a box. "It was given to my father by the late Lord Montgomery many years ago."

Monty opened it and found a gold pocket watch. Taking it out of the box, he turned it over and found the Alexius pledge and his father's initials beneath.

"It is a gift I will treasure always, Your Majesty." Monty's throat felt tight with emotion.

"Now it is time to shed Lord Plunge and become Lord Montgomery," the monarch said. "*Veritas scutum tibi erit.*"

"That is my wish, Your Majesty. *Veritas scutum tibi erit.*" Monty bowed. Everyone in the room clapped loudly. It was both embarrassing and humbling to be acknowledged by so many.

When the king had returned to his guests along with the

other members of Alexius, Monty moved to Iris's side and took her hand in his.

"What now, Monty?" Forrest asked, shaking his hand.

"Now, we set about letting society see you for who you really are," Gabe said. "Come along, there is no time like the present to start."

They rejoined the fete and other guests.

"You are still wearing lavender and yet no heels or silly hair style," Iris whispered to him.

"I did not want to shock them too much." He acknowledged the other guests, who were giving him curious looks.

"I say, Plunge. Have you done something different with your hair?" Lord Cagney asked.

"No indeed, Cagney." Monty lowered his voice slightly. Not quite his voice yet, but he would get there with the help of his friends and the woman he loved.

He walked, talked, but stayed at her side. Yes, people noticed, but few commented. He overheard Zach saying Monty had been unwell, and Iris, his dear old friend, had nursed him back to full health.

Nathan said loudly that it was wonderful to see their dear Lord Montgomery in good spirits again and so close with the lovely Lady Challoner.

By the evening's end, there were murmurs and whispers. Some had heard the king had called Plunge by Lord Montgomery, and they would soon follow suit.

No one really knew quite what to make of the fact that it appeared the simpleton Plunge was now different and had seemed to have formed an attachment with Lady Challoner.

There would be lots of gossip tomorrow.

Monty, Iris, and Henry would leave for Monty's estate soon, where they would marry and learn how to be a family. When they returned to London, it would be as husband and wife.

"Well, that was interesting," Iris said when they were alone in the carriage on the way to her town house many hours later. They'd spent the night on display, being watched and talked about, and both were pleased to be out of public.

"Iris?"

"Yes, Theo?" She touched his face, and warmth spread through him.

"I was late today because I had to collect something and visit Henry."

"Why did you visit Henry?"

"I had to ask his permission to marry you."

"What?"

"He said I could." Monty took her hand.

She was beautiful this evening—any evening, but tonight more so. Her dress was rose satin, and her hair was pinned in place with small diamonds. She glowed with happiness, and it looked radiant on her.

His beautiful girl had bloomed with his love, just as he had with hers.

"I also had to collect this." He pulled a small box out of his coat pocket.

"Theo—"

"It was my mother's. I had the band adjusted to fit you, my love."

"It's beautiful," she whispered, staring at the emerald circled with diamonds and shaped in a teardrop.

"Iris Challoner, soon to be Montgomery. I love you and your son, who I would be proud to call my son when he is ready. Please say you will marry me?"

"Yes, which I have already said."

"Then put this on and make it official. I can wait no longer to make you mine."

He pulled off her glove and then took the ring out of the box.

"It's beautiful."

"My mother never took it off, and I know she would be happy that it is now on your finger," Monty said. He slid it on and then caught her as she threw herself at him.

"I love you, Theo."

And right then and there, no more words were needed, because he had Iris in his arms. Monty had finally found his safe place. He was finally home.

THE END

THE SINCLAIR & RAVEN SERIES

From USA Today Bestseller Wendy Vella comes an exciting Regency series about legend, love and destiny, with a hint of magic.

SENSING DANGER

He will fight his destiny

Legend says the Sinclairs heightened senses are a result of a long ago pact between them and the powerful Raven family. To Honor and Protect is their creed, but the current Duke of Raven doesn't make their task easy.

Arrogant and aloof, James, Duke of Raven, is determined to forge his own path and to hell with folk tales that his ancestors created. But when the breathtaking Eden Sinclair saves his life by risking her own, their past resurfaces, and with it comes the uncomfortable realization that they are linked by more than history.

Fate has determined she will protect him.

Eden is forced to see the man behind the cool, haughty

façade when she must use her special abilities to keep him safe. His suspicion of her soon turns into something else, something far more dangerous. Eden is torn between duty and self-protection. Does she have the strength to fight fate, in order to protect her own heart?

BOOKS IN THE SINCLAIR & RAVEN SERIES

Sensing Danger
Seeing Danger
Touched By Danger
Scent of Danger
Vision Of Danger
Tempting Danger
Seductive Danger
Guarding Danger
Courting Danger
Defending Danger
Detecting Danger

LANGLEY SISTERS SERIES

Be swept away by the romance, intrigue, unconventional heroines, and dashing heroes, by USA Today Bestselling Author Wendy Vella's regency romance series.

LADY IN DISGUISE

Will her secret bring her ruin or love?

Desperate and penniless, Miss Olivia Langley is out of options. To ensure her family's survival she and her sister decide to take a drastic step - they don masks and take to the road as highwaymen. Disaster strikes when, inside the first carriage they rob, they find the one man Olivia had hoped never to see again. Five years ago Lord William Ryder had broken Livvy's heart. Now he has returned and she has a bad feeling that if anyone can succeed at unmasking her deepest secrets, it will be him.

Can a rake reform?

Will knew his return would be greeted with both joy and resentment, but after five years of hard living he was ready to come home and take his place in society. He had never forgotten Olivia no matter how hard he'd tried, and whilst he hadn't imagined she would welcome him with open arms, the hostility and anger she displays are at odds with the woman he once knew. Will is horrified to find she's living a dangerous lie and refuses his help. But now that he's back, Will is determined to do whatever it takes to protect her, and finally claim her for his own.

REGENCY RAKES SERIES

Welcome to Regency England — a world of charming gentlemen, elegant ladies, and sizzling passion! Enjoy this stunning read from USA Today Bestselling author Wendy Vella.

DUCHESS BY CHANCE

He believes she betrayed him!

Daniel, Duke of Stratton, learns of his betrothal to Miss Berengaria Evangeline Winchcomb minutes before his father's death. Having gambled his fortune away, all the late Duke had left to sell was his son. To save his family's honor Daniel agrees to the marriage, but society's favorite bachelor is no longer a charming easygoing man— his father's betrayal has left him angry and with a thirst for revenge.

Has she replaced one tyrant for another?

Eva learns she is to wed the Duke of Stratton on the way to the church. Inside she feels a flicker of hope that at last she is to leave her horrid family— however that flicker is short-lived as she faces the cold unyielding man who is now her husband. Has she escaped one tyrant to be forced into marriage with another?

Is there any hope for Daniel and Eva's marriage despite coming from two completely different worlds?

BOOKS IN THE REGENCY RAKES SERIES
Duchess By Chance
Rescued By A Viscount
Tempting Miss Allender

ABOUT THE AUTHOR

Wendy Vella is a bestselling author of historical and contemporary romances
such as the Langley Sisters and Sinclair and Raven series, with over two million copies of her books sold worldwide.
Born and raised in a rural area in the North Island of New Zealand,
she shares her life with one adorable husband, two delightful adult children and their partners, four delicious grandchildren

Find me on www.wendyvella.com

Wendy also writes contemporary small-town romance under the name Lani Blake